Shannon Bowring has been nominated for a Pushcart and a Best of the Net, and was selected for Best Small Fictions 2021. She holds an MFA from the University of Southern Maine Stonecoast and currently resides in Bath, Maine. *The Road to Dalton* was named an Indie Next List Pick and is her first novel.

THE ROAD
TO DALTON

Shannon Bowring

THE ROAD
TO DALTON

Europa
editions

Europa Editions
27 Union Square West, Suite 302
New York NY 10003
www.europaeditions.com
info@europaeditions.com

Library of Congress Cataloging in Publication Data is available
ISBN 978-1-60945-926-0

Bowring, Shannon
The Road to Dalton

Art direction by Emanuele Ragnisco
instagram.com/emanueleragnisco

Cover design and illustration by Ginevra Rapisardi

Prepress by Grafica Punto Print – Rome

Printed in the USA

CONTENTS

For Mom & Dad,
who never said no to one more chapter at bedtime

"He began to think of the people in the town where he had always lived with something like reverence."
—SHERWOOD ANDERSON, *Winesburg, Ohio*

I magine this:
You are driving alone on a road in Northern Maine. Your
head's still humming from the monotonous drone of I-95,
that empty highway. On the radio, nothing but static and out-
dated country music.

A couple miles back, you passed a dingy tagging station
where men in orange wool hats and vests stood beneath a massive wooden scale, bull moose hanging upside down before
them. Dark blood on the dirt. Dead tongue out of the mouth
and flapping. The scene passed by so fast you wonder if you
only dreamed it—all those men, laughing as the moose swung
in the bitter wind.

This is Aroostook County.

You follow Route 212 west until it ends at Route 11, then
you turn right, heading north, at a faded green sign: *Dalton,
42; Fort Kent, 83.* On either side of the potholed road, conifers
and bare deciduous trees reach toward the sky. Stubborn banks
of snow cling to the shoulder. Your stomach sloshes from last
season's frost-heaves. You roll the window down for a quick hit
of decaying leaves and cold clean air.

It takes three-quarters of an hour to reach the tiny hamlet
of Milton Landing. You slow as you pass a scattering of buildings—rusty trailers on cinderblocks, general store, bait and
tackle. To your left, a wide, slow river snakes its way northeast,
blue ice skimming the surface. The sky is heavy with clouds.

You pass a lumber mill, where towering stacks of logs and plywood lie on the ground. You may or may not know this, but most of the men in Dalton and Milton Landing and Portman Lake and Barren make their meager living from trees. They operate kilns in the mill, or they schlep into the forest to mark trees for slaughter, or they drive the 18-wheelers that carry the timbers back here to the lumberyard. The dark and dirty beating heart of an entire region. Inhale the smell—wood pulp and spruce sap and pine resin. Taste it in your mouth; feel the sawdust coat your teeth.

Soon the road widens, the forest retreating to the edge of open fields dotted with clumps of ice and snow. By now the clouds are so low they might as well be sitting on the treetops. No sun. The landscape takes on a depressing palette of gray, white, and brown. You pass no other vehicles. This empty road is eerie, maybe haunted. When you pass an abandoned church with yellowed clapboards and broken windows, serious doubts creep in. You wonder why you took this road at all.

But you've come too far to turn around. And where else do you have to go; what else do you have to do? You must keep moving. Just a little further.

You pass farmhouses and double-wides. Collapsing barns that sink into the earth. Down an unmarked side road, the looming silhouette of a potato house. Trees and more trees. Half-frozen, fallow fields. Another potato house. More trees.

Just beyond a small park containing little more than a metal jungle gym and a horse-racing track, you crest a high hill and pull over to the shoulder of the road. Turn off the ignition and step into the gray chill. Stretch your legs, feel your tired spine crack and settle into its familiar ache. The only sound is the distant thrum of something mechanical, some low-throated throb of chainsaw or motor. Take a few steps further and look around you.

Spread out in the valley below is Dalton. You squint,

counting three spindly church steeples, one blinking yellow light at the bottom of the hill. You see a gas station, an empty dirt lot across the street from a convenience store. A bullet-marred sign to your right assures you that Dalton, population 1309, is a D.A.R.E. Drug-Free Community. Smoke billows out of chimneys on rooftops missing shingles like gaps in nearly-toothless mouths.

Wasteland.

But something like a magnetic pull coming up from the cracked pavement beneath your feet compels you to get back in your car. Put your hands on the wheel. Keep moving forward, slowly and steadily, straight into the heart of Dalton.

1.
A PRIVATE PRACTICE

T rudy wears her best green dress for the party. Creases stand up on the shoulders from the coat hanger, and tiny pieces of lint stick to the soft velvet bodice. The dress is, perhaps, too short for a woman her age, hitting her just above her knees. Trudy either doesn't notice these things or is pretending not to care.

Richard has never paid much attention to his wardrobe. The bottoms of his trousers are usually flecked with mud or crusted over with salt, and it's not uncommon for his shirts to be half a size too small or too large. He knows nothing about what colors work best with his pale Northern Maine complexion. Yet, much as he despises the starchy blandness of the white coat he wears all day at the clinic, Richard wishes he could wear it to tonight's party. At least then he could hide behind something familiar, put up a thin layer of protection between himself and the world.

"Blue or red?" Richard holds the shirts up for Trudy to inspect.

"The blue sweater has a hole in the collar," she says, her voice muffled around a mouthful of bobby pins as she fusses with her ashy blonde hair. "Red one's tight around your shoulders. Wear the black Oxford."

"Last time I wore it you said it made me look like Johnny Cash."

"Did I? Well, I guess a lot of people like that sort of thing."

Neither of them ever looks forward to the Fraziers' New Year's Eve party. Trudy resents leaving the house after dark, especially in winter, and Richard hates the pretentious food Annette serves each year—salmon puffs, pâté. The woman can't seem to take a hint that most of her partygoers would rather eat pigs-in-a-blanket or chips and dip. It's not as if the people of Dalton need another reminder of the divide between them and the Fraziers, whose family has owned the lumber mill for three generations.

But the Haskells are expected to attend the party, which the Fraziers annually host for Dalton businessmen and-women. Richard runs the clinic his father opened in the early '50s and operates the practice as Simon Haskell would have wanted: healthcare for everyone in town, regardless of insurance. Some patients reimburse Richard over time. Others trade check-ups for homegrown tomatoes or manual labor. Because of this, the Haskells' pantry is always well stocked, their gutters clean. Without Trudy's income, though, they'd be in trouble. Her salary at the library is nothing to rave about, but she's managed to set aside a modest sum in her and Richard's savings account.

He used to promise Trudy he'd give her anything she wanted. A nice house, all the books she could ever want, vacations to faraway places. "I'll take you to New York," he would tell her. "Chicago, San Francisco, maybe even Paris."

Richard no longer makes such promises.

They live close enough to the Fraziers' that they could walk—they usually do, if the weather isn't too cold and the sidewalks not too icy—but the wind chill tonight is below freezing, so Trudy hauls herself up into the cab of Richard's GMC. She hates the old truck. Usually when they travel as a couple, they take her Celebrity. But the car's still at the garage, waiting for repairs.

This is the first time they've gone out together since they got into the accident on their way home from supper out at her brother's place a few weeks back. It was a mild night, but black ice coated the surface of Route 11. Trudy and Richard were arguing, which they rarely did, and so they were both distracted, not paying enough attention to the slick road. It happened so fast. Before Richard could react, they were sliding into the opposite lane, bright headlights of Nate Theroux's F-150 coming right toward them. Banged up the Celebrity's bumper. No injuries, though Nate's wife, Bridget, sitting in the passenger seat of the truck, was so shook up that she went into early labor, right there under the stars. Trudy held the girl's hand and cursed under her breath. Nate paced the empty road until salvation arrived in the form of a passing log-truck, whose driver radioed into Nate's colleagues at the police station for help. Richard, calm and in control, sat beside Bridget in the back of the Celebrity and talked about the rising price of gas while he monitored the girl's pulse and breathing.

Neither Richard or Trudy speaks on the short ride over to Rich Tucker Road—or, as most of the town calls it, Rich Fucker Road. Only a few families live in this neighborhood, which long-ago blue bloods built on a hill overlooking Dalton—the church steeples and chimneys, the forests and the fields, the gulley where the Aroostook River meanders its way northeast. The Fraziers' chalet-style house is perched on the peak of this hill, at the end of a long driveway. An enormous Christmas tree dominates the front windows, its blue, gold, and green lights reflecting off the unblemished snow on the lawn.

Richard parks at the crest of the driveway, careful to situate the truck so he can get out easily when it's time to leave.

In the mudroom, Trudy steps out of her boots and slides on clunky heels. Richard, who forgot to bring a spare pair of shoes, and whose trousers are just a tad too long to allow him to walk around the Fraziers' house in his socks, tries to wipe the muck from their own yard off the soles of his shoes.

"Leave it," Trudy says. "Let their floors get a little dirty."

They enter the warmth of the kitchen and are immediately

enveloped in cashmere and the strong vanilla haze of Annette Frazier's perfume as she throws her slender arms around them. "Welcome to 1990!" She laughs. "Well, almost. Is that dress vintage, Trudy? And Richard, what a great shirt."

Behind Annette's back, Trudy offers Richard a half-smile. They used to take bets on how long they could get Annette to prattle on without taking a breath. The record was New Year's '76, when Trudy goaded her into complaining for nine minutes straight about what a letdown the Dalton Daze bicentennial celebration had been that past July.

The living room, a massive space taking up the entire front of the house, smells of spruce and cinnamon. The Christmas tree looks even more impressive under the vaulted ceiling than it appeared from outside. Soft classical music plays in the background, and the carpet gleams an unnatural shade of white, impervious to the footprints of all the people who've ever walked on it. About three dozen people mill around the room, bearing cocktails and hors d'oeuvres. From across the room comes the braying laughter of Arlene Nadeau.

"You two get your cocktails from Mellie here," Annette says, leading them to the drinks table. "I have to check on the food. Ta-ta!"

She turns, the gold threads in her blouse catching the light from the tree as she stumbles into Raymond Fields. The pastor apologizes as he catches her elbow, even though Annette was the one to walk into him, and she gives him a toothy smile before gliding off to the kitchen.

"Insufferable woman," Trudy mutters.

They order drinks from Mellie—scotch for Richard, white wine for Trudy—and make the rounds, stopping to chat with the same people they see every day at the library, the clinic, the Store 'N More. Phil Lannigan pulls Trudy aside to discuss the Dalton Historical Society's next fundraiser, leaving Richard to engage in small talk with Ian Best.

"I hate parties."

"That makes two of us."

Ian clutches a beer in his plump hand. Richard reminds himself this is no longer the child he once treated for bee stings, but a young man who stands to inherit his parents' thriving potato farm. He asks a few questions about how Ian thinks the crop will do next year—"Good enough,"—then wanders the periphery of the crowd, taking small sips of his drink and marveling once again at the height of the room's windows.

"Imagine cleaning all those," he'd said to Trudy that muggy summer day fifteen years ago. He'd just turned thirty; she was twenty-six. They'd come here with a bleach-blonde realtor from Prescott who smacked her gum and stood with one leg crossed in front of the other like a child in need of a toilet.

"I'd get out the extension ladder and do it myself," Trudy said. "And I'd enjoy every goddamn minute of it."

She had been in love with everything about this house from the moment they walked inside: the tiles on the kitchen floor, the soaring ceilings, the fireplace in the master bedroom. Richard warned Trudy not to get her hopes up—he hadn't yet paid off his student loans, and she had only just started at the library. He'd agreed to look at the place because he, like most people in Dalton, had always wanted to see the interior of this house that sat like a jewel atop their town. But seeing how Trudy stood before these huge windows and smiled as the sun streamed in, Richard resolved to find a way to buy the place. Before Richard could even submit the loan application, however, Marshall and Annette Frazier snatched the house off the market. Later that year, as trees shed their withered leaves, Richard and Trudy bought the yellow bungalow on Winter Street across from the grade school, where they still live.

The clinking of glasses echoes through the room. Marshall and Annette stand before the fireplace, surrounded by their children—William, tan from a recent trip somewhere far from here, Craig wiping his glasses with the hem of his shirt, Penny in a tight cocktail dress, and Bridget, hair pulled into a lopsided twist. Nate Theroux hovers beside her, his eyes locked onto the pink bundle in Bridget's arms as though held there by an invisible tether. Bridget, dressed in a gray sweater, looks pale and tired. But Richard would be surprised if any new mother didn't.

As Annette starts in on her usual speech about a new year's unknown wonders, Richard scans the room for Trudy, finally spotting her near the Christmas tree with Bev Theroux, Nate's mother. He watches as Trudy whispers something into her best friend's ear and wonders what his wife is saying. Something caustic, something brilliant? She can be both of those things, often at the same time, and this used to be what Richard loved most about her. He's not sure what he loves about her now. Her familiarity, he supposes. Or maybe that is the thing he can't stand. He can never keep it straight, this delicate act of a discontented marriage, the silent agreements they've made to remain together.

From the front of the room, Marshall thanks his wife for throwing another great party. In his well-fitting suit and high-heeled boots (Trudy claims such shoes for men are in fashion right now, but Richard remains skeptical), he appears tall, distinguished. Having measured him at each of his yearly check-ups, however, Richard knows the man barely clears 5'7".

"And we have a new member of the family." Marshall gestures to the baby in Bridget's arms. "Sophie Caroline Theroux."

The room fills with more clinking glasses. Arlene Nadeau lets out a loud wolf whistle.

Marshall beams toward his daughter. "Say a few words, hon?"

Richard notices that Bridget holds the baby slightly away from her chest, supported and protected by the circle of her arms but without the benefit of her body's warmth. Her exhausted gaze darts up to Nate, who steps forward to address the crowd.

Just then, Richard feels someone tap his shoulder and turns to see Mellie Martin standing behind him.

"Sorry to interrupt, Dr. Haskell," she says. Judging by her breath, Richard guesses she's been doing more than just serving drinks tonight. "But someone's on the phone for you in the other room."

The kitchen counters are covered with trays of food, pitchers of mulled cider, plastic cups made to look like fine crystal. Richard guesses Annette keeps the real stuff locked away in a cupboard, away from greasy fingers. He holds the phone close to his ear. The female voice on the line is unexpected, but not a surprise.

He hangs up and stands in the doorway between the kitchen and the living room, one foot in, the other out. Nate is saying something about his first clumsy attempts at diapering, and the crowd is laughing, but Richard hears none of it. He gazes across the room teeming with people he's known his entire life, or their entire lives, and watches his wife's gaze drift above their heads, lifting higher until fixing on the rafters. Richard doesn't need to follow her line of sight to know what she sees up there. After all these years of holiday parties, he knows the scaffolding of this house like he knows the bones of the yellowed skeleton that lurks in the corner of his office down at the clinic.

If he leaves now, he can be back in an hour. Everyone in the living room raises their glasses in a toast as Richard silently and with great practice makes his retreat from the crowd.

The cold makes the blue stars tremble. Richard eases his truck out of the Fraziers' driveway, coasts down the steep hill of Rich Fucker Road. He turns left onto High Street, makes a quick right onto Howard. The soccer fields and baseball diamond lie silent under several feet of snow, shining white under a full moon. Icicles gleam from the eaves of houses. He turns again, left onto Prescott Road, and within moments is turning onto Pine Street. A dead-end, surrounded by thick copses of birch and evergreen, bowing under the weight of winter.

A single streetlamp glows outside the clinic, spilling buttery light onto the parking lot. Richard's shoes crunch against hardened ice and snow as he makes the short walk from his truck to the entrance. His teeth ache from the bitter wind.

It's warm inside the clinic, dim security lights and red EXIT signs casting shadows across the floor, illuminating the thick glass blocks that make up one wall. Richard waits in the lobby, watches the parking lot. Headlights slant into the room. He stands with his hand on the doorknob and listens to the heavy *thunk* of her car door, her quick footsteps on the walkway. Pulling in a deep breath and reminding himself to keep a neutral face, no matter what she says or how she might appear, Richard opens the door.

"I'm sorry to pull you away from your party," Rose Douglas says, shaking her dark hair free from a wool hat.

"Don't apologize. I was glad to escape for a while."

Rose gazes up at him from behind one teary brown eye. The other is swollen shut from the force of her fiancé's fist. A small cut, coated with dried blood, rests on the ridge of her cheekbone.

"He didn't mean to, Dr. H. He really didn't." Her voice wobbles. "I shouldn't have bothered him is all, not while he was drinking."

Richard gestures for Rose to follow him down the hallway and into Exam Room 1. He flicks on the lights, apologizes when the bright fluorescents make her flinch, and snaps on a pair of gloves as he roots through the cupboard drawers, takes out peroxide, cotton swabs, medical tape.

"What about the boys?" he asks as she settles on the cot, paper crinkling beneath her. She shrugs off her jacket. She's wearing a yellow sweatshirt, acid-washed jeans, scuffed sneakers that might have been white a long time ago.

"I told you." She sniffles. "Tommy never hits the kids. And anyway, they're over at Ma's tonight, so they didn't see anything, thank God. How bad do you think the bruise'll be?"

"Hard to say. You'll definitely have some swelling around the area for a few days. Might be hard to explain at work."

Rose wipes her nose with the sleeve of her shirt. "I got some vacation time built up. I'll say the kids got the chickenpox or something."

"What will you tell everyone else? Your mother?"

"She's never asked about the other bruises."

Richard says nothing. Rose lets out a long sigh and buries her head in her hands. Her hair falls forward, revealing the smooth paleness of her skin, a tiny, dark mole on the nape of her neck.

"I know how pathetic I sound," she says, straightening back up. "God, if I heard any other girl saying this shit, I'd tell her to take the kids and run."

"This will sting." Richard dabs a peroxide-soaked cotton swab into the cut beneath her eye. She sucks in a breath, then leans in, balances her chin on the palm of his free hand.

Richard remembers when Rose would come in here as a child for her annual checkups, how she would swing her mosquito-bitten legs from the cot as he listened to her steady heart. She was one of his favorite patients, bubbling over with tales of fairies and unicorns as her single mother, who could often be found flirting with millworkers over beers at Frenchie's, sat in the corner of the room absorbed in a *National Enquirer*.

When Rose was sixteen, Richard delivered the news to her that she was pregnant with Tommy Merchant's kid. Two years later, he had to tell her again. And not long after the birth of her second child, she came to him with the first of Tommy's bruises.

"I won't tell anyone about this without your permission," he told her. "Not even the police, if you're set against that. But if he hits you again and you need help, call me."

It gets so heavy, the weight of other people's fears and

secrets. "Keep this between us," his patients tell him, and as long as they are independent adults with full use of their faculties, Richard is bound to honor their wishes. Silently he carries with him the intimate details of Gareth Best's hemorrhoids, or Jo Martin's toenail fungus, or Bridget Theroux's teary confession, sitting there in the back of the Celebrity that night three weeks ago, that she sometimes dreamed of misplacing her baby in a building a hundred stories high.

"There's a women's shelter in Prescott I could recommend," Richard tells Rose. He finishes cleaning her cut and reaches for the tape. "You can bring the boys with you. I've heard good things."

She stares at the eye chart on the wall and says nothing. Richard continues his slow art of healing what can never be healed.

As a boy, he had dreams of designing great ships like the ones they build down at Bath Iron Works. But his parents made it clear someone had to take over the clinic after his father retired (none of them guessing Simon would die of a heart attack long before that). Both Richard's father, who begged with kind eyes, and his mother, dead five years now, made Richard believe he owed something to the town that helped raise him. So he took anatomy rather than art class in high school, went to college downstate on a partial scholarship (avoiding serious debt and the draft for Vietnam all at once), and then he went to med school. He did well as a resident, both with the scientific and human aspects of the job. But sometimes, walking the dim, sterile halls of Maine Med late at night, Richard felt a strange sensation, one he experienced again years later with Trudy, when he would begin to suspect their marriage would never become the strong union he'd hoped for. A feeling of something not quite right, like a shoe that fits just a little too small. Mildly irritating and distracting—but not enough to make Richard change the entire trajectory of his life.

Rose sighs again. "I can't leave."

"Why not?"

He's not sure what he expects Rose to say—that she loves pock-faced Tommy Merchant, despite all that's wrong with him. That she couldn't possibly take her children from their father. That she doesn't know any other way, not growing up the way she did, with that mother of hers, in that double-wide trailer out in Barren.

Instead, Rose asks about the party. "Who all went to the Fraziers' tonight?"

"Oh, all the bigwigs," Richard chuckles. "Pretty much all the business owners. A few mill managers. Some teachers . . . Though it seems Ms. McGreevy was too busy casting hexes against the rest of us to come."

"That woman was two hundred years old when I was in her class," says Rose, breaking into a timid smile. "I can't believe she's still alive."

"And kicking." Richard covers the cut on her face with two small pieces of tape.

"Did Nate end up going?" When she says his name, Rose sits up straighter and her one good eye burns bright. "I just wondered because we haven't seen much of him at the station since they had the baby."

Richard removes his gloves, drops them into the waste bin. "He and Bridget were there."

"How did he . . . how'd they look? Is Bridget doing okay? With the baby coming early and all, I mean."

"She looked like any new mother. Exhausted, overwhelmed. I'm sure you remember."

"Yeah." Her birdlike body deflates once more. "I remember."

"We should ice that eye," says Richard.

"I don't want to be any more trouble. You should get back to the party. Trudy must be wondering where you are."

At the thought of his wife waiting for him, Richard feels the same familiar dread that falls on him each time he returns home after a long day spent in this building with its pale green walls and reek of Lysol. When they were newly married, Trudy would greet him at the front door, embrace him as she asked about his day. The kitchen filled with the smell of good cooking, the warmth of her. It hasn't been that way for a long time.

Richard makes himself smile at Rose, the bruise on her face already turning a dark shade of purple.

"Enough of that," he tells her. "Just sit tight. I'll get the ice."

Some of the braver, drunker guests are singing when Richard returns to the party. It's an old song, and though he doesn't know all the words, he understands them anyway, the comfort of them, the familiarity of the refrain.

His face and hands are still cold from outside when he rejoins the crowd, picking up a glass of scotch from Mellie along the way. Annette and Marshall hold court at the center of the living room, Annette's ginger hair flatter than when Richard left, Marshall's face flushed red. Standing near the Christmas tree are Nate and Bridget. Nate nuzzles the baby against his neck as Bridget stares toward the huge windows, the muted reflection of all the life and color in the room behind her. Richard considers asking how she and Sophie are doing. But no—they have their own doctors in Prescott, an OB and pediatrician for all the necessary follow-up. And as all Mainers know, caring is one thing; prying quite another.

Richard moves past Nate and Bridget, past all the people who trust him more than they do members of their own families. Dean Buckley, who, after years of silent suffering, has finally started to consider antidepressants. George Nadeau, sentenced to a life of pain thanks to the Vietnam bullet in his leg. Even Annette Frazier, whose warts have to be burned off her pretty fingers every other month.

Trudy and Bev stand alone in the corner, half-hidden behind

a ficus draped with silver lights. Richard watches as Bev, over a foot taller than his wife, brushes a piece of lint from Trudy's shoulder. He watches as Bev's hand lingers there, as her fingers graze his wife's collarbone. Watches as Trudy giggles—he can't remember the last time he heard that twinkling little laugh— and leans into Bev. Watches as she presses her cheek against Bev's arm, as she gazes up at her best friend with the same look she used to shine on Richard.

"Sing louder, everyone!"

At the sound of Annette's shrill voice, Trudy and Bev step away from one another. Though he tries not to notice, Richard knows the two have performed this casual falling apart countless times before, at bake sales and book clubs, town meetings and school plays.

When Trudy confessed to Richard, about seven years into their marriage, that she might be developing feelings for her new friend Bev, Richard teased her. It was the late '70s, and that sort of thing was becoming more common, in other parts of the country if not in Aroostook County. He figured it was just a crush, a somewhat peculiar but perhaps inevitable, delayed result of Trudy's conservative upbringing. She was a virgin when they married. Had only kissed two men before him. So Richard told Trudy, "Play around, get it out of your system." Never believing she would actually try anything.

But then—

"What do you mean you *love* her?" Richard asked one August night as he and Trudy sat on their front porch. She and Bev had just returned from a girls' trip to Bangor, and his wife looked different. Brighter, softer. Completely unfamiliar.

"You know damn well what I mean," Trudy said. "I'm sorry, Richard. Chrissake, I don't understand it myself. But now that I know, I can't pretend not to."

It's not like divorce was an option. Richard running the clinic, and Bev still married to Bill, and Nate just a kid, and

Trudy trying to make a career for herself at the library . . . it couldn't happen. It's not as though anybody would chase them out of town with the proverbial pitchforks and torches. It would be worse than that. If Bev and Trudy ever tried to live openly as a couple, they and their families would be cordially tolerated, the same way people in town treat people From Away— Southern Mainers, out-of-staters, anyone different. Richard's patients would drive to Prescott to see the more expensive doctors there, just to prove a point. The message in Dalton would be clear—*You're not one of us, not anymore, not ever again.*

So Richard and Trudy agreed to silence. She wouldn't talk about Bev, and he wouldn't ask. They would stay married. They would keep their jobs, Trudy's one that she'd always dreamed of having, Richard's one that he was good at and used to (that sensation of not-quite-fitting hovered at the periphery, but he learned to push it away). Neither of them wanted children, so that would never be an issue. All of it could work, they reasoned, so long as they both kept quiet.

But sometimes one of them breaks the pact. Tonight, it's Trudy, standing a little too close to Bev. Three weeks ago, it was Richard, letting himself get angry at Trudy for something insignificant that represented something so much bigger, this silent something always looming over them. At her brother's house that night, over boiled dinner, Trudy had taken the last roll without offering it to Richard. Ripped into it with her clean fingernails. Shredded it to pieces with cold butter.

"You didn't even ask if I wanted it," he snapped at her on the ride home.

"For Chrissake, it was only a roll."

"You know it's not just that," Richard said, taking his eyes off the road to stare over at her, sitting rigid in the passenger seat, staring out at the snowy fields, blue-white beneath the stars. "It's never not just—"

And then the Celebrity's tires lost traction, and they went

into a skid across an invisible surface. The bone-cracking sound the car made when it collided into Nate Theroux's truck, and the yellow glare of headlights on clean snow.

Annette again, shrieking from across the living room. "Last verse! Make it *count*!"

Richard watches as Bev drifts away from Trudy and heads toward Nate and Bridget. He takes a few steadying breaths, then wanders over to stand beside his wife, who scowls up at him.

"Where the hell did you run off to?"

"Got called to the clinic."

"You promised you wouldn't work tonight."

"And you promised," says Richard, "to be a little more discreet."

He downs the rest of his drink and watches as, over near the Christmas tree, Bev reaches for her granddaughter, taking the baby from Nate's gangly arms while Bridget continues to look away, toward the darkened window.

The new year's song swells around them, all those drunken voices singing, lifting, rising, hoping. Richard and Trudy stand there at the edge of it all, silent as the last word drifts like snow up into the rafters.

2

BOILED DINNER

O n a frigid January evening, Bev knocks on the door of Apartment 4C at the Whispering Pines Retirement Village. The dark green plywood is slightly warped and hollow, and Bev wonders, not for the first time, how much it might cost to replace the door with something more substantial, something better up to the task of blocking out the Northern Maine winters.

Nora answers the door, letting out the briny smell of boiled cabbage and corned beef. The stout old woman is dressed in trousers, a sweatshirt embroidered with chickadees, moccasins half a size too big for her feet.

"Come in out of that cold, deah. You'll catch 'monia if you're not careful."

Even after years of knowing Nora, Bev is still amused by her thick Maine accent—the lilting cadence, a tendency to drop r's, to skip over entire syllables of words. Plenty of folks in Dalton and Aroostook County have a touch of the telltale accent, but it's more pronounced in those of Nora's generation.

Bev hangs her parka beside the door and slips off her boots. Both are relics of a splurge she allowed herself after receiving the L.L. Bean Christmas catalog a decade ago, shortly after she was promoted to director of the Pines. She'd never paid so much for clothes in her life, and the allure faded quickly. Whenever she wears the coat and boots, she feels awkward, as though she's trying to prove something that doesn't need proving. But she's got too much pride to return the damn things.

"What can I help with?" Bev asks.

Nora waves a liver-spotted hand in Bev's direction as though batting away a blackfly.

"I can't just watch you work."

"You're gonna be pigheaded about it, you can pour the iced tea."

They have the same good-humored argument every week. Nora usually gives in and lets Bev do something meaningless. Refold the gingham napkins, top off the salt and pepper shakers—the same kind of tasks Bev used to give Nate when he was a child.

She and Nora have had supper together almost every Sunday for the past two years, ever since that mud season night Bev brought down a fresh pack of toilet paper for Nora after the old woman called up to the office saying she'd run out. As soon as she entered the apartment that night and smelled the familiar, childhood aroma of New England boiled dinner, her stomach rumbled. "Stay for suppah," Nora insisted, and Bev, in no hurry to get back home after dealing with payroll up in her office all day, was happy to accept.

By now she feels as comfortable in Nora's kitchen as she does her own. White eyelet curtains hang in the windows; in the corner, a pine bookshelf holds Nora's treasures—chipped tea set, old jelly glasses filled with pinecones and dried lilacs, paperbacks that bear *Discarded from the Dalton Community Library* stamps inside their velvety covers.

Bev sets the pitcher of iced tea on the table as Nora brings over the casserole dish, filled with steaming corned beef, cabbage, potatoes, and carrots. She still hasn't grown tired of this meal—the salty bite of the corned beef, the sour cabbage.

"You'll never guess who's coming for a visit," says Nora. "Rogie." Her eyes are bright, cheeks flushed with excitement.

In the four years Nora has lived at the Pines, her son, Roger, has rarely made the nearly-six-hour drive up from Portland, where he works for some bank or insurance agency; Bev can never remember which. Nora says he rents an apartment near the hospital. "If he opens the window, he can smell the ocean," Nora says. This sounds like a nightmare to Bev, who used to gag at the fishy, low-tide funk that hung over Bar Harbor, where her family took summer vacations when she was young.

"That's wonderful." Bev slathers margarine on a heel of Nora's homemade sourdough. "Is he bringing Alice?"

Nora's jaw tightens. "Can't see why he'd leave her behind."

"This the first time you'll actually meet her?"

"Mm-hmm. First time."

As they eat, Bev wonders about Roger's new wife. Alice Something, an aerobics instructor. Roger sent his mother some Polaroids last June, which Nora showed to Bev. The pictures had been taken outside the Portland city hall after his and Alice's wedding. Roger wore khakis, boat shoes, a pale green Oxford shirt. His going-silver hair was cut close to his scalp. Alice, pressed against him on the granite steps, was dressed in a white and navy striped skirt suit and blue pumps. With her bright skin, tousled chestnut hair, and petite frame, Alice looked even younger than twenty-seven. Bev hadn't been surprised that Nora wasn't thrilled about the age difference between Roger and Alice—he was old enough to be the girl's father, for God's sake—but she hadn't expected Nora to toss the photos of her son's wedding day in the drawer of her white hutch, on top of a pile of spent crossword puzzle books. "It could be worse, couldn't it?" Bev had asked. "I s'pose," said Nora, a hard glint in her eyes. "He could be one of them bachelor types."

As Bev begins to clear the table, popping one last chunk of corned beef into her mouth, she asks Nora how long Roger and Alice will be in town.

"Friday to Monday. Guess you and me won't be able to have Sunday suppah."

The same instinct that used to kick in whenever Nate wanted to have friends over for a birthday party or movie night sparks up in Bev. How long has it been since she hosted anything, since she invited anyone other than Trudy to the house?

"Why don't you bring them to my place? Let me cook for you."

"That's too much fuss."

"No, it's not. I'll invite Nate and Bridget, and Trudy and Richard, too. We'll make it a real occasion."

Nora gnaws at the inside of her lip as she rinses their plates. Soap suds cling to the dull gold wedding band she still wears.

"I guess that'd be all right," she finally says. "But I'm bringing scotcharoos. Rogie loves those, you know."

* * *

Back at home, Bev checks the answering machine. The first message is from Trudy: *I tried making your so-called foolproof custard pie and it fell all to hell.* She laughs and moves on to the next message, from Nate. *Hey, Mom. Just checking in . . .* There's a sound as though he's crumpling candy wrappers against the phone. Background commotion—Sophie crying, Bridget saying something. More crumpling, then Nate's back on the line. *Sorry. The baby's been cranky today. I'll come by your office tomorrow for lunch. Order whatever you want from the Store 'N More and I'll pick it up around noon. Love ya.*

Bev slides her feet into the worn-out slippers she keeps near the front door, then pads into the living room, where Bill sits sprawled in his recliner, an empty Bud and a discarded ice pack on the end table beside him. An old episode of *Rawhide* flickers on the television.

"You can't even get up to answer the phone when your son calls?"

"Didn't know it was him calling."

It strikes Bev as bleakly ironic that Nate used to drop everything to answer the phone when Bill would call home while he was out on one of his trucking jobs. The boy could be in the middle of homework or building one of those model airplanes he'd been so obsessed with, but the second that phone rang, he'd race into the kitchen to snatch the receiver off the wall. Over the crackling lines of some anonymous payphone, Bill would report all the sights he'd seen on the road. Mountains propping up purple clouds, ghost towns under desert sun, steel-ribbed cities whose bright lights blocked out the stars.

Bev goes into the kitchen, where she settles at the table with a pack of Virginia Slims. Cradling the phone against her shoulder, she tamps the pack against her palm, strikes her Bic, and inhales. Instant relief, relief doubled by the sound of Trudy's snippy voice.

"Screw custard."

Bev grins. "I told you, Tru, you need to be patient with that recipe."

"To hell with patience. Are you smoking?"

"Course not."

"You're a lousy liar. How was it tonight? Nora doing all right?"

She tells Trudy all about it—the corned beef, the watered-down iced tea, Roger's visit up north with Aerobics Alice.

"I invited them to supper on Sunday," Bev says. "I want to do boiled dinner. I'm going to ask Nate to bring Bridget and the baby. You, too. And Richard."

"I'm not big on that sort of shindig, Bevy."

"Yup, I know."

"Weekends are my time to be *away* from people."

"Mm-hmm."

Bev stubs her cigarette into her ashtray and lights another. The kitchen light is warm and yellow. The irritation of seeing Bill sprawled out in his chair starts to ebb from her veins. He's been such a wallower ever since he had to go on disability for his back a few years ago. To hell with it. Let him sit there, let him wallow. Everything in this little kitchen feels solid and right and familiar, and that familiarity stretches out and makes her smile wider as Trudy lets out a theatric sigh, because even before her best friend speaks, Bev knows what she's about to say.

"So what time should I get there?"

* * *

The following Sunday evening, snow spits from the dark sky in little bursts, falls in glittering streaks past the porch light. Bev glimpses it out the window as she pulls a tray of rolls from the oven. Trudy, who arrived an hour earlier, sets the table. She looks like a proper librarian tonight, dressed in a pale pink blouse and tweed slacks that emphasize her narrow waist and hips, her blonde hair gathered at the nape of her neck. Bev, in jeans and a plain green sweatshirt, dark hair frizzing out around her face, feels sloppy in comparison. But too late to do anything about it now.

Bev pops the cork on a bottle of pinot grigio, the nicest she could find up at Bergeron's at a whopping six bucks. "You think Alice is one of those wine snobs?"

"Christ, we better hope not."

There's a muffled cough from the bathroom, where Bill is getting ready. He'd gone along with tonight's plans willingly enough once he found out Nate and Sophie and Bridget would be here. Bill might have never been a great husband, but he's always been a good father to Nate. Is already a good grandfather to Sophie—he held her so gently the first time Nate and

Bridget came by after she was born. Like breathing too hard might break her.

Headlights sweep across the yard as Nate pulls into the driveway.

"Here comes that handsome boy of ours," says Trudy. She joins Bev at the window and slips an arm around her waist.

Growing up, Nate knew that in a crisis, he was to call 911 first, his mother second, and Trudy third. On his Emergency Contacts in school, he listed her as his aunt, and even though the teachers knew there was no common blood between the Therouxs and the Haskells, none of them questioned whether that mattered. Everyone in Dalton was related somehow, even if that relation wasn't strictly genetic. And everyone in Dalton knew that Bev and Trudy were best friends. *Joined at the hip and ankle and funny bone*, as Bill used to say.

If only they knew the whole of it.

She and Trudy stand pressed together while they watch Nate step down from the truck. He walks over to the passenger side to open the door for Bridget, who holds her jacket tight around her chest as Nate fumbles with the bulky car seat in the back of the truck. The new little family all glowing yellow from the porch light as they walk toward the house.

As soon as Nate has set the car seat and a diaper bag on the kitchen floor, he envelopes Bev in a rib-crushing embrace. His flannel shirt smells of wood smoke, a hint of sour milk. He lets her go and rests an elbow on the top of Trudy's head while Tru smacks playfully at his ribs, their usual, odd way of greeting one another. At 6'2", Nate stands only a couple inches taller than Bev, but over a foot above Trudy, and the sight of them together is as comical as it is endearing.

"Where's Richard?" Nate asks.

"Caught one of his patients' colds," Trudy answers. "Thought it'd be best not to infect the rest of us."

Bev stoops down to free Sophie from her car seat. The

sleeping red-haired infant nuzzles against her neck, puffs out tiny warm breaths against her skin.

"Hello, sweetheart," Bev says to Bridget, who stands by the door with one sneaker off, the other still on. "Glad you came out. You must be tired as hell."

The reek of curdled milk is stronger on Bridget. It clings to her gray blouse, her greasy, strawberry-blonde hair. Bev remembers the smell from her own days as a new mother, taking Nate to her breast in the middle of the night while Bill snored in the other room. Nate has mentioned that Bridget's had trouble nursing—sometimes Sophie won't latch. Other times, she refuses to let go. Bev wishes she could hand down some sage advice. But Nate was an easy baby. Never fought her on anything. Even his birth was unremarkable, just a few hours, no surprises. Nothing like Bridget's labor.

Bill enters the kitchen at the same time the front door opens, the doorknob pushing against Bridget's spine and making her cry out. Nate tries to catch her, but she stumbles into the wall, knocking Bev's *No Bitchin' in my Kitchen* sign askew. Bill rushes forward to help, trailing the scent of Old Spice after him, and there's a chorus of confused greetings and apologies as Nora, Roger, and Alice squeeze their way inside.

"I'm fine," Bridget insists as she finally removes her other shoe and drops it on the mat beside Bill's steel-toed boots. She presses against Nate's arm like she wishes she could use him as a windbreak. "Really, I'm okay."

It's not until Bev ushers everyone further into the room that she gets a good look at the newlyweds. Roger, though taller than his mother, looks a lot like Nora: hazel eyes, nose just a little too big, ears just a little too small. Dressed in jeans and a denim shirt, he seems more like a real Mainer than he did in the wedding pictures. His smile grows wider every time he glances at Alice, who appears completely at ease by his side. Her hair is pushed away from her face, free of any makeup, and her eyes are like the hemlock trees that grow behind Bev's house—green and alive, sparkling as if caught by the sun. She wears dark slacks, a blue sweater.

After everyone has settled down, Roger clears his throat.

"Everyone, this is Alice. Alice, this is Trudy Haskell. She works over at the library—"

"*Director* of the library," corrects Trudy. "Pleased to meet you."

"—and Bev Theroux, director of the Pines; her husband, Bill, their son, Nate, and his wife, Bridget."

"The-*row*?" Alice repeats. "When I saw the name on your mailbox, I thought for sure it'd be pronounced The-*roo*."

"You're technically right," says Bev. "But here in the County, we tend to butcher our French namesakes."

They tell her about some of the other major offenders in town—Beaulieu (*Bowl-yer*), Gagnon (*Gone-yer*), Saucier (*So-sure*)—and then Bev hands Sophie over to Bridget and invites everyone to sit down. She smooshes in between Trudy and Nate. Even with the extra leaf, it's a squeeze to fit everyone in. There's more than the occasional elbow-bump as they dig into the meal, laid out in mismatched dishes on the Moosehead table. Bev feels a pang of shame when she bites into the corned beef and discovers it's stringy and tough. She's even more embarrassed when everyone tells her how good it is.

"Wine?" Trudy holds the bottle out to Alice.

"I actually can't stand the stuff," she says. "I'd take a beer, though."

Bev gives Tru a secret smile.

Everyone settles into chitchat about the weather (not bad for this time of year), the price of groceries (rising all the time), and world news (official end of the Cold War, but what does that mean for them, and what exactly was the Cold War, anyway?).

"I love your blouse," Bev tells Nora. "The little yellow birds. It's so cheerful."

"Ma's always liked her birds." Roger selects two rolls from the basket Bill offers him and hands one to Alice. "Used to put those red hummingbird feeders all around the farm."

Nora spears a pile of corned beef onto her fork. "Surprised you remember."

Roger asks Nate what it's like to be a cop in his hometown, and Nate starts in on a story about a bull moose that wandered into town with brainworm early last fall. Bev knows he has better, sadder stories than that—drunks and wifebeaters, speeders and junkies. And she's heard rumors he's got his eye on Tommy Merchant, who may or may not be selling drugs out of his uncle's garage down on Main Street. But her boy's too decent to spill the details of his fellow townies' lives.

Alice smiles at Bridget, who holds the baby awkwardly between her chest and the table. "I don't think Roger said when he was introducing everyone—what's this pretty girl's name?"

"Sophie."

"How old?"

Nate grins as he reaches for the baby. "Seven weeks," he says. "I'm surprised she hasn't woken up yet—usually she's really alert."

"More than alert." Bridget nibbles at a chunk of potato. "Squirms a lot. Cries a lot."

"She's just spirited." Nate lands a kiss on Sophie's pink, shell-shaped ear.

"Well, sometimes they grow out of it," Trudy says. "Or so I hear."

"Do you not have children?"

Bev tries to find the usual condescending tone in Alice's voice that other women use whenever they ask Trudy this question. She glances at the young new wife, sitting there on good birthing hips in the prime of her baby-making years. But there's no judgment on Alice's face, no expectation.

"Kids are great," Trudy answers. "I just didn't see the need to make any of my own."

"I hear you," says Alice. "I've never wanted any, either. It's so unfair to assume we all want babies, you know? Not to mention old-fashioned. And misogynist."

A look flashes through Nora's eyes that Bev's only seen once before, when Nora shoved the wedding pictures of Roger and Alice into that drawer. That look reminds her of ice on the river, quick and sharp and gone.

Before the silence can grow bigger, Trudy asks Alice if she enjoys teaching aerobics.

"It's not the career path I dreamed of," she says. "My God, the *outfits* I have to wear. But I set my own hours, and that's helpful with my writing schedule."

"You're a writer?" asks Nate.

"I've published some short stories."

Not Aerobics Alice. *Author* Alice. Much better.

Nora turns to Roger with a smile that doesn't reach her eyes. "You told me she's workin' to be some kinda journalist."

Roger stabs a sliver of carrot onto his fork. "I never said that, Ma."

"You told me, you said *journalist*. Like that Barbara Walters. Or the other one, the Oriental."

Beneath the table, Trudy's foot presses against Bev's.

Roger wipes his mouth with a paper towel. "You know her name's Connie Chung, Ma. And I never told you Alice wanted to be any kind of journalist. I told you she writes fiction."

A strained silence follows, during which Nora stares at Roger through narrowed eyes as he continues eating.

"So," Bev says, turning to Alice. "You working on anything now?"

"A novel. Or what wants to be a novel, if I can get out of the way."

Bev's impressed by how calm Alice sounds, as though Nora

isn't scraping her fork against her plate like a child getting ready to throw a tantrum.

"Well," says Trudy. "Once that sucker's published, you'll have to debut it at the library. We'll have an Alice McGowan book signing party."

"Actually, it's O'Neill. I kept my maiden name."

"She went modern," grins Roger.

Nora makes a small, pained noise not unlike the mouse Bev recently trapped beneath her kitchen sink.

"I guess you could say I went halfway modern." Bridget twirls the silver wedding band on her ring finger. Christ, she looks tired. "I hyphenated. Frazier-Theroux."

After everyone has finished eating, Bev turns to Nora. "Did you leave the scotcharoos in the car? I don't remember seeing you bring them in when you got here."

"Didn't bring them. Burned the chocolate," says Nora. "Meant to call and tell you, but I forgot. Guess I'm just old and stupid."

"Ma." Roger rubs the back of his neck. "Don't talk like that. No one thinks that."

"Think we still have most of a Sara Lee in the fridge," says Bill.

Bev and Trudy collect everyone's plates as Nora stares at a painting Bridget gave Bev a few years ago, which hangs on the wall beside the white hutch. The meadow behind the house in spring, all the wildflowers bursting into life.

After they've handed out pieces of poundcake, Bev and Trudy squeeze back into their seats between the table and the wall. Sophie, still in Nate's arms, wakes with a whimper, her round blue eyes darting around the room, and starts to cry. Bridget lets out a long exhale, then excuses herself to go nurse her in Nate's old bedroom.

"So, how'd you two meet?" Trudy asks Alice.

"At the movies," she says. "I'd been stood up for a date,

and Roger was there on his own. We started talking about how much we love Good & Plenties. Then he asked me to watch *Road House* with him. The movie was awful . . ."

"It wasn't *that* bad."

"It was terrible. Anyway, after that, we went out for Chinese and just talked for hours."

"I knew right away." Roger smiles at Alice. "I realized people might have something to say about the age difference. I didn't feel great about it either, at first. But there she was."

"And it was the same for me," says Alice. "He was it."

Bev thinks of Trudy. Her sleet gray eyes. Her reluctant laugh, her tiny feet.

"Sounds like the real deal to me," she says.

"Age is just a number, anyway," Trudy adds. "To hell with what other people think."

There's a clatter as Nora drops her spoon onto her plate before slumping back in her chair, arms crossed over her chest.

Bill asks Alice what she thinks about Dalton. "Must seem like the boonies compared to the big city."

"I like it here. There's so much sky. So many trees."

"Actually, we didn't just come up for the hell of it," Roger squeezes Alice's hand. "We spent all morning today looking at houses."

Murmur of excitement around the table.

"Anything promising?" asks Trudy.

"Well, there was this cute little farmhouse out in Milton Landing . . ."

"Mickey Cloutier's old place," Roger says. "The one on seventy acres, goes all the way down to the river."

"No kidding," says Nate. "That's just down the road from me and Br—"

"You told me you were just out drivin' around," Nora interrupts, glaring at her son. "You told me you were just gonna show Alice the sights."

"We wanted it to be a surprise, Ma. We didn't want to say anything until we knew for sure."

Nora's lips pinch together. "Well, you're saying somethin' now, so I guess I should assume you're serious about this *cute little* farmhouse?"

Bev wonders how Alice holds so calm and still under Nora's venomous stare. Roger's leg starts to bounce up and down.

"Yeah," he says. "We're serious. We put in an offer."

This seems awful fast to Bev. Everyone knows you shouldn't buy the first house you see. Then again, if you know about a place, you know. If you know about a person, you know. She reaches for Trudy's hand under the table.

Down the hall, Sophie continues to cry, Bridget *hush-hushing* her in a slightly off-kilter rhythm.

"What about your job?" Nora asks Roger. "You're just gonna walk away from everything at the bank and do God-knows-what for a living?"

"Christ, Ma, I hate that job."

"It just don't make no goddamn sense."

Alice lays a hand on Roger's arm as he takes in a few deep, steadying breaths.

"Nora." Alice's voice is low and even. "Roger and I both need a change. You have no idea how much he misses home. How much he misses you."

"*Tabarnak*. If he missed me, he should've acted like it. Come to visit once in a while."

Down the hall, Sophie still crying.

Roger's leg stops bouncing. "Well, I'm coming home now, Ma. I thought you'd be happy about that."

Nate and Bill wear identical expressions of discomfort—neither of them has ever been great with emotional outbursts. Under the table, Trudy's fingers squeeze against Bev's.

"You've never even been here," Nora says to Alice. "Why would you live somewhere you've never been before?"

Alice holds her gaze on Nora's. "Because," she says, "Roger means everything to me. I'd do anything for him."

The hitch in Alice's breath as she says that last word—Bev knows that sound. It's the sound she made the first time Nate took a faltering step on his block-shaped baby feet, and again eighteen years later when he walked with those same legs, suddenly so long and steady, across the stage at his high school graduation. It's the same sound Bev made when Trudy tripped over a piece of loose asphalt on one of their walks a few summers ago, landing on her ankle with a sickening crunch.

That breathless, involuntary sound—it can only be love.

* * *

After everyone has left, Bill takes an ice pack from the freezer, presses it to his lower back, and shuffles off to the living room. Trudy buttons her coat and slips on her clogs, scuffed old things she wears just as often to the grocery store as she does in her garden. Bev shoves her feet into her slippers and shrugs on her jacket. "I'll walk you out."

The icy air punches them in the throats the moment they step out onto the front porch. It's stopped snowing. Light from the kitchen spills across the white-blanketed yard like pats of melted butter.

"Nice dinner party," says Trudy.

Bev lets out a snort of laughter as she lights a cigarette. "We should make it a regular gathering."

"Well, now that they're moving up here, we can. We can do just that."

"Next time we'll go to your place. Let Richard do the cooking."

Now Tru laughs, tossing her head toward the sky, heavy with after-snow clouds. Maybe by morning those clouds will be gone. Maybe by morning the sun will be shining again.

"I like her," Trudy says. "Alice."

Bev takes a pull off her cigarette, careful to aim the smoke away from Trudy. Tendrils of smoke rise into the night. "I like her, too."

"Guess Nora can't say the same."

"Guess not."

"What do you think it is? The age thing, the no-baby thing, or the writer thing?"

"Probably all of it."

Bev stubs her cigarette against the railing and pockets the butt, knowing how Tru feels about her flicking the spent ends onto the lawn. Though they're well out of sight of the living room window and the rest of the dead-end street, Bev instinctively checks to make sure no one is looking before pulling Trudy toward her. She inhales her familiar aroma—old books and Ivory soap, hint of lavender shampoo.

"What do you think that old bat would think of you and me?" Trudy wraps her arms around Bev's waist.

Bev remembers the way Nora had said she was glad Roger wasn't one of those *bachelor* types. That inflection, that mean look in her eyes.

"Oh, that we're bound for hell, no doubt."

After all these years together, Bev's heart still cartwheels against her ribs at Tru's touch, the feel of her mouth warm and soft against her own. It was never like this with any man, not even Bill back when he was lean and long-haired and always laughing. Bev had no idea it could be like this. She followed along with what a life in Northern Maine had taught her—you grow up, marry a man, make at least one baby, work hard, pay your taxes, and don't ask too much out of life. Marriage could be about love, but (judging from her bitterly celibate parents, aunts, and uncles) it certainly wasn't about passion. Bev hadn't even thought to be bothered about any of it. Never considered there was more than that.

Until Tru.

First it was just friendship, a bond that began in spring '77. Trudy had grown up in Dalton, but Bev didn't move over from Prescott until after she and Bill were married. Between raising Nate and working at the Pines, she was too busy for much socializing. But eventually the itch for new company had grown too strong, and so she joined Trudy's book group at the library. She showed up ready to talk about a novel she hadn't had time to finish and to take advantage of the promised free refreshments.

Bev had marveled at how familiar Trudy felt as they sat there that night talking about bell bottoms and beef stew, as though the sharp-tongued librarian were a shadow self that only at that moment decided to step into the light.

She began to think about Trudy late at night, long after Nate, a teenager then, slept in his room down the hall. She thought of Tru's hair, the way the ends of it sent little electric shocks through her when the wind brushed it against her cheek. Tru's ability to coax so much life from her garden. Tru's kindness and generosity, both of which she liked to hide with sarcasm. And she thought of Tru's loyalty to Richard. A loyalty that remained, in its own way, even after Bev and Trudy shared their first kiss at that hotel down in Bangor.

It was only supposed to have been a fun girls' weekend away. Instead, Bev's entire life had burst wide open, grown bigger than she'd ever imagined possible.

Bev knows Trudy and Richard have a strained agreement about their marriage. If Bill has suspicions, he's never brought them up to Bev. They'd stopped having sex long before Trudy came into the picture, and Bev, thanks to all those phone numbers Bill had left in his pockets, knew he had slept with random women he met out on the road. They never discussed it. Because that was another thing Aroostook County had taught not only Bev, but everyone who grew up here—silence. The silent, constant guarding of one's biggest feelings, regrets, and desires.

With Tru, though, she can always say whatever she wants.

"Well, Bevy." That voice in the dark. Clear and bright. "Guess it's time I get back home."

"Mm-hmm. About that time."

Down the dead-end street, Ollie Levasseur's terrier barks and howls, barks again. Such a lonely sound. Bev and Trudy kiss again, and then once more, two bodies shivering alive together beneath the February sky.

3

COLD BLACK RIVER

Supper on Friday night is salmon and rice with slimy ribbons of zucchini. All of it in a runny white sauce Greg's mother says is supposed to taste like lemons (it doesn't).

"Yuck," says Aimee. She scrunches up her nose. "This fish smells dead."

Sarah twirls her new senior class ring on her finger, the small green stone catching the light that hangs above the round dinner table. "Every piece of meat you've ever eaten is a dead animal."

"Girls," says their father. "Stop talking about dead animals."

There's a few minutes of clinking silverware, forks on plates and teeth. The spongy pink taste of fish makes Greg's gag reflex kick in. The kitchen's too hot, all the windows steamed up like no world exists outside these same walls he's been looking at his whole life. Fourteen years of mustard yellow.

"No way this can be fresh, Mom." Sarah pries apart the salmon with her fingers. Plucks out tiny bones. "The ocean's, like, three hours away."

Their mother sighs. "It's good for you, Sarah. We could all stand to be a little healthier in this house."

Greg takes another bite, mostly to avoid looking at his sisters, who've been pissed at him ever since his new diet took away their favorite foods—spaghetti and meatballs, cheeseburgers and poutine. He imagines the feast waiting for him up in his bedroom—Charleston Chews, Oreos, cream soda that's probably gone flat by now, just the way he likes.

At Greg's physical last fall, Dr. Haskell had raised his eyebrows as he jotted down Greg's weight—a way bigger number than it had been the year before. "Are you being bullied at school?" he asked.

"I just like eating," Greg answered.

"Did someone of authority put you in a . . . vulnerable position?"

Greg wondered who'd actually tell Dr. Haskell if something messed up like that had happened to them. There was a smudge of what he hoped was ketchup on the old guy's white coat.

"Seriously," Greg said. "I just really, *really* like eating."

Then Dr. Haskell had called Greg's mother in from the waiting room to talk to her about diabetes. She stopped baking muffins and whoopie pies after that, put Greg on this stupid diet with a lot of boneless skinless chicken breast and steamed broccoli. She went through the pantry and threw out the soda, the leftover Halloween candy, even the chocolate-covered raisins. It was like a nightmare.

But his parents don't know he's been hoarding his birthday money and spending it on junk food at the Store 'N More (so long as Ruthie, who mans the cash register, keeps her word and doesn't rat him out). And they definitely don't know about the loose floorboard in his bedroom closet. Or about the flashlight he keeps in there to find his way through the pile of foil wrappers and Humpty Dumpty bags late at night.

Greg doesn't think Dr. Haskell—or anyone else—needs to know why he can't stop shoving candy bars and potato chips down his throat. He doesn't totally understand it himself. He just knows that when he's eating, the bad thoughts, the ones that tell him what he is and who he might (or might not) want to kiss quiet from a confusing roar to a numb, white buzz.

"So, Gregory." He can tell by his mother's big smile something bad's coming. Something especially maternal. "I hear you're taking Angela to Kristin Pray's ice-skating party tomorrow."

Aimee laughs. "Greggie and Angela, sittin' in a tree."

Greg glares at his mother. "How'd you hear?"

"Molly Lannigan. I saw her up at the store this afternoon."

This stupid town. All those gossipy mothers always running into each other at the Diner, the post office, the toilet paper aisle in Bergeron's.

"K-I-S-S-I-N-G . . ."

"Do we need to have The Talk again, son?" Greg's father chuckles.

"Shut up, Aimee. And Jesus, Dad, no. We're going to a stupid party together, that's all."

Greg's mother has that look on her face he's been seeing a lot lately—that Worried-My-Son's-a-Fat-Loser look. "It's been too long since you had Angela over here for supper," she says. "I should call her up, invite her for sometime next week."

"God, Mom, *no*."

Aimee giggles. "First comes LOVE, then comes MARRIAGE . . ."

"But if you're friends, why wouldn't you want to bring her here, sweetheart?"

Their father drops a piece of zucchini on the laminate floor, where it lands with a *splat* and leaves a wet trail like a slug. Aimee's dancing so hard in her seat that her blonde curls bounce as Sarah snorts with laughter and joins her to shout the last line of the song. *ANGIE WITH A BABY CARRIAGE*!

"You've got to be kidding, right?"

* * *

He lies awake that night trying to ignore the craving for chocolate, replaying it over in his mind. Angela coming up to him before English class this morning, asking him if he'd take her to the party.

"With Kristin and all those guys?" Greg had asked. "Why would you want to hang out with them?"

"They're not all bad," Angela said. "Come on. It'd be fun. Like, you know . . . a date." She glanced away from Greg, then back, eyes all bright and fluttery.

"Well," he said, looking around the classroom to make sure no one was playing some kind of joke on him. "Sure. Okay."

Other than holding hands with Lynne Bouchard on a field trip to the Prescott planetarium in sixth grade, Greg's never done anything with a girl. Thought about it, sure. He often finds himself staring at Kristin's bouncy blonde ponytail, and he wonders what size bra Denise wears under those tight sweaters. And Angela. Her waist-length black hair, those long legs . . . She and Greg have been friends since grade school, but he has wondered what it'd be like if they were more than that. He never considered asking her out, though. Figured she'd laugh at him, or worse, tell him she thinks of him as a brother and give him that same sad stare she saves for dead birds on the side of the road.

Rumor has it, Henry Covington will be at the party, too. Henry and his wavy, dark hair. Those killer blue-green eyes.

Down the hallway, Greg's father snores. Outside, the moon is bright, almost full. It would be so easy. Three steps from his bed, into the closet, under the floorboard. Anything he wants, no one would ever know . . .

Greg rolls over so his back is to the room. Squeezes his eyes shut.

* * *

All his clothes are wrong. Most of his jeans have stretchy inserts in the waistbands his mom had to sew in so he can button them closed, and his shirts could double as sacks for the potatoes he picked at Best Family Farms a couple falls ago. His blue jacket has holes under the armpits—he can't ask his parents for a new one, when they just bought this one last year. It was wicked expensive, and it was supposed to last until high school.

Maybe he could fake sick. Call Angela, tell her he has a headache or dysentery or something.

But he'd be the biggest asshole ever if he cancelled on her half an hour before she and her mom are supposed to come pick him up. He doesn't get why she's so excited—parties have never been her thing before, and definitely not parties held by Kristin Pray. But he can't bail on her. And part of him feels almost hopeful, no matter how hard he tries not to. Because maybe all those times he was looking at Angela, wondering what it'd be like to kiss her, she was looking back at him and wondering the same thing.

Maybe.

So he's waiting at the kitchen door when Angela's mom pulls into the driveway and toots her horn. He slings his skates over his shoulder and heads outside, glad no one's home to watch him hobble down the slippery driveway to the minivan. His mother took Aimee and Sarah over to the Prescott mall to buy hair scrunchies or Malibu Musk or whatever it is girls buy, and his father's down at the hardware store, selling plungers and flathead screwdrivers.

The back door of the van slides open, and Angela pokes her head out. Her hair hangs down from beneath a pink hat. She's wearing mittens, a puffy red jacket. "Hurry up!" she shouts. "It's frigging *freezing* out here."

Greg half-jumps, half-falls into the van. Cindy turns back to smile at him. Her hair's shorter than Angela's, but the same color, like raven wings.

"You two's all set back there? Let's get 'er rollin', then."

Before Greg can buckle up, she's reversing out of the driveway, whipping past his mother's frozen rose bushes. As Cindy speeds down High Street, Angela looks over at him, grins and rolls her eyes.

"Momma's a maniac."

The van's nice and warm, and it smells like smoke and something sweet—strawberries, maybe. Cindy loads a tape into the deck and a song Greg doesn't recognize begins to play—a spooky-voiced song about rivers and breathing underwater. Cindy mumbles along, taking drags off her cigarette between words.

At the blinking yellow light across from the post office, Cindy slows to let a log truck coming up Depot Hill turn onto Main. The rumble of the truck's massive tires makes the blades of Greg's skates vibrate against his lap.

"Wanted to say thanks by the way, there, Greggie."

He glances at Cindy, driving with one hand on the wheel and the other hanging out the window, flicking ashes off the end of her cigarette with a bright red fingernail. Cold air whips into the van.

"For what?"

"Hanging out with Ange today. I know how much she wanted to go to this party. But these kids that'll be there . . . only way I'd let her go was if she was with someone I can trust. Who better'n you?"

"Don't listen to Momma," Angela whispers to Greg. "She's been smoking reefer again."

He doesn't doubt this could be true. More than once while doing homework at Angela's kitchen table, they've watched her mother, red-eyed and laughing, twirl around the living room to Stevie Nicks. Cindy doesn't seem stoned now, though.

But Angela wouldn't do that. Make Greg believe this was a date just so she could go to some stupid party for some stupid classmates neither of them has ever cared about. She wouldn't do that to him.

Would she do that?

In the front seat, Cindy stubs her cigarette into the ashtray as she speeds over the double-set of railroad tracks just past the Shanty, where Greg's parents used to bring him and his sisters for milkshakes. Before the weight. Before the diet. A soft-serve blackberry twist with rainbow sprinkles—that would be perfect right now. Or a Heath bar Blizzard. Or two scoops of Gifford's mint chip, cold green sweetness filling up his mouth . . .

Cindy turns into the parking lot above the river. The picnic tables are mounded with white; the Aroostook Lodge closed until spring. All the windows of the log cabin are dark; the screen door of the porch half-hidden behind drifts of snow. As the van comes to an abrupt stop near the outhouses, Greg braces his arms against the back of the passenger seat to keep from being tossed forward.

"What d'you say?" asks Cindy. "Think I should quit pumpin' gas and be a race car driver instead? Maybe then my girl here'd finally think I was cool."

"Fat frigging chance."

"Watch that tone. And who's truck is that? I thought Kristin's ma drove a Cavalier."

"She must've parked down at the boat launch," says Angela.

"Well . . . all right. I'll pick you two's up in a couple hours. Be ready when I get here."

"Sure, Momma."

"And don't you get up to nothing stupid, Ange."

"Okay, Momma."

In his rush to get out of the van, Greg nearly loses his footing when he hops onto the crusty snow. Angela lands on the ground beside him with a graceful flourish, then slams the door closed as Cindy cranks up another song. The van lurches backward, then forward, then zooms onto the road, cutting off a Subaru in the process.

"*Maniac.*"

Following a trail cut through the snow, they head downriver. As he and Angela leave the shadow of the spruce trees, Greg hears the laughter of their classmates. Then he sees blue and green and yellow coats gliding across the iced-over river like Jolly Ranchers pinging around on a scratched mirror. Nine in all. Nearly half the class.

"Ooh." Angela claps her mittened hands together. "Everyone came! Kristin was worried it'd be too cold."

She's never talked like this before—like she and Kristin are best friends or something. She's never wanted to be in that group. *Them.* The ones who go to every pep rally and school dance, the ones always bringing home trophies for all the stupid sports teams. Greg would bet a million bucks that after high school, They'll all stay in Dalton the rest of their lives, work shitty jobs at the Store 'N More or the lumber mill.

Screw that.

Greg peers up and down the wooded shore. Other than their classmates, the only sign of life is one person a little ways down the river, a figure in a teal jacket hunched over a hole in the ice. Greg guesses the truck parked near the Lodge must belong to the guy, whoever he is. On the opposite shore, nothing but dark evergreens.

"Where's Kristin's mom?"

Angela stares at Greg with a look that's half-amusement, half-annoyance.

"We're not little kids." She plunks down on a boulder that juts out of the snow to lace up her white skates. "We don't need someone's mommy to babysit us."

Greg doesn't know what to say. He's used to her following all the rules, rolling her eyes right along with him whenever They get a medal for throwing a ball into a hoop.

Angela holds out her hands for him to pull her to her feet. "Your turn," she says, looking down toward the river. At Them, not at him.

There's a sudden empty feeling in the bottom of his belly, the same sensation he had that time he missed a step on the cellar stairs and fell down to the damp cement floor.

"I think I'll wait a bit," he says. "You go on ahead."

"Get your ass *out here*, Muse!" Henry shouts from the ice, waving his arms. Black jacket half-zipped. No hat, no mittens. Too cool to feel cold.

Angela makes a weird breathless sound like she's forgotten how to laugh. She grins, then turns back to Greg.

"Really," he says, "it's all right."

He's falling down those cellar steps all over again. Cold, empty belly. Face to the ground. Splat.

After Angela runs off down the shore, Greg chucks his skates to the ground, where they make a *thudding* sound in the snow. He lowers himself onto the same boulder she sat on to tie her skates and loosens the laces on his right boot, which he tied too tightly as he was waiting for her and Cindy to pick him up.

Downriver, the fishing guy stands, stretches, then settles back on his camp chair, bright orange flag of his tip-up rig pointed down at the dark hole in the ice.

Greg's stomach groans. He lets himself imagine everything he wants right now. Poutine drenched in gravy. Pepperoni pizza with extra cheese. Fresh-made ployes covered with melting butter and real maple syrup.

Down on the ice, Jessica pulls Ben into her arms. Ben clamps his mouth on hers, hands tangled in her curly red hair.

Greg looks away, up to the bare branches of a maple tree where a chickadee chirps. What would it be like to kiss someone like that? No shame, no worry about who might be watching. What it would be like to kiss Angela?

What would it be like to kiss Henry?

Carrot cake with cream cheese frosting. Gingerbread with lemon glaze.

Henry starts to skate toward shore.

"Where you going, Covington?" Ethan shouts.

"Gotta take a leak."

Henry rests on a snowbank at the edge of the river to take off his skates and pull on a pair of boots. As he nears Greg, the wind gusts, carrying with it the smell of spruce and Irish Spring. Winter and Henry.

"What's up, Fortin?"

"Nothin' much," Greg says. He feels stupid, cold, hungry, huge.

Henry plops down on a smaller rock beside him. He shakes his dark waves out of his face.

"Skating not your thing?"

"Not so much."

Up in the maple tree, a second chickadee lands beside the first. Clouds are rolling in fast and thick. Tiny white flakes start to float down.

"Well, you're not missing much." Henry glances at the river, where everyone's playing crack the whip, Angela flying off the end of the line, long black hair streaming out behind her. "Tell you the truth, Fortin, I've kinda been dreading this party."

"But they're your friends."

"That doesn't mean I like them all the time. You know how it is."

Greg doesn't know. "Sure."

"I mean, what the hell was Kristin smoking when she came up with this idea? When's the last time you went *ice* skating?"

"I think I was eight," says Greg. "My older sister pushed me in the snowbank and told me it was covered in dog piss."

"Shit."

"No, just the piss, I think."

The joke flies out before Greg can think about it. Henry claps his hand on Greg's shoulder, his long fingers nearly touching Greg's neck, and laughs so loud everyone on the ice glances up at the shore. Loud enough even the person downriver looks toward them—all Greg can see from here is a pale oval face. Long legs sprawled out from the camp chair.

"Ooh, look at the homos!" Ethan points at Greg and Henry and makes a jacking-off motion. CJ and Marc join in.

"Coupla queers!"

"Faggots!"

All of Them laugh. Even Angela. Greg sees her glance at Kristin, as if seeking approval. And then she looks toward Henry and grins, and Henry drops his hand from Greg's shoulder and grins right back at her.

Greg finally understands.

It was a couple weeks ago. Henry broke up with Missy Cyr during lunch, after a big blow-out that ended with Missy in tears and Henry handing back the tacky gold necklace she'd made him wear for the three months they'd been together. There were rumors Henry was sneaking around with some other girl, though no one knew who. Greg and Angela had watched the whole thing from their table near the vending machines, Angela hiding a strange, secret smile as Henry walked away from Missy, whose sobs rippled through the cafeteria like floodwater.

Chocolate. That's what Greg needs right now. Scotcharoos. Brownies (all edge pieces, no nuts). Cocoa Puffs.

Henry flicks the bird to his friends, then shouts at them to get bent.

Looking back at Greg, Henry laughs. "See what I mean? They're assholes."

"Why waste your time with them, then?"

Right away, Greg knows he's broken some unwritten rule—
Thou Shalt Not Question One of Them.

Henry's smile disappears. "I don't know, man. But it sure as hell beats sitting alone on a rock."

Before Greg can answer, there's a sharp, icy-cold *CRACK* in the air, loud as a gunshot. There's a scream. More screams.

Everything after that moves fast and slow and all at once, the same kind of time-warp Greg usually only feels in dreams.

All of Them stand around yelling, arguing about what to do while Angela clings to the jagged ledge of ice left over from where she fell through. Screaming.

Greg and Henry stand, but Henry doesn't move toward the river. Greg's boot is still unlaced. No time to lace it back up so he kicks it off, races down the snowy slope with one booted foot, one wrapped only in a thin wool sock. His jacket's too heavy, he unzips it, tosses it behind him as he lurches down the bank. He's vaguely aware he can't see the ice fishing guy anymore, but it doesn't matter, because he can't see Them anymore either. Just Angela. Angela's arms, her red jacket, locked onto the shelf of ice. Angela's round white face above the black river.

Greg hurls himself to his hands and knees. Tests the ice near the shore. It creaks and groans, but it holds. He slow-creeps on his belly over the frozen river, the bone-white cold pulsing up through his sweater, his jeans. Angela's eyes are big dark circles, getting closer with each awkward sweep of Greg's arms and legs. Doggy paddle on ice.

Angela's hat is gone, swept under, and her hair swirls in the current that wants to pull her under, too, under the ice and out of Dalton, through the woods, past the potato fields and broccoli fields outside Prescott, up into Caribou, down into Fort Fairfield, across the border and into Canada. Dump her in the Saint John, where no one will ever find her body.

Somewhere behind him, people shout. Snow falls.

After a minute, or a year, Greg reaches Angela. He tries to

take her hands, but her skin's too slippery; the current too strong. She loses her grip. Slips away screaming. Greg pitches forward, submerging his arms in the water to grab her. The black river roars, he never knew a river under ice could be so loud, never imagined there might be all that power there, hidden from the sky. Freezing spray burns his cheeks, lips, nose. Beneath the water, his hands find Angela's belt, and she's screeching in his ear, and the river is so loud, and those birds won't shut up, and why is it so fucking *cold*, until finally he manages to tug Angela onto the ice, wriggling backward to get as far from the water as possible.

He stares up at the big white bowl of sky. Beside him, Angela sobs. Her teeth chatter so hard he worries they might break. Greg wills himself to ignore the razor-like chills shooting up and down his arms.

"Go, Angie."

But she just lies there and cries. His heart is squeezing too hard, too fast. Every inhale hurts. He can't feel his hands. He can't feel his arms. The ice rocks beneath them.

More shouts, and Greg turns his face to see the tall figure from downriver, the failed fisherman, running down the shore. He throws himself onto his stomach at the river's edge, then swims across the ice just as Greg had done.

"Don't move!" the man yells. "Everything's gonna be fine. Just hold tight."

Greg's never heard someone shout and yet sound so relaxed at the same time. Didn't even know it could be possible. Two different things at once—fear and calm. Command and comfort.

As the man gets closer, Greg recognizes him. Nate Theroux. He's not that much older than Greg—ten years, maybe—and he's not like some of the other cops in town, all sharp-eyed and swaggery, like the guys in those lame cowboy movies Greg's father likes to watch.

"Come on," Nate says to Angela, in the same voice he might use to chat up the white-haired ladies the Diner. "Take my arm."

Angela's lips are the color of grape juice, and she's still crying, but that calm voice must work some kind of magic, because she nods at Nate and rolls onto her belly, links her elbow through his.

Nate flicks his eyes over at Greg, quick but sure. "You're okay," he says. "I'll be right back for you, bub."

Snow falls. River roars. The chickadees jabber away, almost like they're laughing. Or maybe it's Them laughing. Laughing at Greg. He's suddenly aware of how gigantic he must look, sprawled here on the ice in his lumpy gray sweater, swollen with water. A beached whale. Too heavy to drag himself to land.

What a pathetic way to die.

More shouts from the shore, where They're all standing around in their Jolly-Rancher jackets, and Greg watches Nate scooping up Angela in his arms like she's a baby, carrying her up to the boulder where Henry still sits. Nate sets Angela gently down beside Henry, who takes off his coat and wraps it around her, rubbing his hands up and down her arms, pushing wet, dark ropes of hair out of her face. Angela's hands clench around Henry's shoulders, bunching up the fabric of his sweatshirt.

"Hang on out there, bub!"

Nate runs back to the river, starts to crawl across the ice. His eyes move closer, two big blue circles inching their way toward Greg. And all Greg can think about is how much Nate looks like Gumby in that teal jacket, with those gangly legs and arms spread out flat on the silvery-white ice.

What a weird way to be rescued.

* * *

First there's the speedy twenty-minute drive from Dalton to

Prescott in Nate's truck with the heater going full-blast, then there's the drama at the hospital. Nate herds Greg and Angela into the bleach-smelling building, makes a big scene about needing help right away, even though it's not like the ER is overrun with sick people. The only other patient is a bored-looking lady lying across two orange chairs, reading a month-old *TV Guide* with Connie Chung and Maury Povich on the cover, staring at each other all lovey-dovey.

The doctors say they will be fine. Mild hypothermia, little bit of shock, back to school in a few days.

"Only fourteen years old, can you believe it?" Nate says to every nurse who walks into the curtained-off section of the ER where Greg and Angela sit wrapped in tinfoil blankets that crinkle whenever they move. "Didn't think twice, just went in after her."

"Don't you have to get back to town?" Greg asks Nate after yet another gray-haired nurse beams at him and pats him on the head. "Pull over some drunks or something?"

"Not on duty today," Nate says. "I called your folks, told them I'd stay here with you."

When Cindy shows up, her eye makeup's smudged, big hands all shaky. "You stupid girl," she says to Angela, who lies on the cot next to Greg's. "What the hell were you thinkin'? You stupid, beautiful girl. Christ, Ange, I love you. And you."

She turns to Greg and throws her arms around him, wrapping him up in that smell of smoke and strawberries.

"If you wasn't there," she keeps crying. "Christ, if you wasn't there . . . Did you thank him, Ange? You better thank him."

"Thanks," Angela mumbles in a small voice. She stares at the tiny TV mounted on the wall, set on a muted episode of *Cops*. On the ride over, she hadn't looked at Greg or said a word to him or Nate.

Then there's all the fuss once Greg's parents get to the hospital. His mother won't stop rubbing his hair while his father paces at the front desk, asking the secretary when they should expect the bill. Nate only leaves after promising to check in on Greg and Angela the next day.

Finally, Greg's discharged. He says goodbye to Cindy and Angela, who still won't look at him. The drive to Dalton is slow. Greg's mother keeps turning back to look at him from the passenger seat. His father jabs at the radio dial until he lands on a country station playing Garth Brooks.

At home, Greg's mother settles him on the couch under an old afghan and hovers around him like a mosquito on speed—should she throw his socks in the dryer? Does he want to watch *MacGyver*? Is he hungry?

And his sisters. God, his sisters. Why does he have to have sisters?

"So you're, like, a big deal now," Sarah says. "You want us to build you a shrine or something?"

"You won't even go *swimming* with me at camp," says Aimee. "I guess you just don't even love me at all."

His mother brings a plate to Greg. Kraft mac and cheese with cut-up hotdogs. He didn't even know she still had any of the stuff for it. Figured she'd thrown it all away in the big purge.

"What about the diet?"

"Oh, don't worry about that. You just eat up."

His parents sit on either side of him on the couch, his father clicking through channels so fast the room flickers white and blue, his mother staring at him with big wet eyes while he picks at the food.

"Would you rather have something else?" she asks. "I could order a pizza."

"I'm not hungry," Greg says. "Just tired."

"Of course, sweetheart. You go up to bed. I'll check in on you in a bit."

"He's not seven, Cheryl." Greg's father's voice is low and soft. "Leave him alone."

As he walks up the stairs, Greg feels heavier than usual. Waterlogged.

In his room, Greg locks the door behind him. Posters of the periodic table and Indiana Jones taped all over the pale blue walls. Green bedspread. Lampshade that always sits a little crooked no matter how many times he tries to fix it. Smell of armpit sweat, laundry soap. Everything familiar.

Greg stares at the closet door, half-closed. Cindy's songs are still playing in his mind. His stomach groans. His mouth fills with spit. He doesn't want to. He won't. He can't.

In four steps, Greg is across the room and kneeling inside his closet, prying up the loose floorboard. He bends forward and thrusts his hands into the dark hatch, feeling smooth, cool foil wrappers and crinkly chip bags and chunky candy bars pour through his fingers. Treasure. Scooping up everything he can, Greg collapses backward, his spine crashing against the stupid broken umbrella he never remembers to throw into the back of his father's truck on Dump Day.

Henry and Angela.

Angela and Henry.

He doesn't know who he envies most. Henry, for getting to run his hands through Angela's long, dark hair; or Angela, for getting to press against Henry's body, fall deep in those blue-green eyes.

Wanting both—what does that make him? Something as simple as the words those guys used at the river today? Homo. Queer. Faggot. Or something worse? Something so freakish it doesn't even have a name?

Greg sits in the dark and starts unwrapping everything, shoving it all in his mouth. Chocolate smears on his chin. His teeth grind up cookies, candy, chips, everything all at once. Washes it down with sucking gulps of cream soda. He doesn't taste any of it, just keeps shoving it in, forcing it down until his stomach cramps and he has to fight the impulse to puke, has to swallow that down, too.

The way Henry smells—sharp and clean and green. The way Angela smiles—little dimple, glittery eyes.

Greg scoops up more food.

On and on it goes.

4.
ROMANCE

O n a rainy morning in April, as Rose cooks breakfast and tries to remember how long it took to get the results back the last time she was knocked up, Tommy steps into the kitchen, the linoleum creaking beneath his feet. The thin muscles at the front of Rose's throat tense when he wraps his arms around her waist.

"Brandon wet the bed again."

She unwraps two squares of orange cheese and throws them on top of the eggs. Butter sizzles in the cast-iron pan, bought for fifty cents from the thrift shop behind the Catholic church just before Brandon was born two years ago.

"You didn't make him feel shitty about it, did you?" she asks. "He's been trying real hard with potty training, you know."

"I told him it was all right." Tommy brushes a strand of Rose's dark hair behind her ear. "I told him his brother used to do the same thing."

The smell of scorched egg fills the cramped room. "We got to fix this damn stove. It either doesn't cook at all or it burns everything. And you shouldn't've said that to Brandon. You know how Adam gets."

Tommy doesn't really know, though. He doesn't see what Rose sees, the way Adam lords his older-brother privilege over Brandon. The way Adam gets so angry at the littlest, stupidest things. Just like his father.

Tommy's grip on Rose tightens, and she braces herself

for an accusation that the boys' bed wetting is somehow her fault.

But he spins her around in his arms so that she's facing him, and gazes down at her with a look she hasn't seen in ages. There's something soft in his face, unguarded, and she remembers now how beautiful his hazel eyes can be when he smiles.

"I think I need to take you on a date," he says. "Tonight, at the Tavern. Or we could drive over to Prescott, go to Luigi's."

Rose can't remember the last time she and Tommy went out. It might've been a year ago, somewhere between Adam's fourth birthday and Easter. Or maybe it was last summer, around the time they discovered Brandon was allergic to strawberries.

"It's awful short notice." She sprinkles salt over the eggs before setting the plates down on the little yellow table where the boys eat all their meals. "I don't know if Ma'd be able to watch the kids."

"I could always get Stacey to do it."

The last time Tommy's cousin had babysat for them, Rose came home to a disaster zone—flour sprinkled like snow over every surface of the kitchen, Brandon's face sticky with syrup, Adam shouting his new favorite four-letter word for hours after Stacey had slunk off into the night.

"I'll call Ma."

"That's what I thought."

* * *

After Tommy's left for the shop and she has talked with her mother, Rose sets Adam and Brandon up in front of the TV and dashes off to take a shower. Standing there in the mango-scented steam, she feels so giddy about her and Tommy's date that she's nearly lightheaded. She takes extra care to shave around her bikini line.

It used to be like this all the time, back when Rose was a

sophomore and Tommy a senior at Dalton High. She was crazy for him, crazy for everything he did. That leather jacket he wore, and the El Camino he drove for a while, until he drank a few too many Boone's Farms and rolled the car into a field out on Route 11. And the way Tommy used to look at Rose back then, like she was the only girl in the world and he was going to have her whether she liked it or not. God, she'd loved that feeling.

She drops the boys off at Marie Robichaud's house, where half a dozen kids under the age of five run around a room filled with plastic toys, and then Rose drives to work. She's so busy planning what she'll wear tonight that she almost clips one of the parked police cruisers as she pulls into her usual space.

Rose settles in at the front desk of the Dalton police station, notepad ready beside the phone, and takes her library book from her purse. The cover features a corseted princess clinging to a bare-chested stable boy. The Chief emerges from his office, a room crowded with a metal desk whose drawers rattle each time he reaches in for his bottle of Maalox.

"Morning, Ro."

"Morning, Peter. Got a fresh pot of decaf brewing for you."

He rubs his gaunt stomach and suppresses a burp. "Think I'll pass. Ulcer's acting up again."

She likes Peter. He doesn't mind that she doesn't have a diploma, or that she dropped out of school to have Adam when she was sixteen. But she's tired of hearing about his digestive tract, tired of running to the Store 'N More to buy him Rolaids and ginger ale.

"Pretty quiet day so far," Peter says. "Dyer's hoping to catch some speeders out on Poor Man's Road. Rossignol got called to a fender bender up at Bergeron's."

"Anything serious?"

"Helen McGreevy hit the gas instead of the brake, smashed up a couple shopping carts."

Rose, who spent second grade cowering under the angry

glare of Ms. McGreevy, can't help but smile. Serves that old hag right.

It's not until Peter's almost back inside his office that she musters up the courage to ask what she's been dying to know since she walked into the building.

"Where's Nate this morning?"

Peter pauses in the doorway. "Theroux's taking some time off," he says. "Bridget's not doing so well."

"Oh?"

"Guess the weather's got her down or something. Or, I don't know. Something with the baby." Peter holds back another burp. "Anyway, I told Theroux to stay home the next few days. Take care of her and Sophie."

Rose's good mood drops off fast. She'd wanted to brag to Nate about Tommy's romantic gesture. Ever since she started working at the station last summer, just after Nate came on as a rookie, he's been squirrely about Tommy. Rose guesses this is her fault—it'd been too damn hot one August morning to wear long sleeves, and Nate had spotted an orange-green bruise on her forearm. Rose had lied, said Adam got a little too rough while they were playing with his Tonka trucks. Nate's watched her close ever since then. It's been worse since the beginning of the year, when Rose took a week off from work after Tommy gave her a black eye. She told the Chief the boys had the chickenpox that week, and he didn't question it. But when she came back to work (bruises covered skillfully with makeup), Nate seemed to look at her even softer than usual, with that little glint of pity that made Rose feel almost as sick as she'd felt when Tommy knocked his fist against her face.

It'd be embarrassing enough to have Nate know that she lets Tommy smack her around. But what makes it all so much worse is that whenever Rose sees Nate, she feels her heart flicker against her ribcage. And when he smiles at her—God, when Nate smiles with his whole face lit up, his eyes all bright . . . She isn't sure what it is. He's handsome but not *that* handsome. He's smart but, as Rose's mother would say, a bit too simple, a bit too soft. But maybe it's exactly that softness that makes Rose dizzy. Or hell, maybe it's just those blue eyes. Whatever it is, in those moments when Nate grins at her, Rose would do just about anything to fling her arms around him and press her lips against his neck.

She guesses it's the same way Nate must feel about his wife.

* * *

The last of the rain clouds have blown off to the west by the time Rose and Tommy climb into his truck and wave goodbye to the kids, who stand on the cement slab outside the trailer, one on either side of Rose's mother (too skinny, and looking so old with that cigarette hanging out of her mouth). As Tommy heads onto Prescott Road, the evening sun paints the forest and the fields in pretty shades of purple and orange.

She feels self-conscious in her blue dress, which she bought last year from the thrift shop on a whim. Back then, she'd liked it because the color reminded her of the forget-me-nots that used to grow in big clumps behind the double-wide where she grew up out in Barren. But now she worries the dress and kitten heels are way too much for a night at Luigi's, the restaurant attached to the Crown Hotel. Despite its name, the hotel isn't fancy—just a four-story brick building stuck like an afterthought in the middle of the fields that surround Prescott, out near the Tractor Supply and the place that sells waterbeds.

"I'm too dressed up."

Tommy's gaze shifts from the road to the curves of Rose's body. "You're sexy as hell."

Faint nausea rolls through her for the rest of the ride, which is accompanied by a set of hits from Poison and ZZ Top. The queasiness, as well as this vague sense of dread that makes her bones feel weighed down with wet sand, had marked her other two pregnancies. A sense that something terrible is about to happen, something Rose can't predict or control, haunts her. It's an irritating ghost to carry around, especially on a night when Tommy's trying so hard to make her feel special.

Tommy never hit Rose when she was pregnant with Adam or Brandon. Never laid one finger on her, except to rub her feet whenever she told him she felt sick. Sometimes she'd be fine but would lie and say she had a headache or the pukes, just to feel Tommy's fingers squeeze against her toes. Once, when she was pregnant the first time, Tommy placed his hands on Rose's giant belly and called her a goddess. He'd never used that word before. Hasn't used it since. But she still thinks about it some-times, especially when he's out drinking at Frenchie's and the kids are asleep and she can curl up in bed with her novels and her little pink vibrator, which she stole from Tommy's cousin's bachelorette party last summer.

In the half-full parking lot of the hotel, Tommy parks the truck so it's straddling two spots. Rose is surprised when he tells her to stay put until he can hop out, run around the truck, and open her door for her, something he hasn't done since his senior prom. He holds her elbow as she slides down from the cab. It's warm for April in Northern Maine, almost fifty degrees even with the sun mostly sunk below the wooded horizon. The air smells like mud, wet grass, and the faint tang of manure from the cow farm down the road.

With Tommy's strong hand on her arm, Rose feels brave and beautiful, just as she'd felt under the orange lights of the high school gym as they slow-danced to Pink Floyd. All those jealous girls had watched, had curled their lips in Rose's direction, an-gry they couldn't have what she'd managed to claim as her own. Tommy was attractive then and still is now. She stands a little taller when he lands a soft kiss on her lips.

"Let's go through the front," she says as he heads for the side entrance that will take them directly into the restaurant.

"Thought you said this hotel is tacky."

"Still nicer than any place we'll ever stay."

The hotel lobby has high ceilings. On one end of the room is a stone fireplace, decorated with a moose head whose black glass eyes gaze toward the reception desk, where a tired look-ing woman sits reading a *Bangor Daily*. Most of the walls are painted dark green, but there's one wall of knotty pine, covered in stuffed deer heads, antlers, and maps of Aroostook County. Plush blue carpeting silences their footsteps.

In the restaurant, a chubby teenage hostess seats them at a window that overlooks the broccoli fields behind the hotel. In the distance, Rose can see the low silhouette of Marston Hill, where a radio tower blinks its red light every few seconds.

Sitting across from Tommy, without the kids to distract them, Rose realizes she has no idea what to say. He's wearing black jeans and a gray shirt that draws attention to his muscled biceps. He smells like his favorite cologne, which Rose buys for him each Christmas from the K-Mart at the Aroostook Centre Mall. The musky aroma reminds her of the night they made Adam. Five blurry, drunken minutes in the bed of Tommy's El Camino under the blue stars, and Rose carried the scent of his cologne around the rest of the night and into the next morning, when she woke up on her mother's plaid couch and realized she'd forgotten to make him wear a condom.

"Think they still have those breadsticks you like?" Tommy asks.

"It was garlic bread."

"It wasn't garlic bread."

Rose remembers the night Tommy's talking about. She has vivid memories about that bread, dripping butter and flecked with green seasoning.

"You're right," she lies. "Now that I think about it, I guess it was breadsticks."

Their waitress's painted-on eyebrows are crooked, one higher than the other. A nametag on her maroon shirt reads *Fran*. She takes their drink orders—beer for Tommy, Diet Coke for Rose—then sets two menus on the table. "Chicken alfredo's half-off tonight. I'll be back around with a basket of our famous garlic bread."

"Maybe they gave us breadsticks on special that last time," Rose tells Tommy after the waitress is gone.

"Must've," he says, and lights a cigarette.

Rose, who's always hated the smell of Tommy's Pall Malls, lays a hand on her stomach as he exhales a cloud of smoke.

"Shit." He stubs the cigarette out on the edge of the table. "Forgot for a minute. You still haven't heard from the doc?"

"Not yet."

His jaw tightens. "I should call. Complain about how long it takes to hear back about a damn piss test."

The idea of Tommy yelling at Dr. Haskell fills Rose with the same sense of shame she felt that time she lied and said it was the dog that broke her mother's favorite porcelain butterfly. She can still hear the sad howls Patches made all night after her mother locked the dog outside in the cold as punishment.

"I'm sure Dr. H will call soon," she tells Tommy.

Fran returns to take their order. Rose says nothing when Tommy asks for shrimp scampi, though she wonders just how fresh any kind of seafood could be when the sea is three hours south of here.

As the last of the light on the fields outside is replaced by dim gray shadow, Rose looks around the restaurant. In the big corner booth is a mom, a dad, and three little kids who bounce around and blow their straw wrappers at one another. All of them laughing.

Rose watches the dad, a scrawny man with a combover, lean

toward his wife. He pours more wine into her glass and whispers something in her ear. The woman giggles, a sound like a little bell.

"What's the matter with you?" Tommy asks around a mouthful of bread. "You look like you got a hair across your ass."

"Just listen to those kids screech like that," Rose says. "You'd think their parents would teach them some manners. This is supposed to be a nice place."

Fran comes back with the food, more garlic bread, and another beer for Tommy. Rose's chicken is bland, the alfredo sauce a clumpy texture that reminds her of wallpaper glue, or bad tapioca pudding.

"How is it?" asks Tommy.

"Perfect," she says.

She should be glad to be here. But that feeling of dread she's carried the past couple days keeps nagging at her.

"You think the kids are okay?"

"I'm sure they're fine. Your Ma can handle them."

"Adam's been so mean lately. Did I tell you what he did the other day?" Rose twirls her fork through her pasta. "Brandon was sitting there watching *Inspector Gadget* and Adam just ran up for no good reason and started pinching his leg. It took me forever to get Brandon to stop crying."

"Boys get rough sometimes. Brandon needs to toughen up a bit."

Before she can answer, she hears a familiar voice beside her.

"Ro?"

God, that voice. She can't count how many times she's given that voice, deeply masculine and yet so soft, to the kilted warriors in her paperback novels. She turns to see Nate Theroux standing next to the booth. He looks nicer than Tommy, in actual dress pants rather than jeans, and a forest green shirt that buttons at the cuffs as well as down the middle. His eyes are the color of Portman Lake in summer.

"Guess we all had a hankering for food that's not deep fried," Nate laughs.

Tommy stares at him with the same expression he reserves for the spiders that lurk in the cobwebbed corners of the trailer's bathroom. He and Nate were only a grade apart in school, and Rose has heard all about how much of a suck-up Nate was—a goody-goody who never drank or smoked and who made you feel like a piece of shit if you did. "Guy never even went to a pit party," Tommy once said. "Who lives around here and never goes to a fucking pit party? Fucking pussies, that's who."

"Nate," says Rose, blotting her lips with a heavy cloth napkin and doing her best to appear unrattled by his sudden presence. He smells like sun-warmed cedar. "What're you doing here?"

"Bridget and I decided to be impulsive and stay here tonight."

"Stay?"

"At the hotel."

Tommy scrapes his fork against his plate.

"I thought Bridget could use a change of scenery," Nate says. "She's just so tired all the time, you know, since the baby. My mother offered to watch Sophie for the night, so here we are."

He grins as he watches Bridget emerge from the bathroom across the restaurant and walk toward them. Her strawberry-blonde hair is pushed into a lopsided bun, and her cardigan can't hide the fact that her pink dress is way too big in the chest. Rose doubts Bridget can feed that baby of theirs with tits like that, small as a fifth-grade girl's little buds.

"Hello, Rose." Bridget smiles, but her voice is flat. "Hi, Tommy."

"You about ready to go upstairs, sweetheart?" Nate slips his arm around Bridget's waist.

"You're not eating here?" Rose can sense Tommy's hard gaze boring into the side of her neck. She continues to look at Nate.

"We just came down to grab a drink at the bar. We'll prob-ably order room service," Nate says. "Watch TV and go to bed early."

An image of their room splashes across Rose's mind. Plush carpet. Drapes with gold tassels. A king-sized bed with clean white sheets. She tries not to picture Nate and Bridget lying to-gether on that bed. But she sees it anyway, vivid as the scenes in her books—Nate's hands against her pale skin; her hair spilled across the pillowcase. Nate pulling away from her just long enough to look up and ask, in an awed whisper, *What should I do with you next?*

"I'll see you at the station on Monday, Ro." Nate's eyes flick over to Tommy, who tosses back the last of his beer. "See you around, man. Let Rose here drive home, yeah?"

She can sense the same anger pulsing off Tommy as that night in December when she had asked him, in the middle of doing laundry, where the big roll of cash in his oil-stained jeans had come from. There were rumors around town. Something about a shady side business Tommy was running out of his uncle's autobody shop. *Is it really drugs?* she asked, and then Tommy's fist had smashed against her cheekbone so hard she puked all over the stack of freshly folded towels.

"Don't worry," she tells Nate. "No drunk drivers here."

There's an unfamiliar faint blue fire in Nate's eyes, and Rose's stomach clenches as she wonders what exactly he is thinking as he stares at Tommy. Then Bridget tugs on Nate's hand, and his smile returns.

"Right. We're going to turn in. You two take care."

"Nice to see you both." Bridget sounds even less enthusiastic than before, and she's looking away from Rose and Tommy, to-ward the door that will lead her and Nate back out to the lobby, the giant staircase, the room with a bed sized for romance.

Rose and Tommy don't speak again until Fran comes back around to ask what they want for dessert.

"Just the check," says Tommy.

Fran hands him the receipt, but before she can walk away, he slams his hand down on the table, making his empty beer bottles shiver against the silverware.

"This ain't right."

"What seems to be the problem?" Fran's voice is friendly, but Rose, who served cranky old people breakfast at the Dalton Diner for a few months when she was a teenager, recognizes the irritated look behind the waitress's eyes.

"Thought the garlic bread was free."

"The *first* basket was free."

"That's a load of bullshit."

"I'm sorry, sir. Would you like me to get the manager?"

"Do whatever the hell you want. I ain't paying for it."

Fran heads off toward a door marked *Employees Only.* Before she's even out of sight, Tommy is grabbing Rose by the elbow, pulling her out of the booth. She tries to reach into her purse, where she always keeps a spare twenty in case of emergencies, but Tommy tightens his grip on her arm, his fingers digging into her flesh so hard she knows there'll be five cherry-sized bruises tomorrow.

"Don't even think about leaving money for that bitch."

Rose has no choice but to let him steer her out of the restaurant, right past the table with the big family. She catches a glimpse of the mother shaking her head, the father half-rising from the booth before the wife lays her hand on his.

"Not our circus," Rose hears the woman mutter to her husband.

* * *

It happens a little over halfway back to Dalton, in that lonely stretch after Haystack where the woods crowd up to the potholed asphalt and unseen animals slink between the trees.

Tommy is speeding, not saying a word, and suddenly the front passenger tire blows. With the windows down, the sound is like a firecracker.

"Jack's in the bed," Tommy says as he pulls over to the side of the road. "Spare tire, too."

Several moments pass before Rose understands that he expects her to get out and fix it. She stares at him, sitting in the reddish glow from the dashboard.

"It's dark out there."

"Only getting darker."

She clutches the ratty seatbelt, gripping it until her knuckles ache. What will he do if she refuses to get out of the truck?

"There could be bears."

"Prob'ly not."

Rose touches her hands to her stomach, feeling the gauzy material of her dress against her fingertips. "Stress can't be good for me right now, Tommy. I should really take it easy until we know for sure."

He turns up the radio. Lights a cigarette.

The lug nuts are rusty, and it takes all of Rose's strength to pry them free. As she pushes the flat tire down the muddy embankment, an 18-wheeler rattles past, its headlights flooding the cab of the truck and giving her a perfect view of Tommy. She's stunned by how small he looks, like a little kid playing grown-up behind the wheel of his father's pickup. He pinches his mouth in the same shape Adam does whenever Brandon steals his Legos, a shape that reminds Rose of a cat's puckered asshole.

She hefts the donut into place, then rests, leaning against the side of the truck even though she knows the mud will ruin her dress. She thinks of Nate and Bridget and their brand-new baby, who's dressed in yellow or green each time Nate brings her around to the police station. "Look at my little Sophie," he coos, and holds the baby up like a trophy. Rose has never thought the kid is cute—babies with so much red hair freak her out—but she loves to see Nate like that, so happy with his first and only daughter, so seemingly unaware of all that could happen to her. Rose wonders if one day Sophie Theroux will meet a guy like Tommy. Fall in love. Open her freckled thighs and put an end to all the dreams her father has for her.

Rose met her own father only once, when she was eight. He showed up to have coffee with her mother. He was thin with dark hair that brushed against his shoulders, and he had ears that reminded Rose of mashed cauliflower. He gave her a straw hat patterned with pink daisies. "Pretty hat for a pretty girl," he said. It rested so low on her forehead that she had to tilt her neck back to see him. "It don't fit," she told the man who was her father, and then he and her mother disappeared into the bedroom off the kitchen, and Rose fell asleep on the couch waiting for them to finish making their animal noises. When she woke up in the morning, her father was gone. Her mother hung the hat on the fake-wood paneled wall, where it stayed until Rose ripped it down when she was fourteen, not long after she gave out her first blow job under the bleachers at MacGregor Field.

"What the fuck's taking so long out there?"

"Almost done," Rose hollers.

It was important to Rose to give her kids a family with parents who lived together, and so she pushed Tommy to propose as soon as she found out she was pregnant the first time. He was sweet, even saved up his money and bought her a gold-plated ring with a pear-shaped diamond that glints if she holds her hand just right beneath the sun. "Soon," he says whenever she asks to set a wedding date. "Real soon, baby."

Rose twists the last of the lug nuts in place, then carries the tools to the back of the truck. As she does, an unmistakable cramp twists in her lower belly. Ever since she started taking the pill after Brandon came along, her period has been predictable almost down to the hour. The queasiness, the low-hanging dread she's been feeling all night—both signs of pregnancy, but also of PMS, as familiar to Rose as the sour reek of her own breath every morning. She had told Tommy she was waiting for Dr. Haskell to give her the results on a pregnancy test she hadn't taken at an appointment she'd never made.

She just thought it might be nice, even for a few days, to have Tommy look at her like he used to, rub her feet and sit around with her dreaming up baby names and listening to her ideas for an autumn wedding. Sunflowers for her bouquet, Bryan Adams for their first dance.

"If we're not back soon your Ma'll give the kids a bottle of brandy to get them to sleep," Tommy shouts.

Another vehicle approaches, headed east, away from Dalton. Rose squints in the yellow glare from the Subaru's headlights and wonders who might be behind the wheel. A crusty old lady, most likely. Or maybe it's a man about Rose's age, or a little older, with a clean face and a wide smile. Maybe he smells like evergreens. He likes to read, and he dreams of riding horses across a faraway land where mountains rise up like the shoulders of giants. And he's kind, Rose is sure of that, with hands that would never leave bruises that bloom like weeping purple flowers across a girl's skin.

The Subaru slows. She imagines the man in the driver's seat staring at her, standing here in her ruined dress, hair tangled around her face. She must look tragic. Or beautiful. She leans against the truck, thrilled to feel the vibration of the motor against the back of her legs. The Subaru's headlights are bright, but Rose doesn't mind; she likes it, the way that warm light fills her vision and blocks out everything else around her.

Just when Rose thinks the Subaru is going to pull over and that she'll catch a glimpse of the man behind the wheel (he'll have nice teeth, straight and clean), the vehicle speeds up and hurtles on. Pebbles fly up in the car's wake and smack against her bare calves. She watches as the brake lights grow smaller and smaller, until the dark night swallows them whole as if they were never there in the first place.

"Rose!" Tommy's voice is jarring as a shotgun blast. "Get your ass in the truck."

All the way back to Dalton, she thinks about that car. She's sure the driver won't end his journey in Prescott. He's meant for someplace better than here. Within the next hour, that man will reach Houlton, and then he'll have a choice—keep on going east and cross the border into Canada, or head straight for I-95, where the road leads south. Away from the County, away from this state, into the vast unknown that opens up to become the rest of the world.

Of course, Rose must admit to herself as Tommy parks outside their trailer and she sees her boys press their jelly-stained faces against the window, the driver of the Subaru could make another choice once he gets to Houlton. He could continue north. Trace the periphery of Maine and wind all the way back into Allagash, where he might ditch the car, disappear into the forest, and never return. But Rose doubts that. These days, no one goes into the woods unless they have no place else to go.

5.
ROOKIE

It starts on Poor Man's Road, just past the burned-out skeleton of the Morses' old farmhouse, two miles from town. Nate is alone in his DPD cruiser, alternatively listening to the nothingness on the police radio and the somethingness in Seger's voice as he drawls on about long and lonesome highways. The windows are down; late May breeze brushing against Nate's face. Everything smells green, alive. The buds on the maples and oaks hiding the cruiser from the road are finally awake after a long mud season, an even longer winter. Birds singing in the branches. Sunlight, blue sky, first real hint of summer.

There's a squirmy feeling in Nate's stomach that could either be hunger or boredom. Or maybe it's nerves—he can't deny it might be nerves. He's been on the beat (if you can call patrolling the one block of Dalton and its surrounding potholed roads a beat) for nearly a year, but he still feels shaky whenever he's by himself. It'd been easier when Bruce, ten years older with over a decade of experience on the job, was with Nate, sitting in the passenger seat ripping one Marlboro after another. But a couple months ago, Chief Halstead said it was time Nate start earning his keep, policing on his own.

Nate turns off the radio as an AC/DC song starts up. If Bridget were here, she might laugh about what an old fuddy-duddy he's becoming. But he can't help it if he'd rather listen to Seger or Steely Dan—something quieter, a little less in-your-face than most of what they play on the rock station.

Almost no traffic for the past half hour. If only Nate had known how much of this job is waiting. He needs to get up and *move*; he can't stand this sitting still for so long . . .

A black pickup appears at the crest of the hill down the road and in seconds is racing past the cruiser. Nate doesn't need to hold up the speed-gun to know this guy's going 60, maybe 65. Limit's 50 through here. He turns on his flashers and siren, throws the rig into drive, and whips out behind the truck, trying to ignore the sour taste in his mouth and the squeezing in his guts. He's only ever had to speed after someone like this once before, and it turned out to be Molly Lannigan rushing to get her kid home in time to use the bathroom.

The chase doesn't last long—over the railroad tracks and along the forested riverbank, streaked lime green with new growth. Just past the Dump Road, the truck's red brake lights flicker to life and then glow solid as the guy rolls to a careful stop on the shoulder. At the last minute, Nate remembers to park the cruiser at an angle to the road to ensure any oncoming traffic will swing slow around him. Proceed with caution.

He approaches the truck with what he hopes looks like confidence—steady walk, neutral expression—his fingers flicking nervously toward his gun belt. Gravel crunches under his boots. To the right side of the road, dense woods. To the left, broccoli fields.

As he nears the truck, the driver's window jerks down in starts and stops. Nate hangs back until he recognizes the person sitting behind the wheel. Gene Wilkins. Though he's only in his early thirties, six or seven years older than Nate, Gene appears at least fifty. His grayish face is dotted with whiskers and his eyes are bloodshot.

"Going a little too fast again?" Gene asks, voice nearly as shaky as the hands tapping against his steering wheel like restless birds.

Nate steps close enough to the window to smell the sweet,

spicy tang of sawdust that clings to Gene's blue Dickies. "More than a little."

"Shit." Gene turns his face away to let out a string of phlegmy coughs. "Sorry 'bout that. How's about you just let me go, though? Won't happen again, I swear."

Nate's first instinct is to say yes. Send Gene along to his trailer out in Barren, where he's lived alone since Martha left him. Word is she cleaned out their joint account and hitched it down to Augusta or Waterville. Nate imagines Gene sitting in a recliner with the remains of a Hungry Man dinner on a TV tray beside him. Really, what'd be the harm if he just let the poor guy off with a warning?

Then he catches a glimpse of a tiny plastic bag peeking out the breast pocket of Gene's shirt. His stomach squeezes again as a wave of emotion rolls through him. There's pity and mercy in this wave—as far as Wilkins go, Gene's one of the better ones, his crimes of littering and the occasional speeding ticket laughable in comparison to what some of his relatives get up to. But in this wave of feeling is also the sudden recognition that this might be what Nate's been waiting for. A perfect union of luck and timing. This moment, here on the dirt shoulder of Poor Man's Road, might be his only chance to prove what he's long suspected about Gene's cousin, Tommy Merchant.

Proceed with caution.

"What you got there?" Nate asks, nodding toward Gene's chest.

One of the man's shaky hands darts out to cover his pocket. "Ain't nothin'. Just some aspirin, bummed off a guy at the mill. Didn't have no bottle for 'em."

Nate steps closer to the window. "Mind if I take a look?"

On the road behind them, an 18-wheeler stacked high with freshly felled timber rumbles by in low gear. The ground shakes beneath Nate's feet. Quick hit of spruce sap, diesel. Gene falls into another coughing fit, then lets out a long sigh. He looks like a dog waiting for the rolled-up newspaper.

"What if—and I'm not saying it ain't—but what if it ain't aspirin?"

"Well, depending on what it is," Nate says, "I guess I'd have to place you under arrest."

"Shit." Gene gnaws at his lower lip and stares out the windshield, seeming to search for a familiar landmark. But there's only forest here. "I can't go to jail. No friggin' way."

Empty road. Only Nate and Gene and the trees, the almost-summer sun. Nate's guts are writhing now, just like the nerves he used to get before high school basketball games. People cheering him on from the bleachers, waiting for him to shine. Expecting some kind of greatness. He always dreaded those games.

Unlike a lot of the other guys he met at the Academy, Nate didn't want to be a cop to stroke his ego or live his life as one big power-trip. He became a cop because he wanted to give something back to all those people—his home team—who used to cheer him on at those games. Give them a real reason to look up to him.

But right now, he can only think about two things: the unique authority this position offers him, and the imprints of Tommy Merchant's fists on Rose Douglas' delicate, sad-eyed face.

Guys like that, they never stop unless someone stops them.

"There might be another option," Nate tells Gene.

That night, he holds Sophie on his lap while Bridget folds laundry beside him on the couch. Each time she snaps a towel or t-shirt, he catches a whiff of fabric softener. The TV is set on the national news, Andy Rooney back after a strange suspension for something to do with racist—or was it homophobic?—comments.

"Trot, trot, to Boston . . ." With each syllable, Nate bounces

Sophie gently up and down. Her blue eyes squinch shut as she lets out a stream of giggles that shakes her little belly. "Trot, trot to Lynn . . ."

Bridget stretches her arms out over the wide-plank hardwood floor to untangle a pair of Nate's jeans. Pale green glow from the TV on her puffy, tired face. Hair a mess of curls and tangles. God, she's beautiful. As beautiful now as she was when they were seven years old, fifteen, twenty.

"How do you do it?" she asks, adding the folded jeans to the pile on the coffee table.

"Do what?"

"Get her to laugh like that. Cries for me all day, then you come home and she's like a completely different baby."

It's true, Sophie can be a challenge. There have been times Nate's carried her around until her colicky cries made his ears ache. But sometimes, though he'd never admit it to Bridget, he wonders if things are really as bad as she says they are when he's not home. Crying all day, every day, without rest—is that even possible?

Sophie wraps her fingers around the collar of Nate's t-shirt. He buries his face in her copper hair, inhales the sweetness of her scalp.

"So what happens now?" Bridget asks as she untangles a towel from the basket. "With Gene and Tommy, I mean. Won't Tommy kill Gene when he realizes he ratted him out? You know how that family is."

"They're not murderers," says Nate, though he's had the same fear himself, a sense of dread and a blur of vague images borrowed from all the mob movies he's seen. "Anyway, we have a plan."

"Which is what, exactly?"

Figure the damn thing out as we go along, as Bruce so elegantly put it earlier. *Christ, dumber cops than us have figured out harder shit than this.*

"I'm not sure I should be talking to you about it," Nate says to Bridget.

"Who am I going to tell? That baby's the only person I talk to on any given day."

"I just think it might not be right to tell you the whole thing. That'd be like . . ." Nate rubs his hand in small circles against Sophie's back, his fingers snagging on her green onesie. "Bad policework."

Bridget pauses in her folding to stare over at him. "You're shitting me, right?"

"What? Do I sound like a jerk?"

"I don't know." She turns back to the laundry, picks up a lone blue baby sock and tosses it on top of the folded pile. On the TV, the familiar *click-tick-tick-click* of the *60 Minutes* stopwatch. "You just don't sound like *you*."

A week later, Nate once again sits waiting, this time in his own F-150. Bruce is in the passenger seat beside him, lighting a cigarette.

"Don't you ever slow down on those things?"

"Life's too short, Boss."

The smoke makes Nate feel queasy, lightheaded. He cranks his window down to breathe in big gulps of air. Rain in the forecast. Smell of oncoming storm. The lot of Frenchie's, where Nate and Bruce are parked, is tossed with mud puddles that look like smears of black oil in the dark. No drinkers tonight; bar's closed on Sundays.

Across the street, at Stu Wilkins' dingy, flat-roofed autobody shop, a light comes on in a small back window.

Though the Chief has given permission for this, Nate still worries something about it is wrong. Maybe not legally—this is how bad guys get caught—but this whole scheme seems to fall into an ethical, maybe even moral, gray area. Nate doesn't like gray areas. He likes things simple, straightforward. He still remembers reading Ms. McGreevy's notes on his second-grade report card: *A smart enough boy, but he lacks the imagination of his peers. We might encourage him to dream a little.*

Bridget has always had enough imagination for the both of them. And she's always had her own gentle, laughing way of coaxing Nate into doing things he never would have thought of himself. As kids, this took the form of eating penny candy outside the gas station while making up stories for every person they saw going into the Store 'N More across the street. As teenagers, it was drinking strawberry Boone's Farms beneath the radio tower on sticky summer evenings and running barefoot down empty roads. And as adults, skinny-dipping down at the river the night they got married.

Bruce tosses his spent cigarette out the window. "Our guy shoulda been here ten minutes ago," he says in his deep smoker's voice. "Think he's gonna pussy out on us."

"He's probably just running late."

But what if Bruce is right? What if Gene doesn't show, what if they've lost their only chance to catch Tommy in the act? What if Nate's left Bridget and Sophie alone, all day and now most of the night, in that farmhouse on the outskirts of town for no reason? Bridget was so tired when he left for work this morning. Swore she'd be okay on her own, but he can't shake the feeling he should've stayed home.

Then—small miracle—Gene's black pickup appears across the road, idling at the stop sign at the end of Larch Street.

"Hear that rattle-trap?" says Bruce. "Christ, you'd think his uncle'd give him a deal on a halfway-decent muffler."

Nate's stomach is roiling, heart squeezing fast against his ribs. He should've taken a leak before they left the station. He shouldn't have eaten that poutine for supper. The pre-storm air smells like burnt copper. Gene's sitting at that stop sign too long; Bruce was right, the guy's going to wuss out.

Everything, this whole stupid idea, is wrong.

But then, finally, Gene's truck rolls across Main Street and into the lot behind Stu's shop, coming to a stop beside the weedy remains of the orange school bus that's sat there Nate's entire life.

"Showtime, Boss."

"You've got to stop calling me that."

"Hey, Chief says this is your big show." Bruce claps one bear-like hand down on Nate's shoulder and grins. "You're in charge. I'm just here to look pretty."

They watch as the headlights on Gene's truck flash once, then twice, illuminating the rusty back door of Stu's shop. A few moments later, the door opens outward, cutting a swath of yellow on the ground. Nate is sure Tommy isn't going to walk through that door. That he'll stay hidden inside and wait for Gene to go to him. But after a few moments, Tommy appears in that slice of light. Black jeans, black jacket, dark hair slicked back from his high forehead.

"Who's he think he is?" says Bruce, letting out a short puff of laughter. "Danny fucking Zuko?"

Tommy pauses, glancing up and down the deserted Main Street. Nate holds his breath, afraid Tommy will recognize his truck or see him and Bruce sitting here, even though it's dark inside the cab. But it's not uncommon for Frenchie's lot to be dotted with parked trucks just like this one, even on nights the bar is closed, and Tommy doesn't seem to give it a second thought. He strides toward Gene's pickup. The town's so quiet that Nate and Bruce can hear the crunch of Tommy's shoes on the dirt as he crosses the yard, the gunfire rap of his knuckles against Gene's window.

"Went through that last batch pretty fuckin' fast." Voice so clear they hear every word.

Gene opens the truck door and jumps down to the ground. He stands a few inches shorter than Tommy. "Things've been shit since Martha took off."

Though Nate is sure he can hear a nervous tremble in Gene's voice, Tommy doesn't seem to notice.

"You're better off without that cunt," he says. "Wish I could get Rose to leave me."

Nate clenches his jaw until it hurts. Bruce curses under his breath. All the guys at the station think of Rose as their little sister. She's not the best secretary—she's always sitting at the front desk reading what Bruce jokingly calls her smut novels—but she's one of them. Part of the family. Granted, she might not want to be part of that family once she finds out what's about go down here.

"I tell you what she done to me?" Tommy says to Gene, who shifts his weight from one foot to the other, glancing toward the going-nowhere bus. "Bitch makes me think she's knocked up again, then tells me it was a false alarm. Pretends like she don't know any better but I ain't stupid."

Tommy reaches into his jacket and hands something to Gene, who pushes a wad of cash into Tommy's outstretched palm. He counts the money, slow, unworried, right there in the glow of Gene's headlights. Grins and puts the cash in his pocket.

"Got him, Boss," says Bruce, pumping his fist against the dashboard. "What n—?"

But Nate's already opening the door and dropping to the ground. He runs on quick, long legs across the street toward Tommy, who stands there in his all-black clothes looking suddenly like he's dressed for his own funeral. That oily smirk slipping away.

"You mother*fucker*," Tommy says, his fist curling back and heading for Gene's face, just as Nate reaches into his pocket for the pair of handcuffs that's been weighing him down all night.

It happens fast and seems to last forever.

Tommy slips out of Nate's grasp to throw another jab at Gene, who does nothing to defend himself. Nate lurches toward Tommy, tries to slip a cuff on one black-leather wrist. But Tommy's faster. Better. Bright lights are exploding in front of Nate's eyes before he even sees it coming.

It takes a moment to understand the hard thing against his back is the ground. Pebbles bite into his spine. Something warm and wet trickles down his face. All the breath knocked out of him. That sweet-sick taste of copper no longer just in the air, but in his mouth. Hot, pulsing pain between his eyes. Above him, low black sky.

Gene is lying crumpled on the dirt beside Nate, Tommy straddling his hips as he lands punches on Gene's face, ribs, stomach. Nate can hear Gene's wet gasps, Tommy's ragged breath. With each hit, Tommy barks out curses. A rhythm like music, like singing.

"You *ass*hole. You *sonofawhoring*bitch. You *rat*fucking*pussy-*ass*cock*sucker."

On and on it goes, until Bruce's footsteps thunder toward them. Nate feels more than sees Bruce thrust his huge shoulder into Tommy's ribcage and knock him to the ground, where he pins him against the dirt.

"Come on, Boss." Bruce's voice surprisingly calm as Tommy thrashes and roars beneath his weight. "Get yourself up and collar this bastard. He ain't going nowhere."

Jesus, the sky is low.

Nate can't get the angle right on the handcuffs, can't get the lock into place. Then he stumbles on the rights—*Anything you say could or might . . . no, can and will . . .* Then he almost forgets to take the money from Tommy's coat pocket, slip it into a little plastic evidence bag.

Nate wants to call Gene an ambulance—he's bleeding from the nose and mouth—but Gene quietly refuses. He hands the bag of coke over to Nate, ignoring Tommy's hateful stare, and gets into his truck without another word. Drives off slow into the dark, headed south, away from town.

Bruce pigeon-walks Tommy across the street and wrangles him into the cab of Nate's truck, wedging him into the middle where he's forced to sit with his knees splayed to either side of the stick shift. Nate feels the heat from Tommy's body each time he changes gear. It's a nasty feeling, that heat. Animal. Rotten.

"This ain't legal." Tommy's breath is a mix of stale beer and something almost chemical. "We ain't even in a fuckin' cop car."

"Don't get your panties in a knot," Bruce mumbles around another Marlboro.

Nate yields at the blinking yellow light at the end of Main Street and looks both ways, twice. No one's ever hit him before. His mouth tastes like pennies. The ache between his eyes hurts worse with every heartbeat, every too-quick pulse of blood through his veins.

In the station parking lot, Bruce hauls Tommy out of the truck and pushes him into the back of a cruiser, slamming the door shut as Tommy shouts something about suing the entire Dalton police department.

There's only one light on inside the station, a beige clapboard building that also serves as the fire department and town office. Nearly 10:00. It'll be J.D. Sturgeon manning the phones, not Rose. Rose never takes the night shift.

"Boss?"

Nate pulls his gaze away from the lit window to see Bruce squinting back at him.

"If you ain't up for what comes next, I can take it from here. No shame in that, been a long night."

He could drive home, turn off all the lights Bridget's no doubt left blazing, as usual with no regard to their electric bill. Check on Sophie in her crib. Get into bed beside Bridget. Curl up beside her, breathe in the smell of her strawberry shampoo, the faint tang of milk that always surrounds her these days. Pretend this whole night never happened.

But what kind of man lets another man finish his dirty work?

"I'm okay," Nate tells Bruce. "Let's just get it done with."

"Wanna go inside first? Clean up a bit?"

Nate touches his hand to his face and feels flaky, half-dried blood between his nose and upper lip. No one's ever made him bleed before. He takes the keys to the cruiser out of his back pocket, tosses them from palm to palm. There are tissues in the car, he says, he can clean up there. It's a long way to the Houlton jail. Might as well get going.

Somewhere around Haystack, Tommy finally stops threatening to sue and falls silent.

"Thank Christ," Bruce says as he turns up the radio. Something loud, sung in a desperate voice filled with either hurt or hunger. "This okay, Boss?"

"It's fine." Nate tightens his grip on the wheel. The blood is wiped from his face, and the pain in his nose has dulled. But he feels numb and strange, half-asleep. Stuck in someone else's dream. The sky is thick with fat clouds that refuse to break open. What's taking so long? Rain already.

Just beyond Prescott, the small scattering of city lights swallowed in the dark behind them, Tommy says he has to take a piss.

"Can't you hold it?"

"No, fuckstick, I can't."

The sky is so black. Not even the blinking red light of the radio tower up on Marston Hill is visible. No gas stations, no convenience stores. Nothing but fields and forests.

"You want me to piss myself back here?"

"Stop your bellyaching. All right, Boss, let's make a pit stop. I'll get out, make sure he don't try somethin' stupid."

Nate pulls off beside a stand of evergreens that crowds in close to the road. "Should I come out there with you?"

In the backseat, Tommy scoffs. "You wanna watch, too, man? Hold my dick while you're at it?"

Bruce opens the passenger door, letting in a warm, damp breeze. "I got it."

"Holler if you need me," Nate says.

As soon as Bruce slams the back door shut, Nate feels some of the numbness clear from his mind. With Tommy gone, the car feels bigger. There's still that smell, that reek of something rotten, but there's space now. Space for Nate's sense to flow back in. He leans forward and changes the radio station, turning the dial past static and country and more static before hearing Springsteen's familiar voice. He mumbles along beneath his breath. *And then it all comes apart, when out go the lies . . .*

Maybe those are the lyrics, but he's always getting them wrong. If Bridget were here right now, she'd know. She knows every word to every Springsteen song. Will she teach Sophie all those words one day?

God, he should be home with them right now.

Heat lightning flashes to the west, lighting up distant, nameless hills. Nate's stomach twists. Bruce and Tommy should be back by now. Something's happened out there, Tommy's managed to break free from Bruce and is right now running through the woods, will keep on running until he hits Canada, and it will be all Nate's fault; he was distracted, wasn't paying enough attention—

Then there are shadows at the back of the cruiser, and Bruce is opening the door, shoving Tommy inside, and Tommy's laughing. He smells somehow worse now—rot and unfallen rain.

"What's going on?" Nate asks, as Bruce drops his heft into the passenger seat and slams his door shut behind him. "What's he laughing about?"

"Ignore that little shit."

Bruce won't look at Nate. He has never known Bruce to not look at him, even when—especially when—Bruce is telling him some ugly truth about policework he knows Nate won't want to hear or believe. That in Dalton, husbands beat wives and get away with it. In Dalton, parents neglect and mistreat their children. In Dalton, mothers finish a fifth of vodka and intentionally crash their cars into telephone poles out on Route 11. And these are people Nate's known all his life. The same ones who used to cheer him on at those stupid basketball games.

In the backseat, Tommy's still chuckling to himself, softly. The metal of his handcuffs clinks every time he moves, every time he breathes. Nate refuses to look toward him. Keeps his eyes on Bruce.

"Come on, man," he says, "what—"

Bruce closes his eyes, rests his head against the seat. "Just keep driving, Nate."

It's not until they've left Tommy at the Houlton jail and driven halfway back to Dalton that Bruce tells Nate about it.

"That dude's one sick little freak," he says. "He kept talking about Franny. The things he said about her . . . *Christ.*"

Usually when Bruce talks about his wife, it's to complain about her dry pork roast or her constant nagging. As long as Nate has known Bruce, she's always been The Old Broad or just Her. Never Franny. Bruce's voice is strange—quiet, wobbling at the edges.

Nate slows to allow a deer to cross the road. The doe pauses in the bright glow of the headlights, stares at the cruiser for several long moments with big black eyes before bolting back into the woods.

"What kind of things?" asks Nate, easing his foot back onto the gas pedal. "What exactly did he say?"

In the passenger seat, Bruce tugs at his beard over and over. This isn't the person Nate knows. This is someone new. Someone capable of being broken open. It's a shaky, not-right feeling, seeing Bruce like this, the same way Nate felt the one and only time he ever saw his father cry, when they had to put their dog down when Nate was five.

Finally, Bruce drops his hand from his face and lights another cigarette. "Don't matter," he says, voice back to his normal gruff tone. "It was all just bullshit, Boss."

Just like that, Bruce is Bruce again, and Nate drives on.

It's nearly 3:00 A.M. when he turns onto Davis Road. He leaves the radio off; better not to hear anything other than his own breathing and the gentle patter on the truck roof of the rain that's finally pulled itself free from the sky.

He passes the Pritchard Farm, Harvey Trinko's butcher shop, Judy Warren's little log cabin. He passes the Cloutiers' old place, which now belongs to Roger McGowan and his new wife, Alice. All the familiar landmarks, all the familiar people. On clear nights out here in Milton Landing, they can see all the stars, the river, the fields and hills and forest, even the far-off shadow of Mount Katahdin. On clear nights the moon lights it all. But not tonight. Maybe it's the rain, or the low clouds, but it feels darker than Nate's ever seen it before.

He drives steady, slow, along the winding road. It isn't until Nate pulls into his driveway that he suddenly understands—it's so dark on this road because his house, high up on the hill and usually glowing yellow from all the rooms where Bridget forgot to turn off all the lamps and overheads, is dark. Not one light. Not a single room awake, waiting for him.

6.

On the Edge of Town

Bridget used to dream in color—emerald, crimson, indigo; saffron, coral, sunset. But ever since the baby came, her dreams are blanched of color. Only black and gray. Her nightmare images—crooked houses many stories high, buildings collapsing brick by brick—are swollen like wet paper. Soaked through with despair.

Even in her dreams, the baby is always crying.

Nate wakes Bridget early in the morning. His lips soft and warm on her mouth. Down the hall, the baby is finally quiet. Sleeping.

"I have to go to work," he says. His words brim with love that makes Bridget feel heavy. "I could try to sneak home for lunch or supper, but that might be tricky. Bruce and I have to go over the plan—"

"Plan?"

"I told you, remember? Tonight's the night we're arresting Tommy. It's going to be long day. I'm sorry."

His words seem to come to her from a distance Bridget stopped trying to cross days or weeks or maybe even months ago. It doesn't matter. All those words mean is that he won't be home with her today. She'll be alone. Again.

"Maybe you should call my mom, or yours," Nate says. That somber black uniform, clean lines against his broad shoulders, narrow waist. On his hip, the small but heavy gun. "I hate leaving you here all by yourself."

Somewhere inside her, buried as if beneath a dozen feet of snow, all the right words are there. Digging them up takes nearly all the energy Bridget will need for everything else today. Breathing. Leaving this room. Feeding the baby. Changing the baby. Carrying the baby around the house, hours and hours of pacing that never lead anywhere. Carrying the lies, too, the story Bridget's built up over the past six (seven?) months. She feeds one of these lies to Nate now.

"Don't worry," she says. "I'll be all right." She throws back the sheet and gets out of bed, just to show him how normal things are. Normal mothers do this. Normal mothers greet the day, bursting bright with sunshine, and smile. She smiles. Her lips feel like wax.

Nate pauses in the doorway of the bedroom as she slips into her bathrobe and stares at her a moment longer than he usually would.

"You sure everything's okay?"

"I'm okay. Just tired."

His eyes search her face, then he lets out a long breath and nods. Smiles. Smiles because he believes her. That's Nate. Steady no matter what, steady when everything and everyone else falls apart around him.

He reaches out for her, and Bridget lifts her hand toward his. Maybe that one touch could do it. Bring her back to something safe and familiar. It always used to. Her small hand in his, his river-blue eyes keeping her afloat. It's been this way since second grade, when he offered her his moon pie after she dropped her butterscotch pudding on the cafeteria floor. The pudding stained her best pink tights; her mother would be furious, the oversized wooden spoon reserved for spanking might come down from the clean white kitchen wall. Nate didn't know that. He just knew Bridget needed something, and a marshmallow moon was all he had to give. Their hands met as he gave it over, and that one touch broke through something inside Bridget.

"All better?" he asked, and it wasn't—the ruined tights, the punishment waiting when she got home—but in that moment, with Nate beside her, everything felt okay.

She steps toward him now. Only centimeters between them, a shadow, a breath.

Down the hall, the baby shrieks. Nate turns away, toward the awful sound.

After he leaves, the baby cries harder. Bridget stands beside the crib and stares at the red-faced creature sprawled and kicking there. Disgust twists inside her like a parasite. And to think she once longed to be a mother.

The night she found out she was pregnant, Bridget and Nate had a candlelit dinner in their kitchen, still mostly bare of furniture, the fridge containing little other than bologna and leftover pizza from the Store 'N More. Unpacked boxes all around them. Swatches of new paint on every wall—Butter Up in the kitchen, Peachy Queen in the living room, Strawberry Moon in the upstairs bath.

They'd only been married a couple months, but they had been together for most of their twenty-five years of living in this tiny town at the top of Maine surrounded by sky and wilderness. Bridget sometimes dreamed of other places—deserts where earth bumped against heaven, purple mountains that balanced the sun on their jagged white crowns—but she never dreamed of another man. Nate seemed to dream only of what he already had.

"Are you sure?" he kept saying after she told him the news. "Are you sure?" Awed by the hugeness of it. Timid smile in orange candle glow. It was unplanned but not unwanted. Earlier than they'd imagined—but what in this life arrives at the moment one might expect?

"A baby," Bridget said.

"A baby," he said, and kissed her long and slow.

She fell asleep that night and dreamed of colors for the nursery. Not pink, not blue. Something instead to reflect the only land she and Nate had ever known, the one they both loved. Forest, field, river flowing beyond the pines. A shade of green, a slice of life. Something that sparked happiness, something that would wake their baby with wonder and make him—or her—grateful for the earth and all its riches.

Now Bridget stands stretched flat and pale between walls of Verdant Viridian and wishes the baby, still crying, hadn't woken up at all.

Sometime between the second bottle of formula and the third ruined diaper, Bridget's mother calls. As usual, her words are almost kind, but treacherous. A meadow filled with active landmines.

"I miss you, sweetheart. You haven't been out to visit in ages."

"It's only been a couple weeks."

"I'm going to forget what my grandbaby looks like." That jingling girlish laugh—butterfly wings dipped in shrapnel.

"Mom."

"Why don't you bring her over this weekend? Leave her with me and your father while you and Nate go have a date night. You could use it."

"What's that supposed to mean?"

"You don't get enough socialization, out there in the middle of nowhere."

Bridget's parents have only made the three-mile drive out to the farmhouse a few times since she and Nate bought it. During the first visit, her father walked around inspecting peeling windowsills and offering unfounded advice. "You can paint right over that old lead, you know. No need to scrape it all away." Her mother stood wringing her hands in the middle of the living room as though afraid she might brush up against something rotten. "All the money we gave you as a wedding gift," she said, shaking her head.

After Bridget and Nate were allowed to bring the baby home from the NICU, Bridget's mother spent one day and part of a night with them here at the house. Insisted she'd be comfortable in Nate's old sleeping bag on a cot in the nursery. Told them to get their rest, to sleep peaceful knowing Nana Frazier was on the scene. But halfway into the winter night, she left, complaining of mold allergies and frozen toes.

Nate's mother, Bev, is different. She's patient, thoughtful, self-reliant. She's always treated Bridget as her own daughter, but ever since the baby came, her kindness has reached new limits—she shows up unannounced to wash Bridget's dishes, fold the laundry, cook cheese-heavy casseroles. The baby rarely cries around Bev. It's almost a miracle, one that makes Bridget feel as though something inside her has been scraped clean. One that lets a little bit of light peek in around the edges. Then Bev leaves and the baby starts to cry again.

Over the phone, Bridget's mother's voice. "I'm just saying, sweetheart. You should get out of that house. Join the living once in a while."

"I'm just saying, sweetheart. It wouldn't kill you to get out of that house. Join the living once in a while."

Upstairs, the baby shrieks. Bridget hangs up without another word. She stands at the kitchen window and squints in the June sun. Clouds gathering far to the west; maybe there will be rain later today, tonight. Bridget wonders how far she might get if she were to wander into the forest. To the river, at least. The cold, black river.

Sometime around lunch—or what should be lunch, if she had any appetite—the baby falls asleep. This doesn't happen often. It never lasts long. Bridget leaves the nursery and pauses on the upstairs landing, eyes on the closed door at the end of the hall. Her fingers flutter toward the brass doorknob. Nothing good will come of going into the room. But she feels pulled there anyway, like a metal filing up against a magnetic force.

This is the only door in the house that doesn't croak like an asthmatic toad when Bridget pushes it open. The room is lined with windows angled to allow light in at all times of day. All that brightness, blinding.

This room was her studio. The place where color used to burst from her fingers onto blank canvas. Her easel sits before the western window, a drop-cloth spattered with blue and violet and silver beneath her wooden stool. A half-empty canvas stretched on the easel. Her last painting. She thought she'd come back to it—she and Nate were only going out for a drive, a drive in the clear December evening.

They used to do that. Get in his truck and drive around all the roads they knew as intimately as the sound of their own names. All around the little town, to see the Christmas lights strung up gold and red and green. It was cold but not so cold they thought about black ice. The ride was smooth one moment, and then the truck was skittering sideways, Nate's knuckles bone-white on the wheel. Then blood between her legs, the pulse in Bridget's neck so quick, quick, quick it made her puke all over her bright pink coat, and all the stars scattered like someone else's wishes across the northern sky.

Other than the early labor, no injuries from the crash. The vehicles damaged but easy to fix. Lucky Richard and Trudy Haskell were the ones whose car collided with their truck, Nate said. Four weeks too soon, but look, Bridget, look at our girl, tiny but perfect, a fighter. Let's call her Sophie. Sophie Caroline.

Bridget kissed Nate as they stood in front of the NICU incubator. Told him she loved the name. Told him she was happy, relieved. Told him the C-section hadn't been that bad. But what she really felt as she stared at that tiny baby was the numb emptiness of a womb that hours earlier had held an entire universe. The private world she and her unborn child had built together, severed without warning by a doctor's gloved hands as nurses held Bridget down and injected something—poison, it was poison—into her veins. The toxic bubble in her throat. The need to scream, the impossibility of making a sound. The burnt plastic taste of dreams fading from color to gray, life to something else. A terrible in-between.

Bridget doesn't stay long in the studio. The room smells of canvas and paint, turpentine and dust. All along the walls, visions from her life before. Fields of sunflowers, silhouette of Mt. Katahdin. A river winding slow and green, a river rushing wild. Aurora Borealis spilling from the heavens, amethyst and turquoise pierced through with tiny bright white stars. And on the easel her last attempt to capture the wonder of her then-familiar, once-beloved world. The stand of white birches at the edge of their property, awash in silver winter twilight. Blue December snow. A purple sky half-finished, cracked open in the middle.

Bridget never had many friends—the process always overwhelmed her, all those get-to-know-you questions, all those expectations. But she always had Nate and Lori Best, who lived six miles out of Dalton on a potato farm. Lori and her parents and her two brothers wore a lot of flannel and ate every meal together. Bridget was astounded by this. In her own house, she and her siblings flitted through the rooms like forgotten spirits confined to different worlds. Her mother, when she wasn't wiping down every wooden surface with Pledge or vacuuming perfectly straight lines into the carpet, spent most of her days in her bedroom. Her father was rarely around—managing the lumber yard kept him busy, and Bridget suspected he felt more at home in his cramped cedar-scented office than he did in that big house on the hill. But at Lori's place, even though tensions ran high between her brothers and their father, all the family ate together. Every single meal.

She and Lori didn't have much in common other than a shared love of the Bangles and Bonne Bell Lip Smackers. But they made each other laugh, and their conversations were fueled by inside jokes and complaints about everything from math tests to underwire.

Something shifted between them after the baby came. In those winter weeks when Bridget had nothing to do but let her incision heal as Nate carried the baby from room to room, Lori sometimes drove out to visit. Sat at the kitchen table, drank too much coffee and jabbered on about things Bridget couldn't believe she'd ever cared about. Old friends from school, town gossip. Milk leaked from Bridget's nipples, stained all her favorite shirts. Sometime in spring, Lori stopped visiting, stopped calling to check in.

Other than Nate, Lori was always the one person Bridget trusted most. Sometimes she wonders if she could call Lori up and tell her about the dreams that trip through her head each night. The tall, crooked windows from which she hurls the baby with as little care as she'd flick a speck of ash from her collar. The buildings collapsing, all those bricks, that coppery smell of carnage, and Bridget at the center of it all, stuffing the baby under blood-stained debris until the crying stops.

But no.

She can't tell Lori. She can't tell Nate. She can't tell anyone. Who could ever love her or look at her the same again if she were to ever confess the relief she feels in these dreams after the baby is silent? The sensation of a terrible weight lifted from her chest. The grass that turns from gray to green as soon as the baby is gone. All the color, finally returning.

By mid-afternoon the sun is scorched as burned metal. Outside the kitchen, the feeders Nate keeps filled teem with birds—sparrows, robins, chickadees. When a black bird crashes into the window and drops to the lawn below, Bridget doesn't feel anything other than envy. No more hunger. No more fighting, no more struggle.

The baby lets out another howl. Endless hours without a break from that sound. How does such a small thing make such an evil noise for so long?

Bridget stares at the dead bird on the lawn. It would be easy. Quick. It could probably be painless. No one would ever know. All sorts of little lives die without good reason all the time. Death is just a moment. Then comes all the unknown worlds after.

"Colic," Dr. Haskell said back in March, or maybe it was April. Their regular pediatrician in Prescott was on vacation, and Bridget didn't want to wait until he got back for answers. The sky was gray. Dr. Haskell bounced the baby on his knee, rubbed the baby's back with his big, gentle hands. "I know it's rough, but it'll pass. A couple months at most."

And then as the season changed and snow melted into mud, after poking and prodding and listening to the baby's heart and lungs, her pediatrician repeated what Dr. Haskell had said. "Just colic. A wicked case, for sure, but it won't last forever."

That was when Bridget understood there are different definitions of forever.

The operating room lights were cold, blinding. Every sound was muffled. Machines beeped from miles away, erratic rhythms that reminded her of the submarine movies her father watched, those gray radar circles pulsing as danger crept closer, closer, closer. Nurses' voices warbled. There was a strange thick rush in the back of her skull, and the poison in her veins burned up all the light inside her before carrying her off into a velvety darkness.

She hadn't heard her baby's first cries. She hadn't touched the warm pink flesh and held her baby to her breast until their heartbeats synced up. She hadn't pushed her daughter from the safety of the universe inside her into this world.

She failed, she failed, she failed.

"Where's the baby?" She mumbled when she woke up in the recovery room. The walls were too white. At first, she didn't believe Nate when he promised the baby was just fine.

"See?" he said when they went to visit the NICU. "She's alive. She's perfect."

Bridget expected to feel a rush of love and joy and relief when she saw her baby for the first time. But when she looked at the infant lying in that incubator, all she felt was a dull vibration that reminded her of the hum she'd felt deep in her body when she and Nate lay on the grass beneath the radio tower one summer night, back when they were sixteen. All those invisible waves, thrumming in her bones. She sat there and stared at the baby and waited to feel what she was supposed to feel. There was only that eerie hum. A sickening sense that her baby, the one who had moved and lived and dreamed inside her, had disappeared. Vanished somewhere in the ether.

There have been moments when the crying stops and the weight of the baby in her arms is warm and light instead of an anvil pushing her into the cold, wet ground. Moments when Bridget looks down and sees her—Sophie, their child, the one she and Nate created. Copper hair like Bridget's mother. Nate's attached earlobes. Blue eyes that blink up at Bridget with something close to wonder. Or wisdom.

In these moments, love doesn't exactly rush in—it's more a gentle swell, a river slowly, slowly rising as rain weeps down from dim gray sky. But it's enough to make Bridget think that maybe she can do this. Maybe she can be a mother to this impossible creature. Maybe she can feel all the love she's supposed to feel toward her daughter.

The crying always starts again before that river can flood its shallow banks.

Sometimes the dreams cross over into daylight.

The first time was in March, a snowy afternoon—a mistake. Nate at the station, Bridget and the baby alone in the house, when the colic was new. Hours and hours and hours with no relief, until she pressed the baby to her breast to nurse. Held her tight there until the crying turned into a muffled whimper. She could finally hear the radio, set to Rick Dees Weekly Top 40. A song about black velvet, sun like molasses. It was quiet. No crying. And then the baby wound her tiny fingers in Bridget's hair and yanked and Bridget, horrified, pulled Sophie from her chest and smoothed her fuzzy red hair and made sure she was breathing. I'm sorry, I'm sorry, I'm sorry.

The second time was only a few weeks ago. Not a mistake. Nate at work. Rainy morning. The baby was howling, and Bridget had a migraine, and the dishes needed to be washed and the floors needed to be swept and the ceiling in the bathroom was leaking again and the baby kept screeching and the house smelled like sour milk and dirty diapers and the baby needed to be fed, the baby needed to be changed, the baby needed to be burped, and the pilot light on the stove went out and Bridget's head was filled with angry hornets and the hollow hum in her bones was back and the baby was screaming and she couldn't take it, she couldn't take it anymore. She filled the bathtub. She put the baby in the bathtub. She left the room. She closed the door. She stood in the kitchen and didn't know what to do. She stood in the kitchen and realized this was murder. She ran back to the bathroom, flung open the door, snatched Sophie from the water, smacked frantic dry-mouthed kisses all over Sophie's scrunched up wretched face as her shrieks bounced off the bathroom walls and made her ears ache.

I'm sorry, I'm sorry, I'm sorry.

By suppertime the sun is weaker. The clouds creep closer in the strange pre-storm air. The baby cries. Bridget closes the curtains.

Nate calls. She half-listens as he tells her he pulled someone over for speeding but didn't give them a ticket. Just a warning. Too beautiful a day, he says, and it was someone he knows and likes. He knows and likes almost everyone in town. Maybe he's too damn nice to be a cop.

"I won't be home till late," Nate says. "If everything goes the way it should with Tommy, we won't be getting back before two, three in the morning."

He tells her he's sorry. She says it's okay. He tells her he loves her. She says it back. Her voice sounds dull. Everything is far away.

Upstairs, the baby rages for reasons Bridget stopped trying to understand a long time ago. All she knows is she hates that sound.

The feeling has returned—the one she fought back not only in February, not only a few weeks ago, but ever since that night as she bled beneath the stars while Dr. Haskell checked her pulse and told her to hang on. Blood on his hands, blood on her thighs, blood on the backseat of Trudy's car. Help was coming soon, the doctor said. Just one more minute.

She turns the lights off, one by one, moving slow and deliberate through every room. It's better not to see.

She takes care to get the bathwater the perfect degree of warm. How many hours did she spend preparing, excitedly obsessing over things like water temperature and burping methods and the pros and cons of formula? How many different names did she consider for the new life growing inside her? How many mornings did she wake up smiling, counting down the weeks until she held her child in her arms?

Too many. Not enough.

The accident was her fault. Nate was driving but she was to

blame, she distracted him, yanking on his elbow and telling him to look up at the sky. If not for her, he would have seen the ice on the road and the Haskells' car coming toward them, and he would have slowed down, but as always he did what Bridget asked of him. Look up, Nate, look! There. A falling star, a wish come true.

The bathroom tile is white and black. The walls are the color of a summer moon. The baby weeps, desperately needing something she can't give. Everything, all of this, is wrong. Bridget's face prickles with clammy sweat. She opens the windows. The breeze smells of rust and unspent rain.

A long time ago, back when she and Nate were fourteen, maybe fifteen, they made a game for summer nights like this. They didn't have their licenses yet, but it didn't matter, no one cared if a teenager drove their daddy's truck to the outskirts of town when the moon was up and the stars were out. The cab of the truck smelled like Nate's father's cigarettes, menthol-blue and peppermint. The warm air pushed her curls around her face as they sang Bob Seger and Bruce Springsteen as loudly as they could. Night moves, darkness on the edge of town. Dreams and bigger dreams. They parked in the fallow field across from the farmhouse they live in now. The place was well-kept but unlived in, windows dark and empty.

"This will be ours one day," Nate said. "My dad's friends with Trent Donoghue. I'm sure he'd sell it to us."

"We'll paint every room a different color," Bridget said.

"Give you a studio where you can make your art."

"Give you a space where you can build things."

"And someday maybe babies."

She smiled inside the dark. "And someday maybe babies."

Then—and this was Bridget's favorite part of the game, because it was an untamed side of Nate she rarely got to see; he was usually so structured, so contained—then he would drop her hand, kick off his shoes, and run barefoot down the empty road. Wave his gangly arms around his head, unfurl his laughter toward the sky.

"But you have to catch me first," he cried, and that was Bridget's cue to sprint after him. Ribbons of squishy tar beneath her toes. The summer air silky and tinted blue from the million stars above. The moon a yellow wafer, or a glowing pink balloon. They ran beside fields and forest. Unseen but close by, the river; farther away the mountains and the hills. Wild creatures hidden in the folds of the earth.

"Too quick for you, Bridget!"

Both of them laughing because that was the joke. They both knew she had caught him long before. That from the first time he'd handed her that moon pie, he had already decided to never let her go.

Bridget turns off the tap. She lifts the baby from its portable carrier, which she had placed beside the sink, and holds the baby as far away from her body as possible. It pulls in a rattling breath, as if it knows the end is about to fold itself down from the corners of the world, then lets out a wail. The bathwater, smelling of tarnished metal, is clear and still. Deep enough for one pale body. The baby's feet kick two inches, one inch, above the water.

Soon the crying will stop. But the colors may never return, the dream might always be gray and long. Nate will always wonder what happened when he wasn't home tonight, and all the other nights before this, and he'll build his own story from the lies Bridget has told him these past several months. Maybe he'll arrest her. Maybe he'll leave her. Maybe he'll never love her again.

The baby stops crying.

Bridget looks down at the little face, stained with tears. Quivering rose-petal lips. Big, searching eyes that Nate swears will soon turn from blue to green, the same color as Bridget's. And suddenly the baby is Sophie again—still not the baby she dreamed of, not the one she knew before it was ripped from her womb as she slept, but a child she might one day learn how to love. Nate's child—something precious, a gift she cannot steal away from him. That river inside her swelling slow, slow, slow.

And then the baby howls again, louder than ever before. An air-raid siren, splitting the night wide open.

She carries her into the nursery. Sets her in the crib. Pale pre-storm glow pushes through the window. The baby's—Sophie's—eyes are wet and round and infinite, and they stare up at Bridget with something like wonder. Or shame. Bridget turns away. She pulls the door shut and walks alone down the long and dark and narrow hall, into the bathroom.

The sound of the baby's wails squeezes the breath from her lungs. If she waits one more second, she'll go back into the nursery, grab the baby, and run back in here to hold her beneath the surface until that crying finally stops. Just one more second.

She takes one of Nate's razor blades from the medicine cabinet. Undresses. Lowers herself into the tub. The water has begun to cool.

Soon the bathwater is warmer, and pink, and her new dreams are filled with color. The deepest violet, the softest blue, the brightest pure round yellow. Color beyond anything she ever imagined, color that holds this world and everything inside it—all the terror, hope, and sorrow, all the things that might have been—within a brilliant circle. Dreams, and bigger dreams. All sorts of little lives.

7.
NECESSARY ROUGHNESS

At the funeral, everyone crowds around the hole in the ground, stares down at the white coffin. Throws carnations into the void. The maples and oaks are the bright, rich green of early summer; the sky is high and curved. It's a beautiful morning in Northern Maine, and Nate wants to jump into the grave, fling open the casket, and violently shake Bridget's corpse until she wakes up.

Instead, he allows his mother to hold his hand as if he's six years old, and they're getting ready to cross Main Street on their way to the Store 'N More. *Look both ways,* she used to say, even when no cars were coming. *One more time.*

Nate always did what he was told. Always looked again.

Time means nothing. It stopped when he walked up those stairs, in the dark, and found her in the bathtub. CPR was pointless. Sophie was awake in the nursery. Screaming. Nate did what he was supposed to do, called for help—his father, maybe, or 911; he would never remember for sure. Then for several minutes or hours or days he went silent.

But inside—every nerve ending, every muscle, every organ, every shard of bone—screaming.

The parade goes on forever. All of Dalton cheering. Jesus, the sun is bright.

He makes toast. It takes somewhere around twelve years for the bread to pop up, very lightly browned.

Bridget almost always burned the toast.

The roar of the crowd at those damn high school basketball games. The collective shout of his name. Everyone in the bleachers watching him run up and down the court under the orange gymnasium lights, shoving past anyone from the other team who stood in the way. The first time he was fouled for unnecessary roughness, he spent the rest of the game trying to catch the eye of the guy from the Prescott team. Trying to tell him without words that he was sorry.

One day, maybe late June, or early July, or Christ what does it matter, Nate's standing in line at Bergeron's when he sees him. Tommy Merchant. That oily hair, that smirk, strutting down the cereal aisle. It can't be real, no way he's already out, but there he is, standing just a few feet away from Nate. Staring at him over the beef jerky. Smiling. Telling Nate without words that he's not sorry for what he did or who he is. He's not sorry at all.

And Sophie, Christ, what will do this do to her? Growing up with the whole town knowing what her mother did. Telling her about it, asking if any small part of her remembers that night. Or, probably more likely, everyone pretending none of it ever happened.

Off limits:
The upstairs bathroom.
Bridget's side of the bed.
Bridget's studio.
Bridget's car, a used Chevy Nate bought her for her twenty-first birthday, even though—no, because—he knew her

father wanted to buy her a better one. A new one. And something like that should be an act of love, not an unspoken obligation. So Nate went to Cameron Best and worked out a deal and drove the car to the apartment he and Bridget were sharing at the time, that little one-bedroom above the Diner that always smelled like bacon grease, and Bridget ran down the outside stairs that clanged with every hurried step and she fled to Nate and jumped in his arms, buried her face in his neck. And she laughed. No way you can afford this, she said, and she was right. It was the best purchase, up until they bought the farmhouse, that Nate had ever made.

His father. His mother. Trudy. Richard. Everybody. All of them. Dalton. Watching him and wondering. Wondering why. Wondering how he never saw it coming.

There he is again, Tommy, a dark smear on the sidewalk outside Frenchie's. A black leather jacket lurking at the counter of the post office. He carries a feral animal smell. A laugh like razor blades.

Her gardening shed. That's off limits, too. Because one day Nate remembers she wanted to transplant the lilies from one side of the yard to the other. So he goes into the shed and gets all the stuff he thinks he might need, and then he digs up the green stems. They wilt and die even as he's digging. And when he sees the flower stalks shriveling under the sun, giving up without a fight, he feels a rage he's never felt before. Vibrating in every bone. Can you murder a plant? He murders the plants. He rips them to tiny shreds in his hands, tosses their carcasses into the ragged holes he just made. Throws the trowel at the house, where it scrapes against the brick foundation before thudding onto the ground. He won't try to garden again.

Who's going to teach Sophie about periods and training bras?

Sometime after the funeral, Nate stands in the Chief's office counting empty Maalox bottles in the trash can beside the banged-up metal desk. The AC is out. Sweat pours down Nate's face; he shouldn't have worn flannel but it was the only thing that didn't reek of mildew. The Chief says *Paid leave*, and Nate doesn't argue. He hates being here at the station. He hates the idea of sitting in the cruiser out on Route 11, waiting to bust drunk drivers. He hates being at home. He hates his parents' house, the house where he grew up. He hates the big house on the big hill in the center of town where Bridget's family lives. He hates Bridget's family, and he's pretty certain they hate him right back.

"How long?" Nate asks.

"Long as it takes," the Chief says, and Nate doesn't argue. Seven. There are seven empty bottles of Maalox.

"Where's Rose these days?" he asks one of them, Bruce or the Chief or one of the other old timers. "Around," is all they say. All they know. Not family after all. Once she left her job at the station, she was just another townie. Just another girl who got knocked-up young and stuck around Dalton. Just the girl who let Tommy Merchant skulk back home. "I should call and check on her," says Nate, but he doesn't.

Bright day, sun so hot he wants to rip the skin off his face. He has to drive into town. Down Davis Road, past all the once-familiar things. Judy Warren's log cabin. Harvey Trinko's butcher shop. Pritchard Farm. Roger and Alice's place. He could swear he's never seen any of it before.

After the funeral, a few days or maybe weeks, Bridget's mother calls Nate in the middle of the night. Her words slide into one another, and he realizes this is Annette Frazier, prim and proper little Annette, drunk. "You were supposed to watch out for her," she says, and Nate, almost relieved, says, "I know."

Did he pay the water bill?

"Come stay with us, sweetheart. Your father and I are worried. We'll take Sophie for as long as you need, but you can stay here, too. You shouldn't be out there in that house alone. Sophie needs you. She misses you. All of us—we miss you. Come back."

Come back.

He only knows it's the Fourth of July because he gets stuck at the top of Depot Hill for the parade on Main Street with all the same parade-things he's seen all his life, the firetrucks and ambulances and the Chief driving one of the DPD cruisers, and the potato harvesters and massive John Deere tractors and Girl Scouts dancing to some Whitney Houston song and Boy Scouts dragging their heels across the hot asphalt and candy thrown everywhere and sirens and horns and bursts of laughter and happy screams and babies crying and kids demanding more candy, more firetrucks, more everything, and the sun is big and round and yellow, and Nate has to find a different way to get to Bergeron's, where he forgets what he came to town for and ends up buying a quart of Allen's and a box of powdered sugar donuts and that's what he's drinking and eating when, later that night, he tastes blood and hears the distant boom of fireworks down at the river. The echo of red and blue and green.

He thinks about it a lot. Finding Tommy. Tommy finding him.

Springsteen and high-pulp orange juice. Earrings shaped like half-moons. The river a ribbon of black, the sky a starless dark blue, and, like a cloud on the shore, her wedding dress. The smell of strawberries. Strawberry-blonde curls. Strawberries. *60 Minutes*. Poutine and ployes, warm and sopped in butter. Wonder Bread soaked in molasses. Radio towers. Rain. The creak of the hardwood floor in the upstairs hallway. The slap of a screen door falling shut. Soft cotton. Bare skin on bare skin. Dirty easels in the bathroom sink, bright colors swirling down the drain.

And who's going to teach Sophie how to paint a chickadee? A robin, a blue jay, a bright red male cardinal?

After the funeral, there's a reception at Nate's parents' house on Russell Street. The house where he grew up. The living room where he and Bridget stole their first kiss while his father watched *Gunsmoke*. The kitchen where his mother tried and failed to teach Bridget how to cook. The bathroom where fifteen-year-old Nate would stand in the shower until the water ran cold, thinking of Bridget's hair, Bridget's green eyes, Bridget's small, firm breasts, Bridget's smooth legs . . .

She's dead. That girl is dead.

A chorus of I'm sorrys. Over-perfumed hugs. Sloppy kisses from old women who have been old all of Nate's life. Egg salad sandwiches. Tuna salad sandwiches. Ham salad sandwiches. Chicken salad sandwiches.

Whiskey. Jim Beam. Beer.

For every I'm sorry, a drink. For every hug, another. For every kiss, another. His body is numb, maybe he doesn't have a body at all, maybe his body is in the ground with hers, and this is a dream they're sharing, assuming you dream when you're dead. But you're dead. And how can the dead dream?

Someone is sobbing, and someone is throwing up into his

mother's Christmas cactus, and someone is saying everything, all of it, is all his fault, and it should be him that's dead, him who never gets to dream again.

And it's a hot bright day and the sun is an evil thing, hungry enough to swallow this whole town, and Nate's knuckles itch. He realizes, suddenly, that he could kill someone. That anyone could, under the wrong circumstances. That it can be something accidental, like rear-ending the car in front of you or dropping your mother's favorite vase. It's just a moment, and it happens, and then you need to decide what to do with the mess you made.

He'll have to learn how to braid Sophie's hair.

On one of their walks when he was a kid, Nate's mother had let go of his hand for just a moment, to rifle through her pocketbook maybe, or wave hello to someone. Nate looked both ways, then stepped into the road. It wasn't until the truck was a few feet away, horn blasting, that he even realized it was there. His mother hooked her fingers around his collar, jerked him back onto the sidewalk. *Twice,* she shouted, fear in her eyes. *For Chrissake, Nathaniel, I told you to look twice.*

He can take Larch Street, wind along the dirt road behind the Laundromat and come out near the Store 'N More. Take the road to Bergeron's from there. Leave the parade behind.

It's only probation, Bruce tells him, because it's Tommy's first offense, and there's no evidence other than forty bucks and a tiny bag of coke nobody knows how to trace. Bruce says they searched Tommy's trailer, Tommy's truck, his uncle's garage. Nothing. No one in the family is going to talk. Rumor is, Gene Wilkins skipped town the very night Tommy got arrested. So

Tommy got out of jail and came back to Dalton, a mostly-free man.

"He's everywhere," Nate says, and Bruce says, "No one can be everywhere, Boss," and Nate disagrees but can't find a good argument for that, either.

On a rainy morning, his father shows up at the farmhouse with two bags of groceries. "Your mother sent these," he says, and Nate lets his father put the food away. Lets his father wash the dishes and vacuum the floor and do all the laundry Nate hasn't done. Lets his father make grilled cheese sandwiches and wash the dishes again. Neither of them speaks.

Why does a parade have to be so loud? Why does it have to last so long? When they were kids, he and Bridget would stand on the sidewalk with arms out, palms open, catching candy. Bridget's favorite was Dubble Bubble. He caught them all for her.

He dreams of Sophie, her baby-soft skin, white as a cloud. Her copper hair and almost-green eyes. He can feel the weight of her in his arms. Trot, trot to Boston, he says, and Sophie squeals with delight. Again. Trot, trot to Lynn. Again. Careful, young lady . . .

It's not until he's halfway down Larch that he remembers Tommy and Rose live here. That's their trailer right there. The metal siding is stained with rust, concrete slab out front cracked down the middle. And there's Tommy, bent over with half his body hidden in the hood of his truck. Black jeans on a day like this. What's this guy trying to prove?

Nate parks his truck beneath a birch tree. Feels his feet hit the pavement and carry him toward the trailer. Tommy stands up straight. Watches Nate heading for him. Doesn't even flinch.

Did he repay his mother for the electric bill?

Tommy's face is thin, arms bulging with muscle under the tight fabric of his black t-shirt. "Get off my property," he says. Hint of a grin on his face.

"How'd you do it?" Nat steps so close he can smell Tommy's breath. Beer and beef and cigarettes. "How'd you get away with it?"

Heat bugs whine in the spruce trees. On Main Street, parade noise, horns and shouts and laughter. The sun's so hot, relentless.

"I ain't gonna tell you again," says Tommy. "Get off my fuckin' property."

Bridget never cared about the electric bill.

Tommy's eyes are dark and dead. "Heard about your wife." Grinning.

"How the hell did you do it?"

"Can't blame her, you know."

"Where'd you get the drugs? Where do you keep them?"

"Stuck with a fuckin' pussy like you."

"I wasted all that time, that whole night . . ."

"Married to a pussy like you," Tommy says, "imagining a life of just cranking out more ugly babies like that one you got . . . no wonder the bitch offed herself."

He's barreling into Tommy with all his weight. Knocking him down to the dirt driveway, straddling his hips, gravel biting into his knees. Hammering his knuckles into Tommy's cheekbones, Tommy's jaw, Tommy's nose. Jabbing his fists into Tommy's ribs and stomach. Breathless from the effort. Taste of blood in his mouth. The sky so bright. Heat bug chorus. Just beyond the trees, the parade, all of Dalton cheering. Tommy is not a person, just a body, a sack of muscle, blood, and bone.

This violent body is not Nate's body. Nate's body is somewhere else, with Bridget's, maybe—underground.

Tommy has finally stopped laughing.

"Shit, man, enough," he says through a mouthful of blood, "I ain't fighting back so just fucking stop," and there's no more grin in his voice, only panic and fear, and that's when the person who isn't Nate stops punching.

The air is thick with heat and noise. The parade has frozen in place, that moment when all the firetrucks and ambulances and cruisers and potato harvesters and tractors stop so everyone on the sidelines can shout the names of the people behind the wheels and the Girl Scouts and the Boy Scouts swaying from one tired foot to the other in the middle of Main Street. Later tonight the entire town will head down to the river, wait for the big show. Sometimes, not often, Dalton demands fireworks.

"Please," Tommy whimpers.

Enough.

He glances at the trailer. All the windows are covered with heavy blankets patterned with black bears and lone wolves howling at full moons. One of the blankets moves, and he sees Rose's face there, heart-shaped and framed with dark hair. She looks at him. Looks at Tommy, still lying on the dirt, bleeding from his mouth and nose. Looks back at Nate and nods. Maybe almost smiles. Then the blanket falls again, and he wonders if she was even there at all.

Who will keep Sophie safe?

Who will teach her how to love? How to be loved?

There's a hole in the ground and there's a white casket and Bridget is locked inside. When Pastor Fields speaks her name, even her name sounds dead.

The moment never ends, the moment he reaches the top of the stairs and puts his hand on the cool doorknob and stands in the dark knowing something is wrong. Something is gone. Even before he pushes open the bathroom door and sees her in the tub, all that water stained red, Nate knows. He lives in this moment always. This moment never ends.

He has his quart of Allen's and his box of donuts and he sits in the kitchen drinking and eating, staring out the window. Bottle to mouth. Donut to mouth. Another. And another. Dalton is three miles away, but he can see a hint of fireworks down by the river. Muted colors in the sky. Tommy on the dirt beneath him. Tommy, finally not grinning.

Maybe it was a dream. His knuckles taste like blood. Maybe none of it was real.

Stop.
Look both ways.
Again.
Again.

8.
HARDINESS

A lot to look at, but not much to see.

This is the first thought that flits through Trudy's mind when she opens the door to see Greg Fortin standing on her front porch in a B-52's T-shirt. Fourteen years old, and wide enough to block out the sun. A yellow Walkman the size of a brick pokes out the back pocket of his jeans. Light brown hair matted to his temples with sweat. He smells sweet, like the powdered-sugar donuts on display near the cash register up at Bergeron's. By the looks of Greg, Trudy guesses his mother doesn't try too hard to stop him from adding those donuts to the conveyor belt at the last minute. *Impulse buyers.* Trudy has almost as little patience for impulse buyers as she does for people who come into the library expecting her to find a book when they don't even know the title. Or the author. *But I'm pretty sure it's got a blue cover. Or maybe green.*

"Hey, Mrs. Haskell." Greg offers up a shy smile, revealing a line of clean, mostly straight teeth. "Dad said he heard you'd pay a few bucks for someone to help you in your garden."

"No need for that damn formality." Trudy hasn't spoken yet this morning, and the phlegmy sound of her voice makes her feel off-balanced, embarrassed. "I may be married, but I'm no missus. And who said I needed help?"

Greg shrugs. "Some customer, I guess?"

Jim Fortin owns the hardware store, and Cheryl, a stay-at-home mom, makes Christmas wreaths out of her garage. Trudy regularly sees Greg's sisters at the library—Sarah, seventeen, likes Jane Austen, and Aimee, still in grade school, has been stuck on *The Babysitters Club* for a year—but it's been a while since Greg came in. Last winter, maybe, before he saved the Muse girl when she fell through the ice down at the river. Trudy doesn't recall the boy being quite so *rotund* the last time he checked out a stack of books. But she does remember he had better literary taste than the average teen—Steinbeck and Rachel Carson, Baldwin and Louise Dickinson Rich.

Trudy steps onto the porch, pulling the screen door shut so Mycroft can't sneak outside—she can hear him in the kitchen, his double-paws padding across the freshly swept laminate. "Do I seem like someone who needs help? Do I look old? Arthritic?"

Greg takes in Trudy's lounge pants, her bleach-stained sweatshirt. She can smell her hands, the lemon-vinegar solution she was pouring down the kitchen sink when he knocked on her door.

"Nah," he says. "But maybe you could give me some work anyway?"

No, she doesn't want any help, especially not from some kid who probably can't tell a pansy from a petunia. Can the boy even get down on the ground to weed, or haul himself back up again? Then she hears a voice in her head that sounds an awful lot like Bev. *Damn it, Tru, don't be such a grouch.*

"You know anything about gardening?"

"Mom and I tried to grow tomatoes once."

"Were they edible?"

"Not really. But Dad says you need help with flowers, not tomatoes."

"How much do you expect to be paid?"

"Whatever you think is fair."

"And what could a boy your age so desperately need money for?"

"Porn, booze, and cigarettes. What else?" Playful glint in his brown eyes.

Trudy can't help it. She laughs. The boy might have something she doesn't come across often here in Dalton. Fire.

"I'm too busy to teach you anything today," Trudy says. "But if you come by first thing tomorrow morning, I'll let you do some weeding. I might even feed you if you're still here at lunchtime."

"Cool," he says. "I like egg salad."

Trudy watches until Greg reaches the end of Winter Street and turns left onto Howard, that yellow Walkman flashing under the sun. The air smells like dying flowers. Heat bugs whine from the hemlock trees. Summer, dying slowly.

* * *

Most of the time, Trudy is incensed that the library is only open Monday through Thursday. "People like to read on weekends, too, you know," she'd protested when Ollie Levasseur proposed cutting the library's funding a few years ago.

But today, this muggy Friday morning, she's relieved she doesn't have to go to the library. She'd be no use there today anyway, distracted and fidgety as she's been since Mycroft woke her up by batting at her cheek with those big white paws. She's got to keep herself busy here at home until she meets Bev at Frenchie's at 5:00. Finish cleaning, balance the checkbook. Weed the garden, water the garden.

It's not until Trudy's kneeling in the sunshine, hands coated in dirt, that her nerves finally settle. The asters are still going strong, but the hydrangeas have begun to fade, pink petals turning pale green, brittle. Honeybees and butterflies flit around the heliopsis; in the pines, sparrows try to sing louder than the heat bugs. The air is thick and pungent with the growth and decay of mid-August.

Most people assume she's just a bitter, middle-aged librarian, brandishing overdue slips and shushing patrons. And true, she may be a little impatient. Maybe a *lot* impatient. But she's never shushed anyone in her life. And she often waives overdue fines if the person is polite. Almost always if the person is a regular and forgot to return the book because of a sick kid, or a job that takes up fourteen hours of their day.

The real problem, Trudy suspects, the real reason she has a "bit of a reputation," as Bev puts it, is that she's not afraid to voice a strong opinion. And despite the fact that it's 1990, for Chrissake, and the world has supposedly made all sorts of progress, a woman with a mind of her own is still considered problematic. The fact that she and Richard never had kids doesn't help. No one comes right out and says so, but a woman who chooses not to have children can't be trusted, not completely.

But look at these flowers. The bees, the birds, the butterflies. Is this not another way of creating life?

Inside the house, the phone rings. Trudy checks the sun in the blue-white sky—almost noon. No doubt it's Richard, calling on his lunch break to ask her something foolish. *Did you pay the water bill? Do we need milk? What was the name of that agent at the insurance office in Prescott, the one who smelled like pickles?*

All the familiar questions of a marriage.

Sweat rolls down Trudy's spine, under the droopy cotton of her bra. Her back aches from pulling weeds, and there's an empty pang in her belly that reminds her she hasn't eaten anything since her toast this morning. The phone keeps ringing, but she stays with her flowers. To hell with it. To hell with it all.

* * *

Late afternoon, Trudy takes a shower, the cool water picking up soil from her hands and running in brown rivulets down the drain. On the other side of the glass door, Mycroft, a puddle of black and white, lounges on the back of the toilet and stares at her with pea-green eyes. Pity for him. Not much of a show these days. Trudy's been hitting the sweets hard the past couple months, and sometimes the unfamiliar, doughy flesh of her stomach reminds her of bread that wants to rise too fast.

She stands in the lavender-scented bathroom as she dries her hair. At the Shears to You salon last week, she asked for the Princess Diana—short, full, and feathered. Instead, Mandy Thompson had given her something more like MacGyver. She styles the disaster best she can, then sheds her towel and walks into her room, across the hall from what used to be the master and is now only used by Richard.

Flickers of worry and anticipation in her stomach. This will be her and Bev's first date since before Bridget died back in early June. The first time, other than a quick phone call yesterday to set this whole thing up, they've talked to or seen each other since they got into that argument a few weeks ago.

"How's Nate?" she had asked as they had coffee in Bev's yellow kitchen that day. Sophie was in her bassinet beside the table, little rosebud lips twitching every few moments as she slept.

"No better." Bev smoothed a lock of her granddaughter's hair. "He just doesn't have a clue what to do without Bridget."

"Well, he's got to figure it out eventually," said Trudy. "The sooner he brings that baby home, the better. You're not doing him any favors."

"If keeping Sophie here with Bill and me is the only way I can help him, you bet your ass I'm gonna do it. You don't understand."

"What don't I understand?"

"Any of it, Tru. You couldn't. You're not a mother."

It was the only time in their long history Bev had ever made her feel bad about her choice not to have children. She'd always treated Trudy as an equal partner in parenting, sharing all the joys and fears of raising Nate while Bill spent so much time out on the road. And even though Nate has never seemed to catch on to just how deep the love between her and Bev runs (the boy is sweet, but gullible), he's always known Trudy would be around for him. Hell, she's still one of his emergency contacts.

"I might not be a mother," Trudy had said, rising from her chair so fast her blue mug rattled against Bev's tabletop, "but I know what enabling looks like, and that's what you're doing. Just enabling Nate to wallow in his misery. And making yourself a martyr in the process."

Then she dumped her nearly-full cup of coffee in the sink and stormed out without even kissing Sophie goodbye. Regretted it as soon as she slammed the door shut behind her. But if she went back in that kitchen, she might say more stupid, mean things, or start blubbering like a child. So she got in her car and drove away and didn't talk to Bev for nineteen days. Bev didn't reach out to her, either.

That was the worst of it—the waiting. The silence.

And then finally, Bev called yesterday to ask if Trudy would meet her at Frenchie's tonight.

"Got to get some things straightened out," she'd said.

As Mycroft hops up onto the pink-and-white quilt she bought at a craft fair years ago, Trudy rummages through her closet, fingertips grazing cotton, wool, the pilly velvet of her green party dress. She settles on a cream-colored blouse with thin blue stripes, a pleated, knee-length azure skirt, and white flats.

"What do you think?" she asks the cat as she twirls in front of her warped full-length mirror. "Am I a modern woman or what?"

Mycroft twists around to lick his privates.

Down in the kitchen, the phone rings again. Trudy doesn't bother running to answer. It'll be Richard again, calling to tell her he'll have to work late. She's already left him some meatloaf in a Pyrex dish in the fridge. Just how it goes.

* * *

The heat of the day has let up, and a cool breeze cuts through the humidity. Across the street, children laugh and shriek as they run through the wooden playground, built to resemble a castle. "I'm the King and I grant you no trespass!" Trudy can't see who that is standing in the highest turret, but by his slight lisp, she'd guess the boy is a Bergeron. The brown clapboard siding of the one-story school building glows in the early evening light.

The smell of fresh-cut grass and charcoal hangs in the air, reminding Trudy of those not-so-long-ago summer afternoons when Bev used to come over. They'd grill up red hotdogs, sit on the porch, cans of PBR in a cooler beside them, and gossip until the blackflies drove them into the house, empty with Richard up at the clinic. Once inside, away from the eyes of the neighbors (especially Ms. McGreevy, that nosy old crone), Trudy and Bev would go inside. Shed their sweat-sticky clothes, both of them laughing. White lacy curtains billowing in the warm breeze.

Walking past the dilapidated Masonic lodge, Trudy feels as though a hole's been punched through her throat. All the blissful summer days—none of it endures.

Nothing lasts.

Everything stopped when Bridget died. Bev quit the old folks' home. Bev's told Trudy that unless he's playing with Sophie or puttering around the yard, pretty much all Bill's done the past couple months is lie in bed watching TV.

Even now, two months after the funeral, everyone in town still skirts around the subject of how Bridget died, as if afraid it's a virus that might spread. Suicide is for old people with cancer, or retired millworkers who piss away their meager life savings on beer and guns. Not for twenty-six-year-old mothers. Not for the youngest, brightest daughter of the only rich family in town.

Annette Frazier used to come to the library often (bland suspense novels), but she stopped showing up after Bridget died. Stopped leaving that big fancy house up on Rich Fucker Road altogether, or so Trudy hears. Bridget's siblings scattered; her brothers to Fort Kent or New Brunswick, her sister somewhere down on the coast. And Bridget's father, Marshall—well, he's still managing the lumber mill, because what else can he do? Even if your daughter's dead, you still need to make a living.

As usual, barely any traffic on Main Street. In the dusty, diesel-scented parking lot of Frenchie's, Trudy doesn't see Bev's gold Lumina. But Bev's always a little late.

The bell above the door jingles when Trudy enters the bar. This early, it's dead—the rowdier drunks won't be in for another couple hours. George Nadeau and Phil Lannigan shoot pool, neither saying much. Ian Best sits alone at the bar, staring dully at the TV, set to the Channel 8 local news. Good potato crop this year, or so the reporter says. Lining the fake-wood paneled walls of the bar are beer signs, deer antlers, a stuffed moose head whose glass eyes stare mournfully across the room. At Christmastime, Frenchie Pelletier hangs blue and green lights off its massive rack and balances a Santa hat on its head. The place smells like yeast and old sweat.

Trudy slides into the cracked vinyl booth of her and Bev's table, tucked in a corner at the end of the bar. Mellie Martin, heavy-footed and sallow-skinned, shuffles over.

"Haven't seen you in a while."

"You know how it's been."

"Carl went to school with her." Mellie fiddles with one of her red plastic earrings. "Knew her since kindergarten. Had a crush on her but never tried nothing. Prob'ly a good thing—he might be my cousin, but he's not much to look at, I don't mind saying so."

Trudy tries not to cringe at the familiar County butchering of the word *cousin*. "Bridget was wonderful," she says. "We all miss her. Awful, just awful."

She's panicked to hear that her voice has a hollow ring to it, as though she's reading from a script. Luckily, Mellie doesn't seem to notice.

"Bev meeting you here?"

"Should be in soon."

"Two beers?"

"Oh, hell. Why not make it a couple gin and tonics?"

The bell above the door chimes. Trudy watches as gap-toothed Stacey Trinko and her husband, Neil, walk in and sit down at a table by the window. If Stacey's been freed of her secretary duties at the clinic, maybe Richard's left by now, too. More likely he's stayed on alone. The beloved Dr. Haskell, tending to the needs of the community.

He's a good man. Weak, unimaginative, a people-pleaser. But good, and generous, and intelligent, and before she understood who she really was, Trudy believed he was the one for her. Thought they'd have the happy marriage her own folks never did.

He deserves better. But then, maybe Trudy does, too. And Bev, and Bill. Maybe they all deserve better, or at least something different, something they won't ever get in this town. But leaving is impossible. Family, memory, identity—all of it is right here, in Dalton.

"You ever feel like you're drowning?" Bev asked Trudy once. Bill was on the road again, hauling something big somewhere far away. It was so long ago, before Bev and Trudy had admitted to themselves, let alone each other, that the love they felt for one another ran deeper than friendship.

"Only every goddamn day," Trudy said, thinking of the growing silence between her and Richard, the lack of thrill she felt when he kissed her.

Mellie returns with the drinks, then lopes back to the bar. Across the room, Stacey feeds a quarter into the jukebox, and a Rush song starts to play. Trudy sips her G&T—too weak, but she supposes that's better than too strong—and glances at her watch. 5:10. Any minute now.

She tries to drown out the high-pitched, girlish screams of Geddy Lee. If Bev were here, she'd march right over and load the jukebox with Dolly Parton songs. Sometimes on their Girls' Trips down to Bangor, they'll play those songs at bars where no one knows them, and Bev will lead Trudy in a faltering, laughing two-step as Dolly guides them along the sticky dance floor. They've never danced like that in Dalton. Not in public, anyway.

5:14. AC/DC. What did Bev mean when she said they had to straighten things out?

5:18. Van Halen's ear-piercing guitar makes Trudy want to slam her glass against the wall. She tries to practice the slow breathing she uses when someone saunters in and takes their precious time perusing the bestsellers five minutes before she closes up the library.

5:24. Lynyrd Skynyrd. This, thinks Trudy, is cruel and unusual punishment for a crime she can't remember committing.

By 5:31, just as she finishes her drink and starts on Bev's, the bell above the door chimes again.

Trudy looks over to see Nate walking in. She hasn't seen him in several weeks, and she's shocked by how thin he is—he's always been gangly, but now he looks plain sickly. He used to kind of bounce when he walked, an awkward-but-endearing way of moving through the world. Now Nate trudges toward the bar as though slogging through wet cement.

Trudy waves her arms manically until she catches Nate's eye, then beckons him to join her. He drops into the seat where Bev should be. His eyes, usually bright blue, are bleary and underscored by dark bags that make him look twice his age. He smells of unwashed laundry, towels left to mildew.

"Oh, Nathaniel," she sighs. "It's been hell, hasn't it?"

Without waiting for him to reply, Trudy flags down Mellie to order Nate a drink and a plate of French fries. Then she starts telling him about her garden, and Greg Fortin, and the possibility of a drought in the next couple weeks. Nate sips his beer, says nothing. He's always been more of a listener than a talker—one of the reasons Trudy's always liked him, even when he was a teenager. Too many people say too much and don't listen at all.

"Anyway," Trudy says to Nate, "I was supposed to meet your mother here. But I guess something came up."

She hopes he doesn't hear the bitterness in her voice. Or the fear.

He flashes the same guilty look he had when Trudy caught him and Bridget smoking one of Bev's cigarettes when they were fifteen. No doubt it had been the girl's idea, but Nate had covered for her, said it was his. He tugs at his hair, in need of a cut.

"You can blame me for that," he says. "I was supposed to bring Sophie back home today, but I kept seeing ants in the kitchen. Had to bomb the house, didn't think she should be around all those fumes."

Bev and Bill were only supposed to watch Sophie for a week after Bridget's funeral. But every time Bev tries to bring the baby back to Nate's old farmhouse, he has a new excuse—he needs to repaint the downstairs bathroom trim or fix the ceiling fan in the nursery or change the batteries in all the smoke alarms.

Things have been unbearable for Bev since Bridget died. Trudy knows that. But it's been hell for Trudy, too. Unable to ease Bev's pain, unable to convince her what happened to Bridget wasn't her fault. Watching while Bev puts her whole life on hold for Sophie and Nate, who, guessing on how he looks right now, staring at his plate of fries like he's forgotten how to eat them, will never be the same again.

Trudy's never felt more alone or invisible than she has these past few months. She doesn't blame Bev for the distance that stretches between them—she doesn't want to, anyway. But this new, strange silence is like deep water she isn't sure how to tread, and she's getting awful tired, flailing around all by herself.

"I'm sorry." Nate dabs a fry into a watery puddle of ketchup. "I'm sure Mom wanted to come out, but Dad's back's bothering him again, and she didn't think she should leave Sophie . . ."

God, the hurt stamped on his face—it kills her. Just kills her. She lays a hand on Nate's arm until he looks at her, those eyes, so much like Bev's, drowning in the kind of grief no one should have to suffer. Certainly not someone so decent, someone she considers her own.

"Listen," she says. "None of this goddamn mess is your fault."

"I should have seen it. I should have known." The words are slightly muffled as he rubs his hand across his mouth. Back and forth, back and forth.

"None of us saw it. Bridget didn't want us to see it."

"But I should have—"

"You did nothing wrong, Nathaniel," says Trudy. "Sometimes life is just a goddamn bitch."

He lets out a wobbly breath and pretends to scratch at his unshaven face. She pretends not to know he's actually brushing away tears. She walks up to the bar and orders two more drinks. Tells Mellie to make them stiff ones.

* * *

Later, after the stars have come out, Trudy sits on her porch. Inside the house, upstairs, Richard is asleep. Her and Richard's property abuts MacGregor Field, which is divided between a meadow of timothy grass, a baseball diamond, and a kind of no-man's land where the town keeps extra dirt stacked up into cone-shaped hills children climb and slide down like snow-banks. On summer days, Trudy is just as likely to hear the wooden crack of a baseball bat and the answering applause as she is to hear the back-up beep of dump trucks, gravel popping under massive tires. But tonight, there's only the hush of wind through leaves and a chorus of crickets that reminds Trudy it won't be long until all her flowers die away.

Her belly churns with gin and the four peanut butter cups she finished off when she got home. She misses Bev. She's angry at Bev. She wants to shout at Bev, or maybe kiss her. She wants to tell Bev how selfish she thinks Bridget was, ruining all their lives like this. Changing everything. Stealing everything Trudy cares about. And she does blame Bev a little, too, if she's being honest with herself. Blames her for letting all of it be stolen so easily.

But enough of this festering, this build-up of the silent bitterness that buzzes between her and Richard, and Bev and Bill, and nearly all the couples she has ever known, including her own parents. That resentment might be tolerable (maybe even expected) in a marriage, but what she and Bevy have is better than any damn marriage.

Dressed in sweats and a baggy old t-shirt, Trudy gets into her Celebrity and starts up the car. In the lamplit living room window, Mycroft stretches, an eerie silhouette that reminds Trudy of those Poe stories Bridget used to borrow from the library when she was in high school. "Sure you don't want something cheerier?" Trudy would ask, and Bridget would tuck her curls behind her ear and grin. "Where's the fun in that?" she'd say.

To think, Bridget had gone into labor right in this car. When the sun's out, Trudy can still see the faint outline of bloodstains on the backseat, which Stu Wilkins scrubbed clean after repairing the damage to the bumper that occurred after Richard lost control of the vehicle and slid into Nate's pickup out on Route 11. Crashing into those two that

December night—sometimes Trudy wonders if that's not what started all of this. Put all this grief in motion. She remembers Bridget squeezing her hand so hard that night that she thought her bones would shatter. The poor girl's green eyes flitting everywhere, blood trickling down her thighs. "Don't fret," Trudy told Bridget as Richard monitored her vital signs. Took everything Trudy had not to vomit from the rusty smell of blood, the sharp tang of Bridget's sweat. "It'll be all right," she kept saying. "Babies are born early all the time, and they turn out just fine." Never considering that between mother and child, the child wasn't the one in danger.

Russell Street is dark save for a small pool of yellow light outside Bev's house. Trudy parks behind Bill's pickup and gazes at the dark windows of the one-story ranch house she knows as well as her own—the moss-green paint on the living room walls, the loose tile under the bathroom sink, the sound of the furnace kicking on in the damp basement.

Before Trudy can decide if she should just walk inside, as she usually does—she'd hate to wake the baby if she's sleeping—the kitchen door opens, and Bev steps onto the deck. She's dressed in plaid boxers and a sweatshirt, her hair a sloppy pile on top of her head. She strides across the lawn in her bare feet.

She opens the passenger door and slides into the car, pulling the door softly shut behind her. They squint at one another in the dome light until it fades away. Bev's eyes are rimmed with red.

"Nate called, told me he saw you at Frenchie's."

Trudy fiddles with the radio until she finds an old country station. She turns the volume down low. "Christ, Bevy, why didn't you call to let me know you couldn't make it?"

"I did," says Bev. "Around noon. And again at quarter past 4:00. I left messages. Why didn't you check them?"

The ringing phone, Trudy's refusal to answer. *Damn it.* "I figured it was just Richard."

"Well, you should've checked. That's what that machine is for."

Bev's irritated voice makes Trudy feel the same way she used to whenever her mother would scold her for sleeping in too late or forgetting to iron her younger sisters' dresses. Afraid, alone. Unforgivable.

"I'm sorry," she says. "You're right."

A too-long silence, until finally Bev lets out a tooth-paste-scented sigh.

"No." She lays her hand on Trudy's knee. "I'm not right. I'm tired and cranky and sadder than shit. But I should've found a way to get there tonight."

Bev's hand on her knee, the grassy smell of the summer night, the trill of crickets—all of it is as though they've fallen back into better days, their lives before Bridget's death.

"I really am sorry, though, Bevy."

"For what?"

"Being so selfish," Trudy says. "Wishing I could have you to myself all the time. Christ, what kind of woman is jealous of a motherless baby and widowed twenty-six-year-old?"

"An honest one."

Trudy rests her head on Bev's shoulder, and they hold hands, Trudy's pearl-pink nails brushing against Bev's palm. They stay like that for a while, saying nothing.

Finally, Bev sighs again. "I have to check on Sophie."

Trudy brushes Bev's hair from her face. "Yes, you do."

"Coffee tomorrow morning?"

"Will have to be afternoon," says Trudy. "Greg Fortin's coming over in the morning to work in my garden. You believe that? Someone's been going around saying I'll pay young men to do my weeding for me. As though I'm infirmed or something."

Bev lets out a long roll of laughter, a sound Trudy hasn't heard in months. "I never said *infirmed*."

"Damn it, Bevy, it was you? Why the hell are you sending teenagers to my house?"

"You need to work on your people skills," Bev says, her eyes glinting in the dashboard glow. "Figured you should start with someone about your maturity level."

"Oh, for Chrissake."

* * *

Greg is right on time the next morning. Today he's wearing a Talking Heads shirt and gym shorts. No yellow Walkman this time.

Trudy leaves Richard reading the *Bangor Daily* in the living room. "Who's that so early?" he asks from his recliner, but she can tell by his flat voice he doesn't care. He's been distant and subdued since Bridget died.

These goddamn hero complexes. Nate thinking he could've saved Bridget if he'd been home the night she slit her wrists in the bathtub; Richard convinced he should've seen the signs she was depressed when she came into the clinic to get Sophie checked for colic; Bev believing it's all up to her to rescue Nate and Sophie from the grief they're meant to endure. Why can't people accept not everything can be salvaged?

Trudy steps onto the porch. "Well, come on then," she says to Greg. "Going to be a scorcher today. Sooner we get started, sooner you can get home and sit in front of a fan."

He follows her across the lawn—he kind of bobs when he walks, not unlike Nate used to when he was a kid—and she steps inside the potting shed while he hovers in the doorway. Trudy breathes in the comforting aromas of the shed—plywood, fertilizer, sunbaked rubber from the garden hose.

"Everything you need is in here," she tells Greg.

"What if I can't find something?"

"Then you look harder."

She grabs a trowel, two sets of gloves, a five-gallon bucket. "Don't see you in the library much these days."

"I've been busy. Summer, you know. Chores, babysitting my little sister."

Trudy notes he doesn't say anything about friends but doesn't press him on it. She leads him to the backyard, adjusting her usual brisk pace to match his short, bouncy steps.

"Richard—Dr. Haskell to you—couldn't get me the house I wanted, so he bought me an extra acre of land here."

"What house did you want?"

An image of Bridget's childhood home up on Rich Fucker Road flashes through her mind—all those tall windows drinking in the morning light before it warms the rest of the town.

"Doesn't matter," she says. "The point is, I ended up getting something with a different kind of value."

She leads Greg through a footpath at the edge of the yard, their arms scraping against holly bushes. When they step into the garden, Greg lets out a breathy little sigh of surprise. She tries to see it new, through his eyes. A riot of color—purple, white, blue; pink, yellow, red, all fading now but still hanging on, waiting for the sun.

After a few moments, she pulls on a pair of gloves and hands the other to Greg, relieved when they fit over his sausage-like fingers. Kneeling on the ground in front of the leggy remains of the peonies, she gestures for him to join her.

"You're going to find some worms," she says. "Ants. Spiders. So let's hope you're not squeamish."

Greg smiles. "Guess we'll find out, won't we?"

One day a few years ago, she and Bev were weeding in this very spot when Bev found a Buffalo head nickel buried in the dirt. A hot day just like this, sky bright blue, bee-buzz all around as she unearthed the coin and held it out beneath the sun. Grinning as she gently placed the treasure in Trudy's palm.

"That's the thing," Trudy tells Greg. "You just don't know what you'll turn up until you start digging."

She watches him break through the dry soil with the trowel.

Sweat is beading on his temples, and his belly jiggles with each movement, but he looks determined, ready to wrestle any weed that gets in his way.

While he works, Trudy breathes in the scent of August and lets herself imagine. Allows herself to believe they're still living in the before time, and Bridget is alive and Nate is happy and nothing has been stolen from any of them. And in just a few hours, she'll go over to Bev's house. They'll sit at her table and drink decaf and talk about the people they know and like (or dislike) here in town, or books, or world news ("What the hell're we going over to Saudi Arabia for?"). Bill will be mowing the lawn, or better yet he won't be home at all, and Trudy will have Bevy all to herself. And maybe they'll break out their stash of butter cookies and coffee brandy. Maybe Bev will be wearing that purple tank top she knows Trudy likes. And maybe there will be just enough time to—

Inside the house, the phone rings.

9.

FRESHMAN

On the first day of school, Greg is disappointed (but not very surprised) to learn ninth grade isn't going to be much different from eighth. Same single-story building, same gym and cafeteria, same class of the same other nineteen kids he's known since kindergarten. The one long hallway of the high school wing is a mirror image of the corridor he roamed on the other side of the building last year. His locker even sticks like his old one did.

All of Them are the same, too. Stiff new blue jeans, different haircuts, bigger boobs, but as a group, They're still who They've always been. Well, with a couple exceptions: Henry is taller and cuter than ever. Angela's black hair is nearly down to her butt now. The two of them are still together, and they won't let anyone forget it. Holding hands in the hallway, playing footsie under the lunch table. Disgusting.

By the last period of the day, Greg's more than ready to leave this godawful building that smells like teenage sweat and floor wax. He told Trudy he'd go straight to her house after school. Early September, but the asters and roses are still going strong, and she expects Greg to make them to stay that way until the first frost.

Just one more hour.

He files into the Bio room behind Henry and Angela, who head for two desks in the back corner near the windows. Perfect place for some more footsie, probably. But before they can get there, Mrs. Kalloch's reedy voice rises above the din of ninth graders. "Not so fast. Seats will be assigned according to last name." There's a groan of disappointment around the room.

Greg, who tries not to throw up when Angela kisses Henry goodbye as if he's headed off to war, squeezes his way past the crowd toward the desks. Tries not to throw up again when he realizes he's in the first row, middle of the room. No way of hiding here.

He's not as fat as he was last February when he pulled Angela out of the river. All the work he's been doing in Trudy's garden, plus the diet his mother started back up again once she was sure he wasn't going to die of delayed hypothermia, has helped. He's down thirteen pounds. But he's still the biggest kid in class.

After everyone settles down, Mrs. Kalloch announces their first-quarter project. "A scavenger hunt," she says. "You'll have a list of objects to locate around town—seed pods, owl pellets, lichen, that sort of thing. You will then collect, label, and present your findings to the class."

She passes out lists of items, unbothered when Derek Sturgeon makes a farting noise against his hand as she walks past him. "This is a group project," she says. "I'll be assigning the groups. And this counts for twenty-five percent of your final grade, so I suggest you all find a way to work together."

Another big groan around the room. Greg hates group projects. He doesn't want to get stuck with any of these kids. Lazy, stupid, sloppy. Except maybe Lisa J. or Paul. They'd be okay. Nice enough, and smart. Not to mention Greg's never imagined kissing either of them, so there'd be no distraction there like there would be with, say—

"Henry Covington," Mrs. Kalloch announces, squinting at the roster in her hands, "you'll be with Angela Muse—" Wolf-whistles and *bom-chicka-bow-bow* noises through the room— "and Gregory Fortin."

Derek makes another fart noise. More laughter. Greg

wonders if there's a way to will your own body into dying. Just close your eyes and concentrate with everything you've got and make yourself dead.

"Take ten minutes to talk with your groups and get a plan in place," says Mrs. Kalloch. "Then we'll hand out textbooks and start class."

There's a loud scraping sound as everyone pushes their desks together over the tile floor. Henry stays put. Waits for Angela to come to him, which she does quickly. Then the two of them stare at Greg, Angela's smile fading as Henry gestures him over to his desk.

"Come on, Fortin." His voice is friendly, but there's something in his blue-green eyes that warns Greg not to think this makes him one of Them.

Greg hauls himself out of his seat and plods over to them, dropping down at an empty desk. Listens and scrawls their shitty ideas in his new spiral notebook and says nothing even when they start going on about how they're sure to find owl pellets in the scraggly patch of woods behind Angela's house. There are no owls there, Greg wants to tell them, but he doesn't. He watches as Henry plays with Angela's hair, as Angela strokes Henry's knuckles.

Wishes don't come true. Greg's not dead. He's very, very not dead.

The worst part about being a hero is that everyone expects you to go on being one. In the days and weeks after Greg pulled Angela out of the river, teachers and parents all around town would stop to tell him how brave he was.

Greg figured out fast that no matter how much you try to tell people your bravery was just a fluke, no one believes you. They insist you're something special, and they assume you'll do more heroic things, and you can't do anything to change their minds.

This is what you can do: Play *Super Mario Bros* late into the night and try to ignore the junk food under the floorboard in your bedroom closet. Give in and eat the junk food under the floorboard in your bedroom closet.

You can also pull weeds.

"For Chrissake, you've got to be aggressive," Trudy barks at Greg as he kneels beneath her front porch working on a patch of purple asters that day after school. She's barely five feet tall, but in the low afternoon light, her shadow could belong to a giant. "Weeding isn't a gentle business. Give the bastards hell."

Trudy has never treated Greg like a hero. If he weren't sure she'd cuff him on the back of the neck and call him a damn fool, he might thank her for it.

The plan is to meet Angela and Henry at Angela's house on Saturday morning. Greg had suggested that a few hours this Saturday, and another two or three next weekend should be enough to get the stupid project over and done with. "What a fun way to spend the last days of summer," Henry said, rolling his eyes.

As he works his way through his diet-approved breakfast, Greg seriously considers sticking his finger in the socket under the kitchen table. High-fiber oatmeal and electrocution. What a way to go out. But his mother is at the sink alternately washing last night's dishes and watching him with those all-knowing Mom eyes, so he hurries through his meal, then heads out into the sunshiney morning.

It's not a long walk to Angela's house, just up High Street and down Howard, past the high school and athletic fields. Not even a quarter mile, but Greg takes his time, not wanting to be a sweaty mess when he gets there. There's that subtle change of light in the air that always comes this time of year. Autumn soon, then winter. Seven months of cold and snow and freezing rain. Why couldn't his parents have moved them somewhere warmer? You can run a hardware store in Florida just as good as you can in Maine. That's what Greg and his sisters say to their father every February, when it's the coldest and snowiest and most depressing, and their father always laughs like it's the biggest joke in the world. Far as Greg knows, the furthest south either of his parents has ever been is Bangor. Maybe Portland.

Before Angela turned into one of Them, she and Greg would talk about all the places they might go after they graduated and got the hell out of this town. Angie dreamed of New York City—Times Square, Broadway, the Statue of Liberty. All that crap. Greg wanted to go out west. Colorado, maybe, for the mountains, or California, to see the Redwoods and the Pacific. New kinds of wilderness.

Crazy to think it was just last year they'd hang out and talk like that.

He reaches Angela's driveway, stepping over the grass-filled crack that separates it from the sidewalk. Angela's mother is on the front porch, rocking on a rusty glider that squeaks with every movement. Cindy waves at him with her cigarette hand. She's in jean shorts and a cut-off Garfield sweatshirt, bare feet. Bright red toenails. Hair pulled up in a ponytail.

"Greggie!" She coughs, then sticks the cigarette back in the corner of her mouth. "How's my favorite hero?"

He stands on the bottom step, tries not to squint in the sun. "Okay." Ever since he saved her only kid from drowning, Cindy's been so thankful. He wishes he didn't like her so much. It'd be easier to be rude to someone he didn't like. "How about you?"

"Can't complain. Well, I could. But I won't. Still castin' a shadow, ain't I?"

Stubbing her cigarette out on her thigh, Cindy nods toward the yellow front door. "Ange and Henry are in the kitchen. That's where I told 'em to be, anyways. I told that girl, I says, don't you try to bring that gorgeous boy in your bedroom." She lights another cigarette, takes a deep drag. "Those kids, making ga-ga eyes at each other, no doubt thinkin' all the things I used to think when I was that age starin' at Harvey Trinko . . . Anyways, you keep a watch on 'em for me, Greggie. I know I can trust you."

Feeling like he's been socked in the gut, Greg pushes open the front door. The kitchen's dark compared to all the light outside, and the first thing he notices is the smell of maple syrup. The second thing he notices, when his vision clears, is Angela standing at the stove, expertly flipping a pancake, as Henry sits at the table, elbows pressed into the pink plastic placemat. The third thing Greg notices is that Angela and Henry don't seem ga-ga for each other at all at the moment—they're not even looking at each other. Other than the sizzle from the pancake batter, the house is quiet. Neither of them looks up when Greg walks in, so he clears his throat, feeling like he's interrupted some weird breakfast-buffet funeral.

"How's it going?"

Henry looks up and gives Greg that trademark-Henry smile. Angela lifts her free hand in a wave but says nothing. Ever since Greg saved her, she's barely looked at him. At first, he thought it was because she was dating Henry, hanging out with all of Them, but then Greg started to wonder if it was something more than that. He just can't figure out what that something more might be.

"Want some, Fortin?" asks Henry. He gets up from the table and heads for the cupboard to grab a few mismatched plates. "You made enough for all of us, didn't you, Angie?"

She glances at Greg before turning off the burner. "Maybe. If everyone only has two."

Unzipping his bookbag to hide the flush of heat galloping up his neck, Greg says, "Count me out. I already ate. My mom made French toast."

He drops into a wobbly chair, praying that he doesn't break the thing, as Angela slides three round pancakes on each of her and Henry's plates, then carries them over to the table.

Henry follows with a tub of margarine and a bottle of fake maple syrup.

"My mother can barely pour cereal," says Henry, drowning his pancakes under a thick layer of syrup. "Dad's the cook in our house. Not that that's much better."

Greg tries not to listen to the way Henry scrapes his fork against his plate. The kitchen's too warm, sun blasting in through the windows. Sweat starts to pool in his armpits.

"Probably the fastest way to get everything is to just split up," Angela says, her eyes skimming over the list of scavenger hunt items they need to find.

"Sure," says Henry, "everyone take a different section of town and get whatever they can find."

While he likes the idea of working alone, Greg doesn't trust either of them to find the stuff they need. Angela makes decent grades, but Henry's not exactly the class genius.

"I think Mrs. Kalloch wants us together," says Greg. "I mean, didn't she say that was part of the whole thing? Teamwork and all that stupid crap?"

"Dude," says Henry, licking his syrup-sticky fingers, "that *is* stupid crap."

Angela sighs. "So what do we look for first?"

The three of them fall silent, each scanning the list for the easiest items to find. Out on the porch, Cindy lets out a long roll of raspy coughs.

"I know where we can find a bird nest," Henry says. "You know those woods behind MacGregor Field? Dad says that's where the robins hatch their eggs. Maybe we could even find some old shells."

Greg tries not to stare at Henry, but it's hard not to. Those eyes, that white t-shirt against his tanned skin . . . But Henry must think Greg doubts his knowledge of the habits of robins, because his face gets all pink and he tenses up his shoulders. "My old man likes birds, okay?"

Angela picks up the empty plates and walks them over to the sink. "Whatever," she says. "Let's just get this over with."

The woods behind MacGregor Field are not lovely, dark, or deep (Greg really hopes they can read some new poets in ninth grade English). Unlike all the real woods that surround Dalton, this is just a patch of tangled-up, overgrown trees and bushes between the gas station and the Pinewood Tavern. People come out here to hook up, do drugs, drink. There's more trash than there ever should be in any patch of woods—beer bottles, candy wrappers, and a few deflated condoms, which Greg pretends not to see even when Henry, laughing, points at one floating along the piddly little brook.

They find a nest quickly, right where Henry says it will be, a few feet off the ground in the fork of a spruce tree. The nest is empty, no sign of life, but Greg still feels guilty carefully packing it away in his bookbag. What if some bird, tired from flying around all day, comes back here to find his house has been stolen away from him? But maybe that's just how it goes for birds. You lose a nest, you build another one.

Angela spots the shell, mostly hidden under a pile of bracken at the base of the spruce. She picks it up gently, and Greg and Henry crowd around her to look. The egg is so blue. "Like a little piece of sky," Angela says, and Henry stares at the curve of her cheek with his eyes bright and soft, and Greg, feeling like he might as well be watching them make out, has to walk away. Pretend he's looking for lichen. Imagine he's safe in his room, about to take that first, perfect bite of a Snickers bar.

After a few moments, he looks back at them. Angela's still admiring the egg, but she's stepped away from Henry, closer to a patch of sun. In the light, her black hair is like feathers, a mix of purple, red, and green. Henry stands in the shadow of a sour-smelling apple tree and reaches up to pluck a leaf from a low branch.

"Check it out, Fortin." Henry places the leaf into Greg's outstretched palm. Where his fingertips touch his skin, Greg feels statically charged. "We need one like this, yeah?"

"Yeah," he says, "just like that."

Over the next couple hours, they find about half the items they need. Mushrooms and moss. Owl pellets that remind Greg of the lint balls his mother pulls out from behind the dryer. Pinecones and acorns and seedlings from maple trees that Henry tosses into the air, grinning as they helicopter down to the ground.

"You ever do that, Angie?" he asks. "Watch them spin like that?"

"Maybe in grade school."

She carries the robin's egg all around town, cupped like rain in the palm of her hand. She only speaks to Henry or Greg if they ask her a question. She walks a little bit ahead of them, never looking back to see if they're still following behind.

They part ways at Henry's house on Prentiss Street, after an awkward moment where Greg, assuming Angela will follow Henry inside, says goodbye to both of them only for her to say she has plans with her mother and has to go home. Henry doesn't try to hide the disappointed look on his face but says he understands. Then he lightly slaps Greg on the shoulder. "Catch you later, Fortin. Don't let that nest get all smashed up."

Alone with Angela, walking under the September sun, what Greg wants more than anything else in the world is to run home and attack the pile of potato chips in his closet. Just a little bit longer. One more step. One more.

"What do you think happened to the bird who came out of this?"

He glances at the egg in Angela's hand, then back at the sidewalk. His sisters tell him he walks like a sick horse, head down all the time, but he's afraid of tripping. Has to keep an eye on the ground beneath him.

"What happens to all birds, I guess," he says. "Learned to fly, ate some worms, found a mate, made more birds. I don't know."

"Not *all* birds. Some birds die."

Angela's voice sounds almost as sad as the time in third grade when Kristin Pray, now suddenly her best friend, stuck gum in her hair.

"Well, yeah. Some birds die."

In the weeds along the road, crickets screech. From the hill near the Store 'N More comes the thrum of a jake brake as a log-truck coasts into town.

"Did you go to the funeral?"

Greg doesn't need her to clarify which funeral. This summer, the only funeral that mattered in Dalton, the only one everyone talked about, was Bridget Theroux's. It wasn't just a funeral; it was an Event.

"My parents went."

"I wanted to go," says Angela, "but Momma wouldn't let me. She said fourteen was too young for something like that. But how can you be too young for a funeral? Isn't death, like, the only thing we all have in common no matter how old we are?"

"Sure. We all have to do it sometime."

"Right? At least a funeral could give us some practice." Angela brushes her finger along the curve of the egg, tracing the blue. "For the being sad part, anyway," she adds, "not really the dying part."

Greg wants to say something deep or helpful. But what can you say about death and dying? Nothing new.

Neither of them says anything else until they get to Angela's house. When Greg starts to tell her goodbye she tells him, without any hint of sadness in her voice, that she's going to dump Henry.

"And soon," she says. "But don't tell him, Greg. Don't say a thing."

Then she takes her perfect blue egg and leaves him there alone on the sidewalk, crickets shrieking in the grass beside his feet.

A few minutes later, at Trudy's house, Greg finds Dr. Haskell out barbequing, sending the smell of charcoal over the neighborhood. The doctor offers a burger to Greg.

"No, thanks," he says, even though his stomach is squealing with hunger. He glances up at the front porch, where Trudy has just stepped out in a pair of jeans and a pink t-shirt. She stares back at him, hands on her hips. "I should really get to work."

Dr. Haskell leans down to the green cooler at his feet. He takes out a beer and cracks it open. "My wife likes to boss people around," he says. "But life's short and the weeds just keep growing. So if you want a burger, son, eat a burger."

Greg suddenly can't shake the image of Dr. Haskell sitting in one of those windowless exam rooms up at the clinic with a Bud Light in one hand and a Big Mac in the other, grease splotching all over his white coat.

"I don't mind being bossed around," Greg says, and heads for the gardening shed, leaving the doctor alone with his overcooked beef.

Trudy pulls weeds alongside him today, both of them kneeling on cushions in the garden tucked behind the backyard. Greg misses the flowers that were here just a month ago—dianthus and iris and geranium. He's still learning all the names and all the colors.

"You're awful quiet today," Trudy says. Little gray birds flit from the maple branches to the feeders. "Something big and important on your mind?"

"Just things."

"Ah. *Things*. I know about things, you know. Not all things, but some things."

Greg rips a handful of weeds from the dry ground. It hasn't

rained in days, and the colors of the flowers are all wrong. Faded.

"You must've gone to the funeral, right?" The question is out before he can stop himself.

Trudy pushes a strand of blond hair away from her face, leaving a smudge of dirt on her forehead. "Of course I went. Nate's mother's my best friend, you know."

"I know."

"It's hell, but you show up for tragedies like that."

"Sure."

There's a flurry of wings at the feeder, and they watch without speaking as a big black bird swoops down to push all the littler birds to the side.

"I've never been to a funeral," Greg says.

"You know what that means?" asks Trudy, bending back to her flowers. "What that says about you?"

"What?"

"That you're goddamn lucky."

That night, Greg plays *Super Mario* until his eyes burn. He can't stop thinking about Angela dumping Henry. Why would she tell Greg about it? Is he supposed to be her friend again just like that, like she hasn't been pretending he doesn't exist for the past seven months? And how's he going to talk to Henry on Monday and act like he has no idea the guy's about to get dumped?

The whole time he's thinking this, the whole time he's racing through the Mushroom Kingdom to rescue Princess Toadstool, he's resisting the pull toward the loose floorboard in his closet. Underneath are four Snickers bars, two mini-bags of salt and vinegar chips, and one unopened box of Twinkies. He wants it all. But he keeps playing, eyes fixed on the brightly colored pixels in front of him. He falls asleep with the controller still in his hands.

By Wednesday, Greg is sure Angela's changed her mind about the whole dumping-Henry thing. At school, the two of them are just as nauseating as ever—kissing in the hallway, sitting close and giggling like they're in on a big secret at lunchtime. Greg overhears Kristin Pray saying that Angela and Henry are *total lifers*, and Angela just blushes and nods and laughs.

Then on Thursday, after Henry has left with the rest of the soccer team for an away game in Houlton, Angela finds Greg in the hallway after last period.

"Who do you think they were?" she asks, nodding at the initials in Greg's locker. *R.K.D. + T.L.M.'*

"No idea." He pretends to look for his history book, even though he already stuffed it into his bag. She smells like vanilla, and her hair is braided thick as rope, hanging straight down her spine.

Angela leans against the wall, her pale-yellow blouse blending in with the cinderblocks. "Whatever," she says. "Look, have you said anything to Henry?" She lowers her voice as a pack of laughing upperclassmen streams past them. "You know, about what I told you?"

"No," says Greg. "Why?"

"Seems like you guys are getting to be, like, friends."

It's true, Henry's been nicer to Greg than he's ever been before. He nods at Greg in the hall, lends him a pencil in algebra class, picks him for his softball team in gym without any hint of pity. But that doesn't make them friends.

Greg drops the act of hunting for his book and turns to look Angela straight on. "He's just being nice to me because he thinks you and I are friends."

"Aren't we?"

"We used to be," he tells her. "I don't know what we are now."

The loudspeaker pings twice, signaling all the buses are gone and it's time for the walkers to leave the building. Angela stares down at her nails, chipped with blue polish. Greg swings his bag onto his shoulder and slams the locker shut, feeling a little thrill of something mean when the sound makes her jump.

When she speaks again, her voice is small. "Look, it's weird, okay?" she says. "Knowing I, like, owe my life to you, or whatever."

It's the first time she's ever talked about the river. Greg feels himself softening towards her. A little.

"Nah," he says. "If it'd just been up to me that day, we both probably would've died of hypothermia. If you owe anyone, it's Nate Theroux. Not me."

They're the only ones left in the hall, and Greg is late for Trudy. But he stands there with Angela until she angrily swipes at her eyes and reminds him not to breathe a word to Henry about the soon-to-happen dumping. He keeps standing there for a couple minutes after she has hurried out the heavy double doors without saying goodbye.

"I'm sick of weeds," he tells Trudy later that afternoon. A pile of them lies beside his knees. He's sweaty and tired and hungry. The sun's too bright. "It never ends. You kill one, another two take its place."

"It's a garden, Gregory. What did you expect?"

They work in silence for a while, Greg tearing out weeds as Trudy waters the sunflowers. Chickadees at the feeders today. Clouds like slow, fat marshmallows.

"How's that school project coming along?"

He glances up at Trudy, who doesn't look back at him. Just keeps watering the plants, moving steady. She's in the same jeans she always wears, holes in the knees and old grass stains on the butt. A purple shirt today, way too big for her small frame.

"We should have it done this weekend," he says. "If Henry and Angela don't break up before then, anyway."

"And why would that happen?"

Resting back on his heels, feeling his thigh muscles stretch and burn, Greg lets out a long breath. "Angela told me she's going to dump him. I don't get it. They're all over each other at school. Like they're madly in love, or whatever."

Trudy sets the watering can on the ground and stares down at him for a few seconds, her mouth twisting like she's eaten something sour. Then she picks up a pair of shears and turns back to the sunflowers.

"Let me ask you something, Gregory."

Shit, here it comes. The question every adult asks a four-teen-year-old boy sooner or later. *Tell me, son, do you have a girlfriend?*

"Do you like being paraded around town as the goddamn knight in shining armor?"

Greg can't help it. He laughs.

"Hell, no," he says. And then, knowing that anything he confesses in this garden will never leave this garden, he adds, "Sometimes I wish I'd left her out there. Waited for someone else to go pull her out of the water."

"Of course you do." Trudy clips at the dead parts of her flowers with the same energy Greg has when he rips open a new bag of chips. "All that fanfare, everyone talking about you all the time . . ."

"It's an actual nightmare."

"You know that and I know that," says Trudy. "But don't you think most people believe you have it great? Don't you think they're jealous of you, saving the day like that? Doing what they could never do themselves?"

Greg plucks at the weeds beside his feet. "I really doubt anyone'd ever be jealous of me."

"Don't give me that self-pity," Trudy says. "You know I'm right. Everybody wants to be a hero. But the real heroes know it's a curse, not a blessing. So the next time you see those two acting all lovey-dovey, you remember this: it's always different on the inside."

Greg watches a chickadee flit from branch to branch. "They just seem so happy."

"Believe me, Gregory," says Trudy, turning back to the dead bits of her flowers, "people are rarely as happy as they seem."

The plan is to meet at Henry's place today. Greg finishes his Saturday breakfast of champions—Corn Flakes in watery skim milk—and heads out, walking down High Street. It's a lot cooler this morning than it was last week, sun hiding behind dark clouds.

Henry's house, a tidy blue ranch, looks deserted when Greg gets there. No cars in the driveway, curtains closed on all the windows. What if Angela dumped Henry and Henry's in there listening to shitty country breakup music or something? Or worse, what if Angela didn't dump him, and the two of them are hidden away in Henry's room, all wrapped up on his bed?

The door next to the driveway opens, and Henry steps out onto the brick steps. Gym shorts, no shoes or socks. Wet hair. No shirt. Drops of water clinging to his skin.

Aware of how huge he must look in his husky jeans and baggy Talking Heads shirt, Greg tries to suck in his belly. "Guess I'm early," he says. "Sorry about that."

Henry opens the door wider. "It's cool. My folks just left for their big Prescott grocery trip."

The kitchen is small but clean. No pictures or paperwork on the fridge. No clutter on the countertops. Henry leans against the stove and peels a banana, the sharp smell cutting through the odor of bleach.

"What do we have left to find?"

Greg sits down at the round oak table and takes their list out of his bookbag. Busies himself reading it, trying not to stare at Henry.

"More plants, mostly," says Greg. "Nothing too hard to find. Except maybe chert."

"What the fuck is chert?"

"A type of rock. There might be some down by the river."

Henry tosses his banana peel in the sink, then lifts it back out and places it in the trash can instead. Noticing Greg watching him, he laughs. "My old man hates messes."

The phone rings, and Henry dashes for it in a very un-cool, un-Them way.

"Hello? Angie, hey . . . Yeah, he's here, and . . . No, you didn't tell me that." Henry's voice changes. Happy to hopeless. "But the project . . . Fine. Will you call—"

Greg can hear the dial tone answering Henry's unfinished question. He stares at the list, eyes tracing the word chert over and over again. Chert. Chert. Chert.

Henry gently places the phone back on the hook. "So, no Angela today," he says. "She's got some family thing. Her aunts and cousins just showed up at her place."

"But all her family lives near Orono."

"Guess they drove up for the weekend," Henry says. "Whatever. Let's just go. Faster we get started, faster we can finish."

Greg, who hasn't been alone with this guy since they were the last two in line at the water fountain in fifth grade, feels his cereal trying to claw its way back up his throat. He swallows it down. Just get it over with. It's only a couple hours. Then Trudy's garden, and then home, and then all the junk food he can eat.

After Henry puts on a shirt and a pair of sneakers, they head out into the cool morning. They don't talk as they cross from Henry's backyard into the parking lot of the Diner, filled with pickup trucks. The smell of bacon punches through the air as they walk past the restaurant. At the intersection near the post office, an old lady in a Subaru waves them across the street beneath the blinking yellow light. It's a steep slope down Depot Hill, and Greg doesn't dare lift his eyes from the ground. He can feel the weight of his body wanting to topple forward, send him bouncing down the road.

Beyond the tracks, they walk down the path that leads toward the Aroostook Lodge, gravel crunching under their feet. Greg hasn't been here since that day with Angela, and the landscape feels like a foreign planet. Whenever he thinks of the river, he thinks of broken ice and roaring dark water and a cold so deep it could shatter bones. But this isn't that river. This is a late summer river, shallow and barely moving.

They set off upstream, passing under the bridge just as a log-truck trundles across the river. Greg can feel the vibration deep in his chest. The river smells strangely sweet. They search along the shore and find most of what they need—dead fiddleheads, rocks flecked with false gold that would flash like pennies if the sun were shining. But after nearly an hour, they still haven't found any chert.

"You think Mrs. Kalloch's messing with us?" asks Henry, dragging a stick through the reeds. "Making us look for something that doesn't even exist?"

Greg peers down at the ground, squinting to find any rock that might be the right thing. His desire for a good grade is outweighed by impatience to be done with this useless treasure hunt. "Maybe we should call it," he says. "We found everything else."

But Henry shakes his head. "We can't give up."

"It's only worth five points."

"It's not about the stupid points, Fortin. We just need to find it."

There's an edge to Henry's voice, and his eyes look almost frantic.

"Okay," Greg says. "We'll keep looking."

They trudge further upriver. In a half-dead oak tree, a murder of crows is making a big fuss, squawking and flapping their wings. The clouds are thicker now.

"You and Angie been friends a long time, right?"

Surprised, Greg stops walking and stares at Henry, who chews at his bottom lip.

"Since grade school," Greg says, "but not so much anymore."

"But you still, like, *know* her, right?"

Greg leans down to pick up a round, flat rock, hoping Henry doesn't notice how hard he has to work to stand back up. "What do you want to know?"

"Is she all there? You know, mentally? Or is she kind of, like, crazy?"

Greg might not have gone to the funeral, but he knows how Bridget Theroux died. *Crazy* is one of the nicer words people have been whispering about her ever since.

"Are you asking me if Angela wants to off herself?"

"Fuck," Henry says, staring at Greg. "No, that's not what I mean. Jesus, dude."

"Well then what the hell are you asking?"

"I don't know." Henry gazes downriver. "I just mean that every time I think she's happy with me, she gets all weird. Especially lately. She's been acting really weird lately. Like . . . canceling plans on me and not calling me back. Crap like that."

Four big crows hop from branch to branch, screaming at nothing.

"It's like, she thought I was one thing," Henry continues, "but then I wasn't. Or she was hoping I *could* be something, and I can't."

"Something like what?"

"Some kind of Prince Charming who saves people from dragons or warty stepmothers or some shit like that."

It's none of Greg's business. It's not his relationship. But for the first time ever, he feels sorry for Henry. All the things Henry doesn't know about what being a hero really means. What a hassle it is; a load to carry.

Henry drags his hand through his hair. "Forget it. Maybe I'm just imagining things."

Greg tosses the stone into the water, and they watch it skip across the surface five, six times before disappearing. "You're not imagining things," he says.

"She's gonna dump me, isn't she?"

"Yeah." Seeing the hurt on Henry's face, Greg adds, "Look, she's dumb, okay?"

"No," says Henry. "She's right."

Greg remembers that winter day here at the river. How they both heard Angela screaming for help, how Henry stood still while Greg went running.

Rain starts to fall in big, fat drops. Henry turns to run back toward the bridge, Greg doing his best to keep up without tripping and crashing to the ground. Once they're under the bridge, they stop, Greg panting. The rain is a solid gray wall of water. The crows keep shrieking.

"Man, I wish they'd shut up," says Greg as Henry begins digging through a pile of rocks beside one of the bridge pylons, graffitied with veiny dicks and phrases like *LedZep 4LIFE* and *Mandy W has crabs*.

"Dude." When Henry looks up, he's smiling. He holds out his hand, the black rock resting on his palm. "I think I found our fucking chert."

Greg doesn't know what kind of rock it is, but it's definitely not chert.

"You did," Greg says. "You found it."

It's still raining when Greg gets to Trudy's house about an hour later. He finds her on the porch, tucked under a blanket in an Adirondack chair with a mug of tea in her hands.

She pats the chair beside her. "If we can't pull weeds, we'll just watch them grow."

They sit a long time without saying anything, long enough that Greg's calve muscles, twitchy from the walk back from the river, start to calm down. His heart slows. He breathes in the damp air, the sweetness from the rose bushes next to the house. The only sounds are the rain and the clink of Trudy's wedding rings against her mug.

Greg thinks about Angela carrying that blue egg all over town. Henry carrying a piece of rock that wasn't the rock they needed.

"Finish that school project?" asks Trudy. "Or did the love-birds break up first?"

"We got it done."

Setting her empty mug on the arm of her chair, Trudy gazes out at the garden, green and glistening with rain. "You'll have your pick, you know," she says. "Once you're old enough, and you're ready, and you get yourself out of this town, you'll have a whole world of Angelas and Henrys to choose from."

The right thing to do—the safe thing—is to deny it. Pretend to have no idea what she's talking about.

Greg rests his head against the back of the chair. He breathes in the scent of roses. "I sure as hell hope so," he says.

They watch the rain a long, long time. All the flowers are the right colors again.

That night, after supper—chicken and white rice, no surprise there—Greg calls Angela. It rings a long time before her mother picks up, coughing so hard he has to repeat himself twice. He can hear what sounds like a bunch of women in the background, all talking over one another.

"It's GREG," he shouts into the receiver.

"Oh, Greggie, you sweet boy. You just hold right on."

There's a heavy clunking sound as if she's let the phone

dangle from the cord onto the orange linoleum of their kitchen, then Angela's voice is on the line, annoyed.

"I told Henry I had family here today, and it's not my fault if—"

"You know that robin egg you found last week?"

"Yeah?"

"I know how much you like it," says Greg, "but could you add it to the scavenger hunt? We could use the extra points."

A pause. In the background, disco music and laughter. "Fine," she says, "whatever. It's just a stupid egg."

"And Angela?"

"What, Greg?"

"If you want to break up with him" he says, "just do it already. Don't keep stringing him along."

Another long silence. Greg imagines her eyes closing, her free hand twirling her hair. Finally, she lets out a long breath.

"Okay," she says.

He hangs up and walks into the living room, where his parents and sisters are sprawled on the couch and love seat, watching *The Fox and the Hound* for the thirtieth time—Aimee's choice, no doubt.

"Come sit with us," his mother says, but Greg says he's tired and heads upstairs to his room.

The usual routine. Lock the door, look around at everything familiar. Green bedspread. Periodic tables and *Indiana Jones* taped on blue walls. Crooked lampshade. Nintendo hooked up to the TV at the foot of his bed. And the door to his closet, halfway open. He's starving. He wants everything hidden under those floorboards, every piece of candy, every last chip crumb. He closes the closet door.

Then he sits down at his desk and unzips his bookbag, taking out all the items he and Henry found today. When he gets to the small black rock, Greg stops. Presses it into the palm of his hand, just like Henry did. Presses it to his face, surprised by how cool it feels against his lips. He opens his mouth, places the stone inside. Closes his eyes and holds the stone there, only for a second. Thinks of bird nests and perfect blue egg-shells and the sound of rain.

The stone tastes like the river. Sweet.

10.
SIT, SPEAK, STAY

I n the forest, the leaves are changing. Pale green bleeding into yellow. The light is faded, as if the sun is exhausted from shining so bright all summer long. Everything smells like dying vegetation. September.

"Willie, please." Alice tugs on the leash and tries to get Willard away from the river, where he's lying in the reeds. "Willie, don't you want to go home? Have a snack?"

The St. Bernard rolls onto his back, exposing his white belly. His enormous paws twitch at the air and he stares up at the sky as if trying to decide whether the clouds look more like Alice's favorite flats (which are now open-toed) or Roger's reading glasses (which Roger now has to wear like a monocle, as they're missing an arm).

"Damn dog."

Willard licks her hand, and Alice nuzzles her face in his soft neck, inhaling the smells of river water, pet dander, and something, like buttered corn.

In the tall grass, crickets sing. The periwinkle sky is huge and close, and the river laps at the shore with gentle, smacking kisses. Forward, retreat; forward. Retreat.

Whenever Roger cooks supper, Nora eats everything on her plate, no matter if the pasta is overcooked or the beef a little too pink. But she barely touches the meals Alice carefully prepares from Nora's own recipe cards, written out in the old woman's cursive and covered in indeterminate stains. Not hungry, Nora claims, and trudges off to her room.

"How long is she going to punish us?" Alice asks Roger as they wash the dishes. Bright kitchen, refrigerator hum, apple-scented air blowing in from the open window.

Roger rinses a Dalton Diner mug—*Good Eats Here!*—and hands it to Alice to wipe dry. "When I was twelve," he says, "she gave me the silent treatment for two weeks after I refused to wear her homemade sweaters to school anymore."

"That's ridiculous."

"That's Ma."

Later, they shut their bedroom door. Alice pulls her t-shirt over her head. Kisses Roger, slow.

"Want me to—"

"You better."

A rhythm familiar since their first night together two years ago, in his Portland apartment down near Maine Med. Back then, their movements made to the occasional wail of sirens, rumble of jets taking off from the airport. Now a different soundtrack: distant boom of lumber tossed from forklift to muddy ground at the mill across the river, Nora's Mack-truck snores down the hall.

Afterward, mumbles in the dark. Water bill due next week. Town gossip (Nate Theroux's still on leave from the police department, but no surprise there, after all he's been through). Plans for tomorrow's dinner—Alice wants to attempt Nora's tourtière.

"Don't put yourself through the effort, Al." "You know she's just going to throw another hissy fit."

"If she'd just give me a chance . . ."

They've had variations of the same conversation for months, ever since the new director at the Whispering Pines Retirement Village jacked up the rent and Nora could no longer afford to live there.

"Maybe I should try to talk to her," says Roger.

"God, no. Then she'd turn on both of us."

"I hate how she treats you."

"I know." Alice watches his chest rise and fall as he breathes. "She did eventually get over the sweater thing, right?"

"Sure," he says. "But this is bigger than a sweater. God only knows how long she'll make us suffer."

On the floor beside their bed, Willard lies on his side, paws twitching in his sleep. What's he chasing? Or is something chasing him? Maybe both. One after the other until they forget how it started, who started it. Circles, all around.

Every morning, Alice heads down to the kitchen. She tries to tiptoe—Nora's such a light sleeper—but Willard has no regard for quiet. He skates his nails against the hardwood, stomps on his metal dish until Alice pours the kibble. She makes coffee. Toast with blackberry jam. Usually by the time she gets Willard inside after he does his business all over the lawn, both the coffee and toast are cold.

She goes to the annex at the back of the house, where Willard claims his spot on the blue love-seat. Always the wash of calm when she steps into this room, all her familiar things laid out how she likes them. Built-in shelves, rainbow of book spines. Windows that look out past the line where the lawn ends and the wild takes over. Goldenrod, Queen Anne's lace, tiger lilies; something purple, something pink. Beyond the flowers, pointed tops of evergreens.

A room with a view. That's what Alice always wanted, and that's what she found in this house in Dalton, all the way at the top of Maine where trees vastly outnumber people. From the outside, nothing about their old farmhouse is all that different from the others on Davis Road—the siding needs to be repainted; the driveway is cracked from decades of harsh winters. She and Roger haven't had time to pour the same kind of work into the place Nate Theroux has put in at his house, half-mile down the road. But inside, the rooms are bright and clean enough. Good air, good light.

Since she and Roger moved into the house in March, Alice has come to this room every morning, no matter how tired she is, or menstrual, or cranky. Even after they adopted Willard and he peed all over the house, even after Nora moved in with her big suitcases and permanently pinched lips, Alice kept this room a priority. Sacred space, sacred time. Everything she needs to write the book she's dreamed of writing since she read *Charlotte's Web* when she was seven years old. Every morning, the sun makes her rolltop desk glow. In front of her, the Royal typewriter she inherited from her grandfather, who had also loved words—mostly those that could be inserted into slightly off-color limericks and read aloud over a glass of Jim Beam.

Fingers on keys. Blank paper like clean snow.

And every morning, nothing happens. Alice stares at the paper. She wants to write a story about a family that isn't hers, a family whole and unbroken. But where do you begin? And how do you know when you've reached the end?

Six months, and not a single word.

Dalton.
Talk about a closed fist.

Six months, and most people here still treat Alice as though she's an alien, or, worse, what she really is: a Southern Mainer. One of them "city types," grew up in Portland, might as well be from Massachusetts. The tight smile, followed by the hard-as-steel stare she gets at the Diner, the post office, Bergeron's.

She didn't expect the town to fall in love with her, but she did anticipate at least a tacit acceptance. Nora's lived in Dalton since she married Roger's late father over fifty years ago, and Roger lived here until he moved down to Orono for college. So what if he kept going south after that, so what if he landed in

Portland? Home is home, no matter how far you wander, how long you stay away. But people here have been treating Roger the same way they treat Alice, with a vague yet palpable air of distrust.

Maybe it's not just the Southern Maine thing. Maybe it's also the twenty-year age gap (which she and Roger tend to forget about, but others probably see as the height of scandal), or the fact that Alice calls herself a writer (not many artist types here). Maybe, quite possibly, it's all of it.

"Do they just need more time?" Alice asks Roger when they're given the silent treatment from other customers at the Store 'N More one afternoon. "They won't always see us as From Away, will they?"

"Maybe," says Roger, as he watches the flannel-clad men standing around the chest freezer full of live bait, "we should have just stayed Away."

And as for Willard, she blames late spring in Northern Maine. Lilacs full and fragrant, hummingbirds at the feeder, snow fading from the distant blue crown of Mt. Katahdin. Nora was still living at the Pines. Everything pointed to permanence, possibility.

"Have you ever had a dog?" Roger asked, as he and Alice sat on the porch one evening.

"Gram and Gramp had a terrier when I was a kid."

"But now you want a big dog?"

"I just think a house in the country needs a big dog."

She could tell Roger was skeptical, but that was his nature. He thought a long time about things before coming to an answer, and even then, he might change his mind. She tended to make bold, quick decisions.

The animal shelter in Prescott was a clammy, ammonia-smelling cinderblock building out near a bunch of broccoli fields. A girl who couldn't have been more than nineteen—baby-fat cheeks, blonde hair held back in a braid—led Alice and Roger through a row of sad-eyed hounds and spotted mutts. In the last cage, there was the sound of teeth on fabric. Alice peered in to see a giant ball of fur. The dog's body quivered as he tore at a red blanket squished between paws the size of teacup saucers.

"That's Buster," the shelter girl said. "The couple who adopted him from the breeder couldn't get him to do anything. Gave up, brought him in. We're working on him, but he doesn't listen very well."

"How long has he been here?" At the sound of Alice's voice, the dog stopped chewing and stared at her, cocking his head to one side. His tail *whumped* up and down.

"About a month. It's been tough to find him a home—people just don't want to deal with a St. Bernard. Sweet but *huge*. This one'll rip your arm right off the first time he sees a squirrel if you don't know how to handle him."

Alice crouched down. She curled her fingers around the metal squares of the cage, and he belly-crawled over to lick them, staring at her with chocolate eyes the whole time.

Five minutes into the ride back to Dalton, Buster was renamed Willard. About two minutes after that, Willard clambered into the passenger seat, settled on Alice's lap, and puked all over her blue skirt.

That was the same June day Bridget Theroux killed herself. But Alice and Roger didn't know it then. They found out like everyone else, after the ambulance showed up at Nate's house that night, after Nate got home and found Bridget in the bathtub. Anyone with a police scanner in their kitchen and the right connections in town found out what happened and called everyone else who didn't. *Not an accident*, they said. *Suicide*, they said.

Just half a mile down the road. Half a mile. All that pain and sorrow, all that lonely, all too close to home.

A jolt of attraction sizzles along Alice's spine each afternoon when Roger comes back from Best Family Farms smiling and smelling of sweat and sunshine, the back of his neck gritty with dust from the potato fields. She always hated that he worked at that bank in Portland, stuffed in a windowless box eight hours a day. Now, Roger seems more like Roger, as if he's stepping into the person he was always supposed to be.

Alice wants to step into herself, too. She's waiting.

When they had first showed Roger's mother her bedroom, decorated with simple pine furniture and vases of purple lupines they picked for her from a field down the road, Nora just stood in the doorway clutching her suitcase.

"What do you think, Ma?" Roger asked. "Not bad, right?"

She squinted at the light streaming through the windows. "Awful bright, Rogie," she said. "Don't think those drapes are up to the task."

Alice had bought the curtains at the Prescott Kmart. Light blue, like the walls in Nora's apartment at the Pines, embroidered with delicate white birds. They're balled up in Alice's closet now, gathering dust.

Three afternoons a week, Alice shelves books at the Dalton Community Library while Trudy Haskell putters nearby. She likes Trudy, who can go from no-bullshit task master to softhearted librarian at the snap of a finger. One second telling Alice she's shelved the gardening books incorrectly—delphiniums don't plant the same as dianthus, everybody knows that—and the next, pulling a pigtailed little girl aside to whisper excitedly about dinosaur books.

One Friday in late September during the afternoon lull, Trudy stops unpacking new books to stare at Alice with steel-silver eyes.

"You're a drinker, right?"

"Excuse me?"

"Oh, don't get all offended. I mean do you and Roger ever get out to Frenchie's?"

"We've only gone once," says Alice.

"Why?"

"I don't know . . . just not our scene, I guess."

The last time she and Roger went to the bar down on Main Street, the Bud-drinking millworkers had ignored them, and the costume-jewelry bartender had stared at Alice as if she were speaking a foreign language when she asked for a Gritty's Pale Ale.

As they close up the library at the end of the day, Trudy turns to Alice. "I haven't seen much of Bevy since Bridget died," she says. "Busy taking care of her grandbaby and all, now that Nate's had himself a mental breakdown. But sometimes the two of us go out to Frenchie's, have a few. Make all those men in there listen to our girly music on the jukebox."

"Sounds nice."

"Good. Because you're coming with us, next time we go."

Before Alice can reply, Trudy ushers her out of the building, locks the door, and struts down the leaf-strewn path that leads to the parking lot, which is shared by the grade school. Along the way, she shouts at a group of teenagers clumped near the rusty swing-set to stop sneaking those goddamn cigarettes and get back home to their mothers.

Say what you will about Trudy Haskell, but that woman knows how to make an exit.

Another attempt at dinner. Nora's recipe for stroganoff. "Not hungry," the old woman says, and trudges up to her bedroom.

Alice and Roger wash the dishes in silence. When he drops the Dalton Diner mug and it shatters on the linoleum, she doesn't help him clean it up. He tries to glue the broken ceramic back together, but it's no use. *Good Eats Here* becomes *God Eats Her.*

"Maybe we need to stop trying so hard to make her happy," says Roger as they lie in bed later that night. "Maybe we just stop feeding her and let her sulk."

"That's what you do with children," Alice says. "Send them to bed hungry so they learn their lesson."

Slight smile on his lips, worry in his eyes. "I don't know if you've noticed," he says, "but my mother *is* a child."

About six weeks after Nora moves in, Alice leaves her writing room after another morning of not writing. At the kitchen table, Nora plays solitaire. It's past 11:00, but she's still in her purple housecoat, white hair coiled up in rollers. Usually, she doesn't emerge from her room until Alice leaves for the library after lunch. Alice finds evidence of the old woman's movements through the house—cookie crumbs in the sink, crossword puzzle books on the table. Strange that she's here now. Alice doesn't want to scare her off. No sudden movements.

As she makes herself a turkey sandwich, Willard pressing his nose against her hip, Alice hears Nora's stomach let out a drawn-out growl.

"You want lunch?"

Silence. Then the old woman's voice, small and resigned. "I s'pose," she says, "if you have enough."

Alice spreads Miracle Whip in an even layer all the way to the crusts. She stacks tomato (blotted so the juice won't run), cheese, and turkey (leanest slices in the bag) on a crisp, green square of iceberg. Cuts the bread on a diagonal, just like her Gram used to do for her when she was a kid.

Nora stares at the sandwich as though Alice has just handed her a pile of Willard's shit.

"Can't stomach this whole-wheat stuff," she says, pushing the plate into the center of the table, next to yesterday's copy of

The Bangor Daily News—Bush and Gorbachev urging Iraq to leave Kuwait. "You know, there's nothin' wrong with plain old Wonder bread."

"We don't have that."

"Guess I ain't hungry, then."

Get out now or say something Alice knows she'll immediately regret. Something that will backfire on both her and Roger. She leaves her own sandwich on the counter and tells Willard they're going for a walk.

When they reach the river, she lets the dog flop onto his belly in the reeds and sits on the gravelly shore while he laps at the water. The snap in the air makes her think of foggy nights and Jack-o-lanterns.

There's a splash not far downriver. Willard lifts his head and growls, a guttural rumble that seems to come from deep inside a barrel. Alice's heart stutters. No other person should be here. This is her and Roger's land, thirty acres of pure, untamed river frontage.

Another splash. Pebbles crunching beneath human feet.

There could be anybody out here. Rapists with guns. Poachers with guns. Rapist poachers with guns. And what is she against thousands of acres of wild woods? Nothing. Like this river, just energy flowing through for a moment before it disappears forever. Just half a mile down the road, Bridget Theroux had felt that same powerless insignificance. A different kind of fear, an internal one, but a fatal one all the same.

Alice doesn't try to hold Willard back when he lunges forward. He sprints past a fallen white birch, rounds a bend, and his barking abruptly stops. She waits, saliva like copper, trying to decide whether to chase after the dog or save herself and run toward the house.

Then Willard comes back into view, his mouth open in a grin as he trots beside Nate Theroux. Alice's heart slows; her muscles relax.

The last time she saw Nate was a few weeks ago, at Bergeron's. She was buying aspirin, coffee, oranges. Nate was in line ahead of her, clutching a bottle of Allen's in one hand and a plastic deli container in the other. A freckle-faced teenage boy bumped into Nate, who dropped the container on the floor, egg salad splattering the orange tiles. The kid ran off, past the wall of locally crafted signs that boasted grammatically questionable phrases such as *Mamas Alway's Right* and *Lifes Better Upta Camp*. Nate wouldn't let Alice or the cashier, an old lady with blue eyeshadow, help him clean up the mess. "My fault," he said.

Alice walks toward Nate and Willard, who took off with his leash and is now dragging it through the shallow water that laps at the shore. "Hello, there."

Nate returns her smile, but there's no light in his sapphire eyes. He's dressed in jeans, faded plaid shirt, sneakers. His brown hair sticks out over the tops of his ears. In one of his hands, a pile of stones.

"Hope I didn't scare you," he says. "I was just skipping these. Used to do it when I was a kid."

He tosses the rest of the rocks into the river, where they land with little splashes. Willard jolts forward to chase them, but Nate grabs the leash, holds firm. "Cool it, bub." Voice soft as the current meandering downstream. Willard stares up at him with lovey eyes, then settles on his belly, back in the reeds.

"How'd you do that?" Alice asks. "When I try to get him to sit and stay, he usually runs away faster."

"I don't know." Somewhere nearby, a cardinal sings. *Chew-chew-chew.* "Do you ask him or tell him?"

"Ask, I guess."

"Maybe that's why?"

When she met Nate this past winter, he stood so tall. And he smiled so often, especially whenever he talked about Bridget or Sophie. Now he wilts like the flowers in the meadow, spent, dreading the winter ahead.

"I'm sorry, by the way," Nate says.

"For what?"

"Being out here, on your land. Our property butts up against yours. Sometimes I forget where the line is."

That word—our. Three months since Bridget died, and Nate still doesn't think of himself as a single my.

"Don't worry about it," says Alice. "No one really owns a river anyway, right?"

"True enough." He hands the leash over to her. "I should be heading back. You take care."

"You, too."

Alice watches Nate until he rounds the bend. The shape of grief—shoulders hunched, head held toward the ground, not one glance up toward the sky.

"Let's go, Willie."

The dog's brown eyes fix on hers, but he makes no move to get out of the water. She tries again, making her voice firmer this time, her hold on the leash loose but steady.

"Willard. Come."

He stands. Shakes water off his fur, lips flapping like wings. He walks beside her all the way home. Only pulls at the leash once, when a chipmunk darts across the forest path in front of them, then settles down when Alice commands him firmly to stop. Back at home, she feeds him the turkey from Nora's uneaten sandwich. Special treat for a good boy.

A week later, Alice sits in a booth at Frenchie's across from Trudy and Bev Theroux. Trudy's wearing a pale pink sweater dress; Bev's in jeans and a green top. She's at least six feet tall, and her curly hair, which poofs out around her head like a storm cloud, makes her look even taller. Alice gets the impression she could pick potatoes or chop wood all day and still have energy left over.

ZZ Top plays on the jukebox, lit up electric blue under a

buzzing Budweiser sign. Staring down at them is a collection of deer and bear faces frozen in placid acceptance of their deaths, along with one huge moose head choking beneath a layer of dust.

"So, Alice. Tru tells me you're doing all right at the library."

"I still can't remember all the Dewey numbers."

"Well, at least you're not shelving philosophy with geography anymore," Trudy says.

"And how's it going with Nora?"

Alice tugs at a strand of her hair. "I don't know," she says. "The same, I guess."

Bev shakes her head. "If I hadn't left the Pines . . ."

"For Chrissake, Bevy," says Trudy. "Stop blaming yourself for everything."

The two women share a glance loaded with love and exasperation. It's the same way Alice looks at Roger when he refuses to throw out the dirty kitchen sponges, the same way he looks at her when she forgets to leave the bills to be paid in the special *BILLS TO BE PAID* folder near the microwave.

Not for the first time, Alice wonders if there's something deeper than friendship between Bev and Trudy—and if there is, if it's a secret to the town, or if it's well known but stubbornly ignored, the same way the weathered millworkers and baby-faced twenty-somethings at the bar pretend not to see the few migrant workers who sit in the dimly lit corner near the bathroom. Roger once told Alice, who was surprised to see the brown-skinned, small-boned men playing soccer at MacGregor Field one summer night, that it isn't uncommon for Hondurans to rent rooms above the furniture store by the season. "Broccoli pickers," he explained.

Mellie Martin appears with gin and tonics for Trudy and Bev. Nothing for Alice. Before she can ask for a Zema (she hates that shit, but she's not a hard liquor person, and she's not in the mood for Bud or PBR), Mellie turns and points a dagger-like purple fingernail at her.

"Got something special for you," she says. She hurries off to a curtained-off room behind the bar, then back to the table, a bottle of beer in her hands. "Gritty's Pale, right? I felt kinda bad that time you came in and wanted one, so I ordered some."

Alice reaches for the bottle and fights back the sudden, stupid urge to cry. "You didn't have to go to all that trouble."

"Yeah, well, you're prob'ly the only one that'll drink it in this crowd."

As Mellie returns to the bar, Alice looks at Bev and Trudy, both of whom stare at her with amused looks on their faces.

"This town," says Bev. "We don't do too well with unfamiliar things here, do we?"

Trudy takes the lime wedge from the rim of her glass and squeezes it into her G&T. "Now *there's* an understatement." She offers the lime to Bev, who sucks at the pale flesh before tossing the rind into her own drink.

"And on that note," Bev says as ZZ Top morphs into Bachman-Turner Overdrive, "I've had just about enough of this music."

Trudy's gray eyes sparkle with mischief. "Here's a couple quarters," she says, reaching into her purse.

Bev heads across the room, barking out enthusiastic greetings to everyone she sees along the way. Some of the men make sour faces as she reaches the jukebox.

"Do they ever try to stop her?" Alice asks.

"Would *you* try to stop a woman that size?" Trudy snorts with laughter as Bev feeds some change into the machine and the familiar intro of a Dolly Parton song begins to play. "No one messes with Bevy."

Or with you, Alice almost says, but stops herself. Something is happening, something she doesn't want to ruin with her own words. Bev and Trudy find each other's eyes across the room as easily as if the bar was empty save for the two of them, and Bev beckons with her index finger. Trudy shakes her head, sips her drink. Bev moves closer, big hips swaying as if rocked by river waves.

"Trudy Elisabeth Haskell." Her voice so loud everyone stops drinking and shooting pool and looking up at the TV mounted in the corner behind the bar to stare at her. "Get your bony ass out here."

"Oh, for Chrissake," Trudy mutters, her cheeks blooming red. "But I s'pose. She'll just keep raising hell if I don't." Then she grins, a wide, pretty grin Alice has never seen in the three months they've worked together at the library.

Trudy walks on tiny feet to the center of the dance floor, where Bev pulls her into her arms, keeping just a little distance between them. The height difference between the women is startling—Trudy might top five feet at most—but somehow they fit together. Bev leads Trudy in a practiced two-step, both of them laughing, breathless, as Dolly sings on.

Everyone else goes back to drinking, or shooting pool, or staring at the TV. But Alice watches the couple in the middle of the room. Sway, step, step, sway. Two bodies in complete sync, moving through the neon glow. On the plywood floor, their shadows morph into one shape, chasing them as they trace their imperfect circle. Sway, and step, and sway. Love, and love, and love.

Hours later, Alice undresses in the darkness of her and Roger's bedroom. He lies sprawled out and half-asleep on top of the blankets. Sweatpants, bare chest, dogeared Leon Uris paperback beside him.

She presses her naked skin to his and kisses him until he wakes, his arms wrapping around her waist. Willard slumps onto his dog bed, grunting like an old man. The inside of Alice's skull feels warm and swirly as it always does after she's had a few drinks. Down the hall, rumble of Nora's truck-driver snores.

"Roger?"

"Hmm?"

"This was supposed to be our life," she says. "Not ours and hers."

"Tell me about it."

All those nights in his Portland apartment, scream of sirens, red-flash-blue-flash through the windows. The two of them curled up on his futon, talking about everything they were ready to leave behind. Long workdays. City traffic. Sweaty aerobics studios where Alice led bouncing, leotard-clad women to the cardio-quick beats of Madonna and Gloria Gaynor.

"I've run out of things to write about," Alice would tell Roger. "I need a new scene. A place I've never been before."

"When I was a kid, I couldn't wait to leave the County," Roger would say. "But lately I can't stop thinking about going back."

She thought *potential*. He thought *home*.

Roger presses his mouth into the hollow above Alice's collarbone. Outside, full moon, diamond-stars, feathered tops of trees. Tomorrow, big plans to drive to Prescott for their monthly run to Ames, where they can stock up on essentials like tampons and kibble. Items too expensive or not available at Bergeron's. Maybe they'll take the long road back to Dalton, wind through the fields behind Haystack Mountain (more of a hill than a mountain), past scattered, rusty trailers, leaning barns.

"I'm mad, too, you know," Roger says. "I wanted to give you something good here. But this fucking town. And my mother . . ."

Alice trails her hand along his chest, stomach, hip. Hush now. Later.

She wakes early one October morning. Familiar routine— feed Willard, bring him outside, back in for coffee and toast. Writing room. Sacred space, sacred time.

Outside, the sun is just a rumor, pale gray-orange glow on the horizon. Alice sits at her desk. Rests her fingers on the keys of her grandfather's typewriter. She usually tries so hard not to think of anyone in her family, tries to keep the hurt away.

Sometimes you have to let yourself fall in. Be clobbered by it.

She closes her eyes and thinks back to the conversation she and her grandfather had as he lay dying of stomach cancer five years ago.

"If I don't see you in the future," Gramp said, his gnarled fingers tangled up in hers, "I'll see you in the pasture."

She was his favorite girl, and he was everything to her, but he was ready to be with his wife, who'd died just six months before him from congestive heart failure. And he was ready to be with his only daughter, too. Deirdre. Deirdre, who never married and who gave her maiden name to *her* only daughter, because the father was a stranger of the one-night-only kind, gone by the time Deirdre skipped her period. Long gone by the time she gave birth to Alice. Long, *long* gone by the time ten-year-old Alice went to live with her grandparents, Harry and Marjorie O'Neill, after Deirdre was killed by a drunk driver on I-95, one foggy autumn night in '73, two days after Halloween. Rotting pumpkins everywhere.

Alice's fingers race and stumble across the keys. Every sentence riddled with words that might be wrong but also might be right. What stays and what goes? How do you decide? You decide later. Now, right now, as the sun finds its way above the trees, you sit here and you write them all.

Willard trots at her side, looking up at her often for guidance. Here. No. Leave the chipmunk alone. Stay. The river is low; water so clear Alice can see pebbles on the bottom. Maybe, just down the road, Nate is alone in the farmhouse he shared with Bridget and their baby. Maybe at this very moment, as Alice frees Willard from his leash and lets him run through the cold water, Nate is pacing the rooms of his house, imagining how much brighter they seemed when Bridget was inside them.

Back at home, Alice goes into her closet. She takes out the curtains that briefly hung in Nora's room and spends half-an-hour vacuuming up the dust and scraping off dog vomit crusted on their hems. Then she fills the clawfoot tub with water, kneels on the cold tile floor, and scrubs Dr. Bronner's into the delicate fabric. Willard pants next to her, his nose twitching as he breathes in the peppermint scent.

It's a windy, bright day, and the curtains only have to hang for an hour out on the line before they're dry. Back inside, the kitchen smells of simmering chicken stew, heavy on thyme and garlic as per Alice's grandmother's directions.

She heads upstairs, toward Nora's bedroom.

"What?" says Nora, opening the door and eyeing the pile in Alice's arms. "What're you doing with those drapes?"

Alice pushes her way into the room. She lays the curtains on the dresser. Hauling the chair out from the desk where Nora has piled a dozen crossword puzzle books, she says, "I'm hanging them up."

"I told you, they aren't heavy enough. Don't block the sun at all."

Alice climbs onto the chair and starts looping a curtain across the rod on the window nearest the bed, neatly made with the white quilt tucked over the pillows. A vase of dried hydrangeas on the nightstand sits beside a sepia-toned photograph of Roger's father. Separated by decades, the two men stand the same—slightly duck-footed. And they share the same shy, upside-down smile.

"Then we'll get some blinds to put behind them," Alice says.

"*Tabarnak.* That's too much fuss."

"For Christ's sake, Nora." She turns to face her mother-in-law, who looks tiny from this vantage point. "I chose these curtains for you, and we'll get you some damn blinds if that's what it takes for me to see them hanging up here."

Nora's hazel eyes, so much like Roger's, blink up at Alice.

Her hair is matted on one side, and her housecoat is faded, frayed at the sleeves. Alice wants to apologize, but she won't. Not this time.

Nora plunks down on the edge of the bed and starts bouncing her leg so hard the vase on the nightstand rattles. She presses her lips into a thin line. "Always hated blinds," she says. "Maybe just some of them sheer panels."

Feeling something flutter in her chest, like the wings of one of the birds embroidered on the blue fabric in her hands, Alice turns back to the task of hanging the curtains.

"Panels would look nice," she says.

The smell of Nora's White Rain shampoo fills the room. Alice can hear Roger and Willard outside, Roger laughing, Willard barking in response. Every now and then, the dog appears in her line of sight, tail wagging as he hauls around a stick the size of her arm.

She steps down off the chair and stands beside the bed to admire her handiwork. The sun pours in through the gauzy curtain fabric.

"I'll be damned," says Alice. "It *is* too bright."

At supper that night, Nora barely eats any of the chicken stew. But when Alice comes down to the kitchen early the next morning, she sees that two of the buttermilk biscuits, the ones she'd spent so long making, closely following every command of the neat handwriting on her grandmother's recipe cards, are missing from the cookie jar where Roger stored them the night before. In the sink—crumbs, a dirty butter knife. And a crossword puzzle, half-finished, open on the table.

11

MADE TO ORDER

F or a lot of men—maybe most men—a mid-life crisis means classic cars or twenty-year-old secretaries. For Richard Haskell, it's bacon. And sausage. And beef. The fattier, the better. This after decades of lean, unsalted chicken and fresh green salads.

A mid-life crisis, for Richard, is also the sudden return to a habit he had as a child of writing down his most mundane moments and observations in unlined notebooks, which he gets at Bergeron's, near the cheap birthday cards nobody ever seems to buy.

Forty-five years old. Almost halfway to the grave, and all he wants is greasy, dead flesh and the satisfaction of seeing his own handwriting marching neatly across paper in deep blue ink.

Sunday, Aug. 12, 1990—Breakfast at Diner. Bacon, extra-crispy. Eggs over easy. Pancakes. Coffee with cream and sugar. Corner booth by the window. Busy morning, big after-church crowd. Rose spilled glass of OJ. Hot and sunny, humid. AC still not working, too late in season to fix.

Richard thinks about Rose Douglas a lot, almost as often as he thinks about Bridget. Two months since the suicide, but Richard still spends hours contemplating how she did it. He knows how quickly blood pours from veins, the exact amount of pressure exerted from a heart in its last frantic moments. He knows how many pints of blood are in a human body. What he doesn't know is what Bridget must have been thinking as all that blood stopped flowing.

Enough, he tells himself, and this is when he turns his thoughts to Rose. Time to focus on the living. On the ones who might still be saved.

When Rose comes into the clinic one day in early August for her boys' annual checkups, she's smiling. "You won't believe it," she says as Richard checks Adam's reflexes, the kid's lower legs kicking out, his younger brother, Brandon, giggling from the green vinyl chair in the corner of the exam room.

"What won't I believe?"

"Arlene offered me my old job back," says Rose. "It's just waiting tables, but God, I need this. Did you know I been working nights at the Texaco in Prescott while Ma stays with the boys?"

Richard does know this. He also knows about the job at the Diner, because he was the one who suggested to Arlene that Rose might be a good fit—she'd done the gig before, after all, as a teenager. Surely not much about pouring coffee and serving burgers had changed in the few years since then. But let her think good things come out of nowhere. Let her think whatever god she might believe in is finally on her side.

"I didn't know," Richard tells Rose.

"You ever worked nights, Dr. H.?"

"Not since my residency."

"It's hell."

"Now that," he says, warming his stethoscope in his palm before placing it gently to Adam's chest, "I believe."

A week later he starts going to the Diner on a regular basis, after all these years of rarely making an appearance. He just wants a good, hot breakfast, he tells himself, and it couldn't hurt to check on Rose while he's there, make sure she's okay. It's not his fault those things just happen to coincide.

Sunday, Aug. 19, 1990—Sausage. Scrambled eggs. Anadama

bread (dry). First time trying the cappuccino (good). Table near door. Lot of chit-chat. Timothy Fortin having sale on paint & primer. Miz McGreevy doesn't tip (unsurprised). Rose tripped over a chair leg but didn't fall. Little rain. Trudy quiet.

After a long, mostly unhappy marriage, Richard is used to his wife's silence. But it's different now. He used to look at Trudy as she puttered around the kitchen doing dishes or as she knelt in the garden with her flowers, and he'd long to know what she was thinking. Wonder if she ever thought of him, if she remembered when they were young and they would take a blanket and a few bottles of beer down to the river on sticky summer nights. Stars and moonlight, water soft and sweet. The unexpected strength of her hips pulling him deep inside her. Does she remember, Richard used to wonder, does she remember any of that love at all?

But after Bridget dies, whenever Richard watches Trudy moving through the house and the garden as she always has, quick and straight, he doesn't wonder what she's thinking in her sharpened silence. He doesn't have to wonder anymore. It's Bev, he knows. It will always be Bev.

Sunday, Aug. 26, 1990—Bacon & sausage. Belgian waffles, strawberries. Table by soda machine. Nate came in just for a cup of coffee to go. Odd thing—he & Rose acted like they didn't know each other at all.

There have been all sorts of rumors about Tommy Merchant since he skipped town in July. People whispering as they pay for their cigarettes at the gas station, as they pick up their mail at the post office. That rotten bastard, out of jail so fast and then gone again, just like that, no explanation. And did you see him before he left? Face all busted up, two black eyes? Had to be his uncle or a cousin. You know how that family is.

There are also rumors, whispered in lower tones of voice, that Nate might have been the one to leave those marks on Tommy. Not many people around here really believe that, though.

But Richard knows what death can do. After his father's fatal heart attack, Richard went out one day to chop wood. It was his and Trudy's first October in the house on Winter Street. Recess at the grade school, kids out on the playground yelling and laughing as kids are meant to do. The air was almost frozen. The axe felt good in Richard's hands, and he swung it fast and hard. *THUNK. THUNK. THUNK.* With each swing, more momentum and rage for the next one. His father was dead, and the clinic was his, and everyone in Dalton needed him to be the man his father used to be. Loyal. *THUNK.* Sturdy. *THUNK.* Steady. *THUNK.* It wasn't until Richard felt Trudy's small, warm hands on his back that he realized what he'd done. Missed the woodpile, hacked instead into the pine bench she had so lovingly placed near her baby rose bushes. Didn't even notice. Didn't even see. "It's okay" she said. This was before Bev, before their marriage was all silence and unspoken things. "Let me do the rest." And she took the axe from his hands and she swung it not at the woodpile, but at the bench, finishing what Richard had accidentally started.

"I'm sorry," he whispered as she held him late that night. "That was unacceptable."

"Don't be stupid," Trudy said, stroking his hair, so much thicker back then. "That was grief."

So maybe it was Nate who beat the living hell out of Tommy Merchant. Maybe it wasn't. Richard doesn't care. He's just glad someone did.

Wednesday, Aug. 29, 1990—Steak, medium-rare. Onion rings. Dr. Pepper, first in years. Corner booth . . .

"Dr. H?"

Richard looks up to see Rose standing beside his table holding a coffee pot. She's in a black shirt, maroon Dalton Diner apron tied neatly behind her back. Her hair is pulled away from her face. Silver earrings dangle near her cheekbones.

"What're you doing here on a weekday?"

Closing his notebook and capping his pen, Richard says, "Took the day off. Leigh-Anne and Janine can handle the clinic without me."

"I didn't think you ever took days off."

"They say it's good to try new things, right?"

Sunshine coming through the window, brightness in her eyes. "Right," she says. "You want anything else? Dessert?"

"I'll take some apple pie if you split it with me."

The only other people in the restaurant are some of the same old ladies that come in after church on Sundays, a group of them tucked under the red neon clock. Richard can see George in the kitchen cleaning off the grill as Arlene leans against the industrial mixer nibbling on a slice of thick white bread.

"Deal." Rose shakes the coffee pot, contents sloshing. "Let me just put this back."

She returns with an extra spoon and a slice of pie, scoop of vanilla ice cream melting on top, and slides into the seat opposite Richard.

"Cheers," he says, clinking his spoon against hers.

Outside, late summer sun. Hardly any traffic. The yellow light at the intersection blinks. Cackle of laughter from the church ladies' table.

"How are the boys?" asks Richard between mouthfuls of pie. Cinnamon and sweetness.

"Good," Rose says. "Brandon's new thing is dinosaurs. Adam starts kindergarten this week. Ma says he'll be a real quick learner."

"I don't doubt it. And how's everything else?" He thinks back to the strange, charged silence between Nate and Rose here in the Diner a few days back, the way they each tried too hard to pretend like they didn't recognize the other. "Any new romances?"

Rose blushes. It's only then he notices the tiny diamond still on her left ring finger. "Just in my books," she says, and Richard feels ashamed for even imagining. She's not the disloyal type. No matter where Tommy is or what he's done. And Nate—of course not. No way Nate would have moved on from Bridget already. Probably never will.

"I'm sorry," he says. "That was over the line."

After a few moments, she speaks again. "Now can I ask you something?"

"Anything."

"How long since you last took a day off?"

When Richard answers, he doesn't know if he should laugh or cover his eyes. "Never," he says. "I've never taken a day off."

Rose licks ice cream off her spoon. "That's, like, really unhealthy."

"I've been thinking about closing the clinic."

It's not until the idea is out there, floating in the space between them, that Richard realizes how much he wants those words to be true.

"I don't know," he says. "Maybe it's a bad idea."

Rose taps her spoon against her lips, not taking her eyes off his face. Richard feels squirmy and humiliated, like a child about to get chastised for saying a bad word.

"I think that if you *can* do something, you oughtta do it. Life's real short."

"It is," says Richard.

And he thinks of his father, the good doctor, who never ate sugar or drank alcohol or smoked cigarettes, dead at fifty-seven. Bad genetics.

And Bridget Frazier-Theroux, twenty-six-year-old wife and mother, dead in a bathtub, alone. Bad everything.

"Life's just too damn short," Rose says.

Good Christ, it is.

Saturday, Sep. 1, 1990—Drank beer in sun. Maybe too much. Long walk around town. Saw Nate filling up truck at gas station. Didn't say hello. Bunion acting up. If clinic closed people could go to Prescott. It's really not a very bad drive.

He thinks about blood more than he'd like to. He sees vials and vials of it at the clinic before he sends them off to the lab in Prescott. After all these years, it still surprises him how dark human blood appears in those plastic vials. Like the thick grape juice his mother used to make him drink at church.

He specifically thinks about Bridget's blood. Not just what it must have been like in that bathtub—diluted, pink instead of purple—but what it felt and looked like gushing over his hands in the back of Trudy's Celebrity that December night last year. Hot, crimson, urgent. One accident, hardly a fender-bender, and the girl was in early labor. Sometimes it happens like that. The smallest little trauma. But still, it took Richard by surprise how quickly the blood flowed out of her as she lay on the backseat. Her jeans were ruined. When she peeled off her underwear, Richard looked away, giving her the tiniest bit of privacy he could. Like when the nurse leaves the exam room for a patient to get undressed and tie those ill-fitting johnnies around their waists only for Dr. Haskell to go into the room and have them remove the gown again.

"It's too soon," Bridget kept saying that winter night, as Trudy held her hand and Richard counted her heartrate. Blood everywhere, the smell of copper. "It's too soon and I've been having bad dreams."

"What kind of dreams?" Trudy asked, and in that moment, Richard loved his wife madly again, for being so good and so calm in an emergency. For knowing when to talk and what to ask and why the asking mattered.

"There's this building," Bridget panted, tears streaming down her face. Panicked green eyes. Dome light nearly blinding her. "A hundred stories high. And there's all this crying—a baby crying. Maybe my baby? And I'm supposed to do something about it. But there's so many rooms. I can't find the baby. I can't do anything."

"Strange dreams are very common in pregnancy," Richard said as he stared out the back window, watching Nate pace the dark and empty road.

"That's what I hear," said Trudy.

Bridget winced as another contraction tore through her. A marvel, Richard always thought, what a female body can withstand. Then she opened her mouth as if to say something else, but that's when he saw the red and blue lights flashing, reflecting off the abandoned church just down the road.

"It's okay," Richard promised Bridget. "You're going to be okay now."

Sunday, Sep. 2, 1990—Prime rib for supper.

Sitting in front of the TV, ignoring the national news, Richard makes plans. Writes lists, crosses them out, doesn't answer Trudy when she asks just what in the hell he's up to. *HOW TO KILL A BUSINESS*, he writes in all capital letters across the page of his notebook. *Set fire and collect insurance. Sell to lowest bidder. Disappear.*

But he crosses that out. Disappearing is too much like what Bridget did, and no matter how much Richard tries to want the same thing, he always comes back to the inescapable human will to live. To survive, or at least exist. Keep breathing.

Retire, he writes. Better.

But forty-five is far too young to retire, and Trudy doesn't make enough at the library to support them both. Neither of them have any sort of inheritance, no dead-family money coming to them in the near or distant future.

New job, writes Richard. Underlining it once, twice.

The words look alien. Flat blue letters staring up at him in the TV flicker. Accusing him of something ugly which is simply the truth. He's not qualified for any other job. He was born and educated and trained specifically for this one. Other doctors have options. Richard only ever had this clinic and the town's expectations.

Always a shoe that didn't fit quite right.

Not long after the funeral, he stopped wearing his white coat at the clinic. Everyone knows he's the doctor; he doesn't need to put on the damn uniform. The only thing he misses about it are the pockets, big enough to tuck away anything he might need during an exam—lollipops for upset children, extra pens, breath mints. But without the coat, he has more freedom of movement. His arms don't feel pinned down. He can breathe a little easier.

Tuesday, Sept. 4, 1990—Took afternoon off, drove to Prescott hospital. Spoke to Dennis Frost, said they could use me in their family practice dept. Good pay, good hours. Lunch at River Run. Reuben, French fries, Coke. Took long way back to town. Leaves just starting to turn. Dead deer out by the water tower. Big buck. Surprised no one's sawed off the rack.

One hot, dry evening, he runs into Bill Theroux at the meat counter in Bergeron's, both of them reaching for the last ribeye. Bill looks at Richard with hungry, empty eyes. Overhead, fluorescent lights hum. The store smells like freezer burn and fresh bread. "You got here first," Bill says, but Richard pushes the steak into Bill's hands. "I can't take it from you," Richard says. Sometimes he thinks the right thing would be to tell Bill about their wives. But maybe Bill knows already. Maybe he believes in silence, too, and to tell him would be cruel. Bill drops the steak into Richard's green plastic basket. "You're not taking anything from me," he says. "I'm giving it to you."

Thursday, Sept. 6, 1990—Lunch special, beef stroganoff. Two servings. Short-staffed. Rose waited all the tables by herself.

His father used to make stroganoff. The noodles were always a little overcooked, and the gravy wasn't quite thick enough. But it was Richard's favorite meal, because it came from his father's hands, and even as a child, he understood that was something special and rare and not to be ignored.

One time, Richard might have been around ten years old, his father was in the middle of cooking this meal when there was frantic knocking on the front door. His mother answered. Rushed voices in the hallway, then his mother came running into the kitchen with a girl not much older than Richard right behind her. The girl had big blonde hair, and she looked familiar, someone he'd seen around town before. But in the moment, Richard couldn't remember her name.

"You gotta come quick," the girl said to his father, and Simon Haskell, recognizing an emergency when he heard one, turned off the gas stove, picked up his black doctor's bag from the table, and followed the girl out into the night.

"What's wrong?" Richard asked his mother. "What happened?"

She wouldn't look at him. "Mind your business," she said. "One day, you'll understand."

It was 1956. The girl's name, Richard remembered a few days later, was Sally Wilkins. She had an older sister, Mary, seventeen years old. People in Dalton said all sorts of things, but mostly it all came back to this: Those Wilkins girls. They sure do like the boys.

That was the last time Richard's father made stroganoff.

Saturday, Sept. 8, 1990—Diner closed, George & Arlene's anniversary. Grilled cheeseburgers at home. Gregory Fortin over to help T. with garden. Saw Rose at Store 'N More picking up pizza, boys were with her. Brandon had a little plastic T-Rex. Adam tried to sneak candy bar into his pocket, but Rose caught him. No rain in two weeks. Good time for vacation.

He has Stacey cancel a week's worth of appointments and tells a disbelieving Janine and Leigh-Anne to take some well-deserved time off.

One bright morning, Richard locks himself in the empty clinic and stands in every room, lets the memories come. Glass wall in the waiting room Trudy always said looked cheesy but most of the patients, especially the kids, love. In the front office, charts lined up in alphabetical order, some dating back to when his father ran the place. Pink folders for girls and women; blue for boys and men. Richard's father started that up, too, and Richard never had the heart to change it even though he agreed with Trudy that it was sexist and unnecessary. His office is cluttered with paperwork, skeleton in the corner looking dusty and yellow.

In Exam One, he lies on the cot, stares up at the water-stained drop ceiling. This is what his patients see as he tells them they have cancer, or syphilis, or diabetes. This is the ceiling sixteen-year-old Rose Douglas stared at when he had to tell her that all her vomiting wasn't the flu, but morning sickness. It's the same ceiling twenty-five-year-old Bridget Frazier-Theroux saw when he delivered the same news to her.

Just one word, and the whole world changes. *Pregnant.* Rose wept. Bridget smiled.

Monday, Sept. 10, 1990—Breakfast at Diner. Crepes. Hot chocolate. Back for lunch, mac & cheese. Rose not there. Still

no rain. Everything dead or almost dead. Just about time to
start the wood for winter.

He thinks about Bridget and he worries about Rose, but this
is another ugly, simple truth:

Rose is alive, and Bridget isn't, and he can only take credit
for one of these things.

Colic, he told her when she brought Sophie into the clinic
this past spring. Just colic, nothing to worry about, and he
didn't think to look hard at Bridget, to ask if she was really
there for the baby, or for herself.

Born and educated and trained specifically for this one job,
and Dr. Haskell didn't even consider postpartum depression. It
never crossed his mind.

Mon, 9/10—Luigi's for supper. Bacon-wrapped shrimp.
Bloody Mary. Ate at bar, why not. Discharging patients long
process but doable, they'll be angry but what does it matter.
Drive back to Dalton felt longer than usual.

"What is wrong with you?"

He's surprised and pleased to hear a trill of panic in Trudy's
voice rather than the familiar edge of disappointment. He looks
up from where he's hugging the toilet to see her standing in the
bathroom doorway. Pink pajamas. Mycroft weaves between her
ankles, meowing.

"Are you dying?" she asks, and there it is again, that panic,
right on the surface for Richard to acknowledge.

"Not dying," he says. "Bad shrimp."

Trudy gently kicks the cat away and wets a washcloth at the
sink. She sits on the edge of the tub and presses the cool, damp
cloth to his forehead. Nothing has ever felt so good. He closes
his eyes, rests his cheek against her thigh. She doesn't move
away.

"Where did you eat shrimp?"

"Prescott. Luigi's."

"Well, for Chrissake, Richard, what'd you expect?"

The cat settles down beside his feet. Dark outside already, but it's not that late—seven, maybe eight. This time of year the light goes fast.

Downstairs, the phone rings. He feels Trudy's leg tense beneath his face, but she stays put.

"Won't that be Bev?" he asks. "Calling to say goodnight?"

A brief silence. Then Trudy says, "I can call her back later. Be quiet, now. Try to relax."

It's so easy to forget—she is capable of little kindnesses.

"And don't barf on my goddamn slippers."

Her own strange way of loving.

Wednesday, Sept. 12, 1990—Eggs and toast at home. Early to clinic. Steady day, no surprises.

When Richard steps into Exam Two and sees the woman slumped on the cot, for a breathless moment, he thinks it's Rose.

But then the woman looks up, and he understands his own confusion. In all the years he's known her, Annette Frazier has had blondish-red hair, same as Bridget's. Now it's dyed dark brown, almost the same color as Rose's hair. She looks smaller. Diminished.

"Richard," she says, and then she's crying, face in her hands. Her nails are rough and ragged. "Dr. Haskell. Tell me what to do."

He grabs a box of Kleenex from the counter and places it on the cot beside her, then steps back to give her room. Annette's skirt is wrinkled, navy blue shirt splotched with tiny bleach stains near the hem. Hard to believe this is the same woman who used to host New Year's parties in little black cocktail dresses.

"Tell me what to do. Tell me how to make it stop."

Richard considers what a good doctor would say. What his father might say. There are antidepressants he could prescribe, referrals for psychiatrists—not here, there are no reputable ones here in the County, but further downstate. Bangor. Portland. He could suggest grief groups and meditation. Exercise and sunshine.

"You can't," Richard tells Annette. "You can't make it stop. It never stops."

They stay in the windowless room a long time, not speaking. The appointment runs beyond the time allotted; he misses his call with Dennis Frost to talk about potential schedules at the hospital. But Richard doesn't leave the room.

Do you blame me? he wants to ask Annette, but he already knows the answer.

Of course she blames him. She blames everyone. This woman blames the world. This woman is allowed to blame the world. Her child, her baby, is dead.

Saturday, Sept. 15, 1990—Breakfast at Diner. Veggie omelet. Coffee. Finally raining . . .

"Dr. H?"

Richard looks up from his empty plate to see her standing next to his table. Her hair is pinned back in two braids, and she looks so young, so bright, he can feel his heart trying to tear itself apart.

"Rose," he says. "How are you? How are the boys?"

Her smile looks more natural than it used to, like she doesn't have to work so hard at it. "You always sound like you really want to know."

"I do."

"I know—that's the weirdest part." Rose laughs. "Anyway, they're good. And me. I'm good, too."

"I'm glad to hear it."

"I know you are." She looks at Richard, head tilted, a question in her eyes.

"What is it, Rose?"

"I just been thinking," she says, "you shouldn't close the clinic."

"Why not?"

She leans down to clear Richard's dishes. As she does, he notices a pale thin line on her left ring finger.

"I know it must get real busy there. And you should definitely take more days off. But you're good at it, Dr. H. You're a real good doctor."

Before he can answer, Rose turns away, carries his plate to the kitchen. She's too thin. But maybe not so delicate as he's always thought.

The bell above the door tinkles, and Roger McGowan and his wife, Alice, walk in, shaking rain from their jackets. Laughing, they slip into the corner booth.

Richard opens his notebook, presses his pen to the page. Picks up where he left off.

Thursday, Sept. 27, 1990—Bought some of those adhesive pictures for exam room ceilings. Tropical fish, snowy mountains, all that sort of thing.

Sunday, Sept. 30, 1990—Breakfast at home. Oatmeal. Cantaloupe. Chopped wood and mowed lawn, probably last time this season. T. work in garden, Bev by for coffee. Nate w/ her. Wrecked.

Trudy stands beside Richard, admires the uniformly cut lawn.

"Looks all right," she says.

"Not too bad."

The last of the season's crickets are singing. The light is lower today than yesterday; tomorrow it will be a little lower. Trudy glances down at the cuffs of Richard's jeans, which he has rolled up over his ankles.

"New fashion statement?"

"I was trying to keep from getting grass stains and wood chips all over them."

"I should start calling you Prufrock."

Richard has no idea what she's talking about, but she laughs, kindly, and he doesn't ask her to explain.

A few minutes later, Bev pulls into the driveway with Nate in the passenger seat of her car.

"Can't stay long," Bev hollers across the lawn as soon as she steps into the driveway. "Bill's got Sophie and we told him we'd be right back. Just thought Nate here could use some human interaction."

Trudy and Bev sit down on the porch together with two mugs of coffee and start right in talking—years and years of a conversation Richard doesn't belong to.

"Come on," he tells Nate, and leads him down into the garden. Most of the color is gone by, but some of the sturdier sunflowers are still putting up a fight, though even they are starting to go limp.

"I never realized how tall they are," Nate says.

"They're a hell of a plant," says Richard.

Up on the porch, the women laugh, not as loud as they used to, maybe, but still laughter. Still some little joy only meant for the two of them.

Richard grasps for the right words, something safe and familiar.

"It's about that time," he finally says. "You should call the clinic, schedule your yearly physical."

Nate stands among the half-dead flowers and nods. "Sure." He stares away, toward the lawn. "Whatever you say, Doc."

12.
HOME RANGE

They take to the woods—four middle-aged men with back problems and failing eyesight and wives at home who probably won't miss them. They take the things they've carried into the woods for the past thirteen years: Rifles and ammo. Long-johns and flannels. Thirty-racks of Bud. Enough bread and beef jerky to last the duration of the hunt, which used to be an entire week, back when they were young and glad for an excuse not to shower or shave. As their ages climbed and their bellies drooped, their hunting trips dwindled from a week to five days. Last couple years, they've only spent a long weekend at the cabin each November, just enough time to feel like they put an honest effort into bagging a buck. Only Richard and George brought home deer last season. Bill missed his one shot, and Dean fessed up to coming along just to play cribbage.

Bill had hoped this might be the year they finally drop the tradition. But then the wives got involved. He can just imagine the four of them—Arlene and Leigh-Anne, Trudy and Bev—in one of the cracked vinyl booths at the Diner, sipping black coffee, scheming it up. How to get the men out of the house. How to make it seem like everything was normal, like they hadn't buried Bridget five months ago. How to keep all the familiar things alive.

"See ya when I see ya," Bill told Bev before he left early that Friday afternoon. The cluttered yellow kitchen felt chilly even with his jacket on. Damn boiler on the fritz again—he'd have to fix it when he got back on Monday, if Bev didn't get to it first.

Bev held Sophie out to him, and Bill, ignoring the twinge in his lower back, took his eleven-month-old granddaughter in his arms, surprised as always by how heavy she was for such a small thing. He bounced her up and down as she gnawed at his shirt collar. Two teeth coming in. Soft red hair, round green eyes just like Bridget. She'd already outgrown most of the clothes Nate brought the month before, and Bev and Trudy were planning to buy more in Prescott this weekend. Bill wondered if Trudy would be coming back to the house with Bev afterward, staying over after Sophie fell asleep.

"Trot, trot to Boston." As he bounced Sophie, Bill mumbled the familiar song, which he learned from his father, under his breath. "Trot, trot to Lynn. Careful, young lady . . ."

"You better get going," said Bev, reaching to take the baby back. "That sun'll be gone in a few hours."

They take Bill's truck, as always, because his is the only one with a crew cab big enough for the other three men to fold their limbs against the dashboard or the back of the front seat. Leg room isn't an issue for Bill, who barely clears 5'5". The others used to razz him about this when they were young. But now no one talks about Bill's height, or his receding sandy-brown hair, or the fact that he hasn't worked in almost four years.

These days, this annual trip to the woods is the only chance Bill gets to drive any further than Prescott, to feel even half as alive as he did behind the wheel of the rigs he used to drive all through Maine and beyond. Usually his route kept him on the eastern seaboard, but sometimes Bill got to deliver loads of pallets or lumber all the way to Colorado, Arizona, Kansas. Long hours with only the hum of the road and Seger's gravelly voice to keep him company. Cities like diamonds in the night. Deserts the color of blood and bone.

And then there was the occasional stop at a roadside bar. Smell of beer, perfume, cigarettes, women who pressed scraps of paper with their phone numbers on them into Bill's hand. He doesn't miss the drunk flirting of those nights, or the sweaty strangers trying to get him to dance to *Rhinestone Cowboy*, or the yellow bar lights that made everyone look like they had liver problems. He only called a couple of those phone numbers in all the years he spent out on the road. But the possibility was always there, and that was what mattered. Not the chance of a lay (even in his twenties and thirties, Bill worried his libido wasn't what it should be), but the chance that something *could* happen. Something different from his life back in Maine.

Bill eases the truck down the road to Dean's camp, which, once they pass the gate to the North Maine Woods, is mostly dirt. Pines taller than any of the three churches in Dalton creep in close to the path.

"Anyone catch the forecast?" Richard's knees press against the back of Bill's seat as he leans forward to take a can of ginger ale out of a paper bag from Bergeron's.

"Snow tomorrow," says Dean as he thumbs through the Delorme, squinting at a map of Bangor.

"Could be a nasty storm Monday," George says from the passenger seat, where he kneads his fingers into the meat of his left thigh. Sometimes Bill wonders if he can still feel the 'Nam bullet in there, lodged between muscle and bone. Does George remember how and where it happened? Does it give him nightmares, or has he gotten used to the weight of it?

The men don't talk much during the ride. They never did. A fondness for silence and an appreciation of the woods are two things the men have in common. That's one thing Bill always liked about these trips. The quiet, and the trees.

But the silence feels different today. Heavy. Uneasy.

All four men threw dirt on Bridget's casket. All of them went to the reception afterward at Bill's house and watched as Nate drank one beer, then four, then seven, before throwing up and collapsing in loud sobs in Bill's recliner. If it hadn't been so pitiful, the scene might've been embarrassing. But none of the men—in fact, no one who'd been in the living room that June day—said anything about Nate's breakdown then and haven't spoken of it since. Not to Bill, anyway. Far as he can tell, after the first big shock of her suicide passed, no one in Dalton has said much of anything about Bridget, or Nate, or Sophie, or any of the whole damn mess at all. Like it never happened.

Outside the truck, all those trees, all that empty sky. Bill drives on.

They take their time getting settled in the cabin. There's only one bed, which George and Bill share, in separate sleeping bags. Dean and Richard set up two squeaky cots not much softer than the wood plank floor. Snacks and Tums are laid out on the butcher block sideboard. Rifles are propped beside the front door. Extra rolls of TP are brought to the outhouse. For supper, B&M beans on brown bread, potato salad on the side. For dessert, a bottle of Jim Beam. Maybe not the meal Nate would've made if he were here—Bev taught the boy to cook when he was just a kid, mother and son whipping up old favorites like ployes and Yule log while they listened to Fleetwood Mac and Rod Stewart—but a good camp meal.

After supper, Dean skunks George at cribbage, then he skunks Richard.

"Up for it, Bill?" George asks, shuffling the greasy old deck of Bicycle cards.

The fire's going, and the cabin smells of woodsmoke and sweat. Richard and Dean sit at opposite ends of the ratty couch. Dean works on a word jumble, his reader glasses perched on his nose, the +2.5 sticker still stuck to the top of one lens, as Richard skims a *Field and Stream* that's lived on the coffee table the last few years they've been coming here.

Bill and George play a couple rounds, metal pegs chasing each other around the board Dean carved decades ago. In the middle of their tie-breaker, Bill pauses to stretch his lower back.

"Still botherin' you, huh?"

"Every day."

"Yup. Know how that goes." George moves his peg forward. "Skunked you again."

It takes a long time for Bill to fall asleep. Richard put too many logs on the fire, and it's stifling in the cabin. Dean snores. George must've put on a few pounds since last November, because Bill can feel himself rolling over to that side of the bed each time he almost drifts into a doze. His back throbs with a familiar ache that he imagines would give off a glow of white-gold light, if pain was a visible thing you could see radiating off a person.

If Nate's grief were a color, what color would it be? Maybe the same as Bill's—dark blue, river water in winter. Or maybe the mossy tint of Bridget's eyes.

The night drags on.

They take their guns into the cold, sunless morning. There's a milky skim of ice on the shallow edges of the lake. No wind in trees. Smell of woodsmoke from the cabin. George and Dean, who like to sit in the tree blind to the south of the lake, head off together, their orange vests disappearing into the pines. Bill and Richard walk north, along an old game trail that winds through a stand of birches before opening up into a field.

They've had good luck here in the past, in the ground blind Dean keeps set up all year long. Few years back, Bill took down an 18-point, nearly 250-pound buck. Took hours to field dress that sonofabitch, and by the end of it all four of them were covered in blood and half as drunk from the thrill of it as they were from Beam. All of them laughing and taking Polaroids of each other standing with booted feet propped up on the carcass.

Remembering that now makes Bill feel queasy. Or maybe he just needs to eat something.

He and Richard settle into the blind. They ready their guns, unpack their breakfast of leftover beans and a Thermos full of instant coffee.

Richard clears his throat. "Has Nate said anything to you about Marshall?" His voice is careful, even, his eyes fixed somewhere far across the field.

"Nothing," says Bill, not bothering to add that the Fraziers pretty much cut Nate off after the funeral. "Why?"

"Well, I heard this from Stacey Trinko, so take it with a grain of salt," says Richard. "But I guess Marshall's thinking of selling the mill."

The idea of one of the Fraziers ever walking away from that lumberyard is as unthinkable as a winter in the County without snow.

"Who the hell would he be selling to?"

"Some company out of Quebec." Richard takes a gulp of coffee. "Or maybe it was New Brunswick . . . Like I said, though. Probably just a rumor."

They fall silent again. What else is there to say? Marshall's either selling the mill or he isn't. Nothing anyone can do about it; no use harping on about what might happen to Dalton if the Fraziers do sell. Over half the town will either be out of work, or this new company, whoever they are, will keep everyone on and everything will go on just as it always has.

Bill readjusts the cushion he's sitting on, but he can still feel the frozen, lumpy ground underneath him. In the forest, blue jays shriek. The clouds come rolling in.

They wait.

He had stood with Nate on the farmhouse lawn after the flashing blue and red lights of the ambulance and DPD cruisers were gone. It was nearly 4:30 in the morning, and the rain from the night before had cleared. Nate kept saying it was his fault. If he'd only been home. If he'd only paid more attention. Bill led Nate to his truck and buckled him in just like he used to do when he was a kid. It's all right, son. I got you. Sit tight.

He went into the house by himself. Didn't turn on any lights. The second floor smelled metallic and mineral, a smell Bill recognized from his hunting trips. He moved past the upstairs bathroom, not letting himself look in, afraid of what he might see, and went into Nate and Bridget's bedroom. Took a few changes of clothes from Nate's bureau. Did his best to find the suit Nate had worn to his Pepere's funeral three years earlier, but later, in their ranch house on Russell Street, Bev pointed out that he had grabbed the wrong one, the one Nate had worn at his and Bridget's wedding.

Back in the truck, Bill noted someone had left the porch light on. Nate when he got home from arresting Tommy Merchant, maybe, before he went into the house and heard Sophie wailing in the nursery, before he went upstairs and found Bridget in the tub, before he called Bill, who called Chief Pete at the station, after he finally made sense of the garbled words Nate was spluttering across the telephone lines. *Bridget. Blood. I didn't know.*

Bill and Bev had sped the three miles out to Davis Road, where Nate stood with Sophie on the farmhouse porch. Sophie screeching, Nate silent. Bev took the baby and drove Bridget's car back into town. Bill stayed with Nate. Sat with him on the porch swing without saying anything while the cops and EMTs did what they had to do up in the bathroom. Sat with him while Paul Saucier and Linda Vance wheeled Bridget out to the ambulance (as they carried the gurney down the front steps, the white sheet shifted, and Bill caught a glimpse of one of Bridget's high-arched feet, blue under the nearly-morning stars). Sat with him while Pete came down and told them what they already knew.

"Dad."

Bill glanced over at the passenger seat, at his only child, not a child at all anymore but a new father. A rookie cop. A kind, naïve, gentle boy. And now, somehow, a husband whose wife had killed herself.

"Dad," Nate said again, and then the kid started crying just like he did when he was five and they had to put down their golden retriever. Loud, sloppy tears, sobs that made his slightly sloped shoulders jerk up and down.

Bill held Nate best he could over the stick shift. Nate was still in his black DPD jacket, though the Chief had had him hand over his gunbelt for safekeeping. Nate felt so light in Bill's arms. Like air, or water. He held on tight. And then, once Nate quieted down, without saying anything else, Bill drove back toward Dalton. Left the porch light on.

CRACK.

Beside him, Richard has the rifle held up to his shoulder. The air smells like hot metal. Bill squints out at the field, tries to spot a tawny brown pile on the ground.

"Christ, Richard. I don't see nothing out there."

"Must have got away."

"Sure you hit him?"

"Her. We better track her down, find out."

Carrying their rifles, they head off through the field. They find the first drops of blood and follow the splatter in a crooked line into the forest. It's darker here, evergreens blocking out what little light there is in the overcast sky, and it takes a while before they pick up the blood trail again. They stop to drink more coffee.

Richard frowns at Bill, who has his arms twisted behind his torso, trying to work the ache out of his lower back. "You up for this?"

It's the same careful tone Bill used to use with Nate when they were trick-or-treating and Nate's feet were dragging on the sidewalk, his Spiderman pillowcase stretched out with pounds of candy. "Sure you want to keep going?" Bill would ask. "We could head home. Get a head start on that haul before your mother says you gotta go to bed." But Nate would always insist on one more house, just one more, until finally Bill had to carry the boy home, candy sack slung across one shoulder, Nate half-asleep across the other.

"Never felt better."

They head deeper into the trees. The pain radiates from Bill's back down to his hips and legs with every step over the uneven ground. *Sciatica*, the Prescott doctors said. *Herniated disc*, the Bangor doctors said. Whatever it is, it's a slow, never-ending torment.

Before long, the blood on the ground gets thicker, the splotches closer together, often in dizzying circles. They find the doe lying on her side, ribs heaving up and down, under a stand of pines. Blood seeps out of a hole in her stomach and pools on the bracken beneath her.

Richard covers his mouth with one hand. When he speaks, his voice sounds like he's just swallowed a mouthful of sawdust. "I was aiming for her eyes."

"Bit off the mark, there."

The deer whimpers, a sound more human than animal. Bill waits for Richard to finish the job, but the doctor just stands there. "That poor girl," he says. "I can't believe I messed it up so bad."

After waiting a little longer, Bill takes the safety off his rifle. Pretends not to see Richard rocking on his feet beside him as he lifts the gun and aims the muzzle at the crest of the deer's skull. Pretends not to see the look of defeat and relief in the animal's glassy black eyes as she stares up at him.

He pulls the trigger.

The doe dies.

They take swigs from the bottle of vodka Bill tucked into his pack before they left the cabin this morning. He can't stop staring at the deer's empty eyes, or her pink tongue flopped out and hovering above the ridged edge of a fallen pinecone.

After his second shot of vodka, Richard lets out a deep breath. "Best we just get on with it," he says, voice back to his usual low, even tone.

But staring at the doe, knowing what happens next—the flesh and the gristle and all that blood—Bill can't move. His mouth floods, and beneath his orange wool hat, his forehead prickles with sweat. The forest, Richard, the dead animal . . . it's suddenly all grayed out and wobbly, like a TV channel with bad reception.

"Or maybe you should sit this one out," says Richard, grabbing Bill's elbow. He guides him over to a stump, eases him down until he's sitting, then kneels in front of him.

They've never been this close before, noses almost touching. Bill can feel the heat from the doctor's body. He can see every pore on Richard's forehead, one stray black eyebrow hair that shoots off in the wrong direction. Eyes the color of walnut shells.

"What're you doing?" he asks between heavy, uneven breaths as Richard removes his gloves, then Bill's, and takes his hand in his, pressing his index and middle fingers against Bill's wrist.

"Pulse." Richard stares at a patch of snow, his lips moving slightly as though counting to himself. After a few moments, he drops his hand.

"Bad?"

"Could be worse. Your chest hurt?"

"Yeah."

"Any dizziness, shooting pains in your left arm?"

"Don't think so."

"Well, good news is, it doesn't sound like a cardiac event. Seems more like a panic attack."

"Like those women in the old movies with those stupid smelling salts?"

Richard lets out a vodka-scented puff of laughter. "If you want to put it that way," he says. "But what you're experiencing right now—tight chest, hard to breathe, probably feel like you're trapped in a plywood box?"

Damn if that isn't exactly right.

"It'll pass." Richard rummages in his pack for a bottle of water, which he hands to Bill. "It's just your body's way of reacting to stress. I didn't bring any smelling salts with me, so hopefully this'll do the trick."

Bill sips at the water while Richard moves over to the carcass and takes out his hunting knife. Every few minutes, he looks up at Bill, asks how he's feeling, and Bill nods, says he's all right. He tries not to see the worry—or is it pity?—in Richard's eyes. Tries not to wonder if Richard will go home and tell Trudy, who will inevitably tell Bev, because those two tell each other everything, about the sight of him broken and scared shitless on a stump in the middle of the North Maine Woods.

At least there would've been some dignity in a heart attack.

They take a long, slow route back to the cabin, Richard dragging the deer behind him on a blue tarp he stowed in his pack for just that purpose. Snow spins down through the trees.

"Sure you don't want a break?"

It's the third time Richard's asked, and Bill, who's only ever hit one guy in his life, a playground dare when he was twelve, has to push aside the urge to punch the doctor on his hawklike nose.

"It's not a big deal. All sorts of people have panic attacks."

"Yep. Okay."

For a moment, it looks like Richard might want to say something else, then he hitches the tarp higher on his shoulders and keeps walking. The carcass bounces over every rock, root, fallen

branch. Bill's spine feels like a distended bag of hot needles, jos-
tling with every step.

About a quarter mile to the cabin, close enough they can see
the metal roof peeking through the trees, Richard stops walking
and asks for the vodka. Snow sticks to their orange vests, starts
to coat the ground. The doe's stiff limbs poke out of the tarp, its
dainty black hooves pointing back toward the forest.

Richard scratches his chin, pocked by the start of a five
o'clock shadow. "Remember our first fall out here? What was
it—'75?"

"Somewhere around there."

"You shot that ten-pointer, right?"

"Eight."

Richard stares toward the lake. "Whose idea was that first
trip?" he asks. "Your wife's, or mine?"

Bill watches thin curls of smoke rising from the cabin's stone
chimney. "Think the two of them cooked it up together."

You could use some time with the boys. That's how Bev put
it when she suggested Bill go with Dean and George for a week
of deer hunting. She and Trudy sat at Bill's kitchen table, steam
rising from their mugs of coffee. And Bill agreed, because he
was fifteen years younger then, and he wanted the time off from
work, and it'd been too long since he went into the woods.
Then Trudy joined in the conversation. *Think I'll send Richard
with you. He could use a break from that goddamn clinic.*

He imagines Bev and Trudy back at his house right now,
the two of them sitting at the table in the same yellow kitchen
where Nate took his first steps, the kitchen where Bev bakes
whoopie pies every year for Bill's birthday. They had a good
thing going there for a while, he and Bev. A normal life. Then
she met Trudy.

"She's my best friend," Bev said then and still says now.

But somewhere along the way, Bill started to wonder. The
way Bev looked at Trudy, the way she laughed around Trudy,

throwing her head back so hard her dark curls shook. The way she wrapped the phone cord around her wrist and leaned against the kitchen wall, staring out at the backyard with a big grin on her face every time Trudy called to complain about whatever it was she had to complain about that particular day. Bev had been the same way with Bill, once, back when they first started dating. All fluttery and laughing and loud.

He's tried to figure it out from time to time over the years, circling the question with polite conversation. *Trudy and Richard seem happy to you? What'll you two girls get up to in Bangor this weekend? Pretty fancy dress just to go to Frenchie's for a drink with Trudy, ain't it?* Bev's answers are never enough to either prove or ease his suspicions. *Happy as any married couple, I s'pose. Girl stuff—shopping and hair, you wouldn't be interested. You expect me to go out on the town in my sweats?*

"Our wives," Richard says, handing the bottle of vodka to Bill. "They're always cooking up something together, aren't they?"

"Guess so."

If he wanted to, Bill suddenly understands, he could ask Richard right now if he knows the truth of it. Maybe Richard's even waiting for him to ask.

But what good would it do? If he finds out for sure that Bev and Trudy are together, he might have to do something about it. And even though Bill liked the possibility of those nights on the road, in sweaty barrooms thousands of miles away, in the pit of his stomach he knows he's not a man who'll ever make any big sort of change. Change means hassle, risk, uncertainty. No. He belongs in Maine, in the County, in Dalton, in the little house on Russell Street. He belongs there for the simple reason that he wouldn't know how to belong anywhere else.

He finishes the vodka and glances at Richard, standing there with the carcass slung across his back and a dried splotch of coffee on his collar. "We should move on. Get back to camp."

Richard, still looking out toward the lake, nods without looking at Bill. "Okay," he says. "If you're ready."

The deer leaves an uneven trail of red behind them.

They take off early the next morning, none of them keen to stay until Monday in case a little snow becomes a major problem. They take their guns, their ammo, their leftover beer and jerky. They take the dirt road back through the woods and onto Route 11.

They take the carcass to Harvey Trinko's butcher shop near the half-frozen river in Milton Landing. As Harvey helps Dean, George, and Richard heft the deer out of the back of the truck, those stiff limbs bouncing everywhere, that dead tongue lolling, Bill's temples prick with sweat again. Again, his vision gets gray, wobbly.

"Gotta take a piss," he tells the others, then wanders into a thin copse of trees behind the shop.

Leaning against the clapboard building, he tries not to think about Harvey slicing his big, shiny knife into that doe. He thinks about the buck from a few years ago, the almost sexual thrill he'd felt when he pulled the trigger and felt, more than heard, the heavy thud as the animal dropped. *Mine*, he'd thought. Laughing as he wiped still-warm blood on his face. He vomits into the snow.

Harvey takes requests for cuts of meat from George, Richard, and Dean. When it's his turn, Bill declines. "Not a big deer," he says. "You three take what little there is."

He takes them all home. Richard first, to his and Trudy's house on Winter Street, where Trudy's blue Celebrity isn't parked in the driveway. Bill guesses that car is parked in his own dooryard right now, beside Bev's Lumina. George is next, a quick zip down Prentiss Street. He limps across the slushy parking lot and into the back of the Diner. And Dean last, to his and Leigh-Anne's Cape on Depot Hill, where he and Bill catch a flash of a frowning, small white face in an upstairs window.

"That Jenna?" asks Bill.

"Yeah, and she looks pissed. Maybe her mother grounded her again."

"Been acting up?"

"She's almost thirteen. You know how that is."

Nate never had a rebellious stage. Maybe some Boone's Farms on the rides he and Bridget would take all around the back roads of town. But if that ever happened, more likely it would've been Bridget's doing. She was more of a risk-taker than Nate, who was always worried about breaking rules, determined to keep everything under control. Nothing like Bill in his teenage years, which were a blur of pit parties and trouble in school, which abruptly ended when Bill dropped out in tenth grade.

"Jenna's just got this attitude," says Dean, staring toward the end of the driveway, at the detached garage he uses as his carpentry shop. "Won't listen, talks back all the time."

"That so?" asks Bill. Christ, he wants to be alone. This weekend. The doe. All this damn talking. Enough already.

Dean clutches his green canvas bag, picks at an edge of the duct tape that's holding one of the seams together. "Leigh-Anne says it's because of what happened with Anthony."

Bill's frustration softens. They never talk about Dean's boy, who died when he was just a few years old. Even when they all went on their hunting trip together later that fall the year it happened, none of them talked about it. Instead they let Dean wander alone into the woods whenever he needed to or paddle himself around the lake. Ice was late that season.

"What's it been now?" asks Bill. "Six years?"

"Seven."

Bill watches the wind rock the bare sugar maples at the edge of Dean's yard. No sun today, only gray. *Eeyore weather*,

Bridget used to call it. Painted him a picture of it once, a big white sky with fat clouds hanging above an open, snowy field. The picture still hangs in the living room, right above Bill's recliner. Sometimes if he looks really close, he sees faint colors in the snow and clouds—blue and purple, silver and pink. Other times, that field and that sky just look like a big white blank.

"It ever get any easier?" he asks, angry at himself when his voice breaks.

Dean doesn't look at him. "No. Just a little further away."

After Dean's shut the red kitchen door behind him, Bill throws the truck into reverse. Idling at the end of the driveway, his hands grip the steering wheel so hard the dry, cracked skin around his knuckles starts to itch. The thought of going home makes him so damn tired.

Instead of heading back up to the blinking yellow light on Main Street, he drives down Depot Hill, over the railroad tracks and across the bridge, where the river creeps its way northeast. At the end of the bridge, Bill turns left, heads for Davis Road.

He gives Nate all the leftovers from the weekend. Everything except the booze. Better not get his son going on that shit. Better keep it for himself.

"I've got food here, Dad," Nate says as he stacks jerky and cans of beans in a cupboard. "I'm not starving."

Sure looks that way, though. Like one of those skeletons in the haunted house they set up over in Prescott every year. Bone white. Blue eyes dim and hollow.

"Maybe you're not," Bill says, "but I sure as hell am. Feel like making your old man some French toast?"

He sits at the small round table, covered with unpaid bills and old newspapers, and watches as Nate drops the spatula on the floor, struggles to crack the eggs, seems to forget how much milk to add to the mix. He remembers watching Nate in this kitchen the first Thanksgiving he and Bridget bought this place.

He seemed to float around the room then, those long arms everywhere, hands in everything—golden-skinned turkey out of the oven and onto the sideboard, sprinkle of salt and pepper over the orange squash. Not a spill or missed step anywhere, and nothing but a grin on Nate's face as he and Bridget told Bill and Bev about an ongoing, good-humored argument they had about what color to choose for the drapes in their master bedroom.

"Gotta be green," Nate said.

"Blue," said Bridget. "It has to be blue."

By the time Nate slumps into the seat across from Bill, the kitchen is covered with dirty dishes and filled with the last traces of smoke. Nate slides a plate of toast over to Bill, who starts in right away. The bread's too soggy, and he bites into a tiny piece of egg shell.

"How is it, Dad? Did I do okay?"

"You did great, kid. Couldn't've done it better myself."

He gives Nate a hug before he leaves. His son's tall, too-thin body stiffens for a moment, then relaxes, sinking into Bill's arms just like those long-ago Halloween nights when he carried him home under the streetlights. His head droops against Bill's shoulder, a warm, heavy weight like a stone left in the sun.

He holds that weight. He holds it.

13

THE ROAD HOME

For his daughter's first birthday, Nate buys a stuffed Winnie-the-Pooh for her and a bottle of Allen's for himself. He makes these purchases thirty miles away from home—the teddy bear at the K-Mart in the mall; the booze at a dimly lit gas station out near the Northern Maine Fairground, abandoned for winter, the horse track and bleachers left to freeze beneath several feet of snow. He gets the bear gift-wrapped. When the girl at the counter selects shiny red paper covered with candy canes, Nate doesn't bother to correct her. It's early December; everyone's buying Christmas presents. At the gas station, he asks the cashier to place the Allen's in a paper bag, which he tucks into his glove compartment and wraps up in one of Bridget's old scarves to keep safe from the potholes that scar the road.

Later tonight, at Nate's parents' house, there's going to be a party. His mother has invited friends and family for Sophie's birthday. They'll coo at his daughter, give her too many presents, videotape the moment she plunges her face into a piece of cake. After the party, Nate will drive back home, alone. Once again, Sophie will stay with his parents, who won't ask what he intends to do by himself in that drafty farmhouse, his only company the porch light that illuminates one corner of the 1990 F.A. Peabody calendar tacked up beside the kitchen window.

He intends to drink. He won't get drunk. He never does,

not since Bridget's funeral. It was so new then, the reality of her death, and up until that moment, he hadn't had much experience with alcohol. Didn't know his limits. Now, seven months into life without Bridget, he knows just how much it takes to soften the world without blurring its edges completely. He always stops when he feels his cheeks start to warm and tingle, always places the bottle in the cabinet above the stove, and then he goes to bed. And if sleep doesn't come easy—it often doesn't—Nate turns the lamp back on and looks through mildew-spotted repair manuals he found out in the barn. How to bleed an old boiler. How to adjust the mower deck on a '74 John Deere tractor.

When he was a kid, Nate and his dad would take apart car engines or clocks just for the fun of putting them back together. Part of why Nate had wanted to buy the Donoghues' old farmhouse was for all the projects the place promised—crown moldings to square off, windows to seal, walls to insulate. He understands those sorts of things. Problems with solid, knowable solutions.

What he doesn't seem to understand, he only realized after Bridget died, are the problems people present.

But when he reads these old repair manuals late at night, with the slow-burn of booze in his belly and the wind rattling the windowpanes, Nate can fall into a world that makes sense. A world where anything, no matter how far gone it may seem, can be fixed.

By the time he leaves the Prescott gas station, it's started snowing. Three days into December and Aroostook is already buried under a foot of snow.

He decides to take the back way home. There are a few hours to go until Sophie's party, hours with nothing for him to do but wander through the house looking for new projects, ways to keep his mind off Sophie, and Bridget, and the job he hasn't gone back to since she died. Nearly half a year not working. If his wife's death isn't enough to drive a man batty, that sure as hell is.

Nate's mother keeps asking when he's going back to work, and he keeps telling her he doesn't know. But the Chief called Nate last month. Said he could come back anytime.

"Christ knows we could use you," the Chief said. "If I have to hear Bruce bitch about drunkie patrol one more time . . ."

Nate told the Chief he'd think about it. Maybe after the holidays, he said, which seemed far off in the future back then but now feels like a freight train hurtling toward him while he lies tied up on the tracks.

He drives past the rusted back gate of the Prescott airport. Snow is tossed away by the breeze before it has a chance to collect on his windshield. Flanking the road are white-blanketed potato fields, broccoli fields, fields where sunflowers bloom in late summer. Evergreens march down to the Aroostook River and up the northern face of Haystack.

Classic rock plays on the radio. When did the songs he grew up with became *classic*? Just a decade ago, he had aced his driver's test while the man from the Caribou DMV mumbled these same Bob Seger lyrics under his stale-coffee breath from the passenger seat of Nate's mother's car.

When Springsteen starts playing, Nate slaps at the dial as if it's a mosquito, accidentally pushing the volume louder before turning it off.

Sometimes this anger still takes him by surprise. He'll be measuring lengths for new window sills and the rage will come on him, so sudden and so big that he finds himself throwing plywood and nails across the room. And he'll have to stop and sit and breathe and try not to remember that other fit of rage, the one that started and ended in a dirt driveway on Larch Street with Tommy Merchant pinned beneath him.

Nate takes a few deep breaths in and out, slowly. He grips

the steering wheel and tries to focus on every curve and bump of the road before him. Just that. Just the road. One mile at a time.

He and Bridget used to drive this route a lot, back when they were teenagers and desperate to get away from their parents. Bridget had cassette tapes filled with Springsteen songs, the ones they played on the radio and the ones everyone seemed to forget about. Nate hasn't been able to listen to any of those songs in months. It's just one more hole Bridget's death ripped into his world. Since she died, he has been shocked over and over again by these little losses. Springsteen songs. The smell of paint and turpentine. Coming back from town and seeing all the windows of the farmhouse lit up. He'd give anything to drive home and see every single window blazing with warm yellow light.

He thinks about the booze in his glove box. There's hardly any traffic right now, not on a Monday morning when most everyone is out working, unlike him, living this pathetic half-life. No one would see him; no one would know.

As he reaches over to unlatch the glove box, Nate spots a glimpse of red up the road, an odd splash of color in this white and gray landscape. An old Cavalier, parked in a snowplow turnaround with its flashers on. He considers driving by. But barely before that thought has formed itself in his mind, Nate puts both hands back on the wheel, turns on his warning lights, and coasts to a stop behind the Chevy, the same careful movements he'd use if he were in the Dalton police cruiser pulling someone over.

This stretch of road, there's nothing but woods, scattered trailers, a few farms where tractors crouch beside half-collapsed barns. He'd feel safer if he were in his uniform, or at least his DPD jacket, Nate thinks as he uncurls his long legs out of the truck and walks toward the car, shoes squeaking against the snow. He can't imagine he looks much like a cop right now, in paint-stained jeans and corduroy coat that's missing a button.

A gust of icy wind blows snow into his eyes as he raps on the driver's side window, and for a few moments, he can't see a thing. The same frozen-up fear that gripped him that night he found Bridget shoots through him, sour fingers clawing the back of his throat. He hears the window roll down a few inches.

"Yeah, can we help you?"

Rubbing the snow from his eyes, Nate sees a skinny teenager sitting behind the wheel of the car. Her hair is cut unevenly just below her chin. In the passenger seat is a six- or seven-year-old girl with the same blonde hair and short, piggish nose. A pair of fuzzy dice hangs from the rearview mirror.

"I said do you need help?"

Nate stoops down to meet the older girl's brown eyes. "Everything all right here? Where are your parents?"

"We're fine," she says. "I'm eighteen."

He's certain the girl is barely pushing fourteen, but something tells him it'd be best not to argue. That same sense tells him these aren't the type of people who'd feel comforted by the fact that he's a cop, out on leave or not.

"I'm Nate Theroux."

The older girl squints at him and keeps her hands tight on the wheel.

"I live in Dalton," he continues. "Just saw you pulled over and thought I should check it out, make sure everyone was okay."

"Tina," whines the girl's sister. "Let him help us. I don't wanna be stuck out here no more."

"Damn it, Courtney, now he knows my name."

"He looks nice. He's got nice eyes."

"That don't mean shit."

The sisters stare at each other until the younger one's lower lip begins to tremble, then Tina sighs and rolls the window down all the way.

"We were going along fine and the car just quit on us. I don't know what happened."

Nate points at the dashboard, careful not to step too close to the girl's window. "Looks like you're out of go-juice."

Tina stares at the thin needle that points accusingly at the red E on the gas gauge. "*Fuck.*"

Ever since Bridget died, it's been like a dam has built up inside Nate's chest. He let the dam explode once, that hot July day with Tommy's blood on his knuckles. Since then, he has only allowed the dam to release in measured little torrents, because he fears that if he lets go again, that dam will burst completely, leave him broken wide open.

Looking at these girls now, Nate feels the pressure building. Their threadbare coats, the smudge on Courtney's cheek that must be an old bruise. He thinks of Sophie. Even as she finished growing in the NICU, she was so strong, eyes wide open, taking in all the light and movement around her. *She knows me*, Nate thought every time he stood above the incubator, marveling at that skim of copper hair on her scalp. She'd blink up at him and work her little fingers as though reaching for him. *She needs me.*

The closest gas station is almost half an hour away. If he were in his cruiser, Nate could radio for a tow truck. He glances up and down the empty road, stomping his feet to get the blood flowing as snow pelts against his cheeks. If he leaves the girls to go get a can of gas, anyone might come along. You never really know the kind of people who might live out here, in this depressing stretch of land between Prescott and Dalton.

"Listen. I can give you a lift back home. I'm sure your folks are worried sick about you."

Tina hugs her arms around herself. "We're not just gonna get in a truck with a guy we don't know."

"Stranger danger, stranger danger," Courtney sings out in a robot voice.

Nate remembers a game he used to play with Bridget when they were in grade school. The Trust Me game, she called it.

"How about this?" he says. "You ask me whatever you want, and I'll answer. I promise, it will all be the truth. Nothing off limits, those are the rules."

"How do I know you won't just lie?"

"Look at me."

"I'm lookin'."

"*Really* look."

Tina stares at him, his eyes watering from the wind, his hands steady where he holds them folded together in plain view of her. She gnaws at her bottom lip. Nate waits, hoping she'll see that all he wants is to help them. Save them.

"All truth?" Tina finally says. "No lies?"

"No lies."

"You some kinda pervert or axe murderer?"

"No."

"Are you a drunk?"

He thinks of the coffee brandy in his truck. The slow, solitary drinking he plans to do tonight. He thinks back to the night of Bridget's funeral, the fool he made of himself at his parents' house after drinking all that beer, sobbing in his father's recliner like some kind of lunatic in front of half the town.

"I drink when I'm sad sometimes," he says. "But I've only ever been really drunk once in my whole life."

After considering this a few moments, Tina nods. "You don't seem like the type. Just had to ask."

"It's a good thing to ask. What else do you want to know?"

"You married? Got any kids?"

"I have a baby girl," says Nate. "Her name's Sophie. And I was married, but she died."

He looks away, toward the forest. Fresh snow on evergreens. Bridget used to paint scenes like this, and he never understood how she captured all that silver-blue light beneath the snow, the subtle living presence of trees.

"Lookit, Tina. You made him sad."

Tina rests her hand on the windowsill. Her nails, painted metallic blue, are chewed into uneven triangles. "That sucks about your wife."

"Can we go with him now?" asks Courtney. "I'm hungry."

Tina sighs, stares hard at Nate. "You really promise you won't do nothing bad?"

Save her. Save her.

"I promise." Nate holds out his hand until Tina places her small palm against his. He barely grips her fingers, afraid of hurting her. The weight of her hand is no more than that of a baby bird, hollow-boned.

Tina clambers onto the bench seat of Nate's truck between him and Courtney and makes a big fuss about adjusting her sister's seat belt before buckling herself in. Aware of how thin the girls' jackets are, their lack of hats and mittens, Nate turns up the heater to full blast. The hot air puffs against his frozen cheeks. For years, the upholstery of the truck, which Nate bought from a guy who drove it back and forth from a job at the mill, has held the memory of sawdust and menthol cigarettes. These aromas are now overpowered by the new smells that cling to the girls: unwashed scalp, faint tang of milk, and something sweeter—soap, maybe, or the Fast Orange hand scrub Nate's father sometimes uses after working on the lawn mower or raking leaves.

"Where's home?" Nate asks, picking up Sophie's wrapped birthday gift from beside Tina and tucking it beneath his seat.

"About five miles back toward Prescott. Head straight, I'll tell you when to turn."

Now that they're in motion, Tina seems resigned to whatever fate waits for them at the end of the road. She slumps against the seat, her eyes tracing the motion of the windshield wipers.

Courtney sings under her breath, childhood lyrics Nate thought he'd forgotten long ago but that he now discovers still pace a worn path in his mind.

Back to my home, I dare not go . . . for if I do, my mother will say . . .

Though he understands family secrets are not given up easy, Nate needs to know if he's bringing the girls back to an unsafe situation. Depending on what he can get Tina to tell him, he may have to kidnap them after all, drive them straight to the Prescott police department and demand to talk with someone from Child Protective Services.

"Is it just you and your sister?"

"Got a couple half-brothers over in Fort Fairfield."

"Fart Fart-field," giggles Courtney.

"You live with your mom and dad?"

Beside him, Tina's arm tenses. "Our mother," she says. "And our stepdad."

Nate slows for a dark blur on the side of the road that might be a moose. When he's satisfied it's only a fallen log, he presses his foot back on the gas.

"Our mumma's a nurse," says Courtney. "She works at the animal hop-sital."

"All she does is answer phones, dummy."

"What about your stepfather? What does he do?"

"Used to work at the chip plant," says Tina, "till he busted his back up."

She instructs Nate to ease down a rutted dirt road. To either side of them, white fields stretch toward the forest, where clouds' fat bellies slouch against the treetops.

"Ours is that little shack at the end of the lane. That green one."

"Just tell me straight. Is someone at home trying to hurt you?"

"No one hurts us," Tina says. "Not anymore."

Courtney traces lopsided hearts into the fog on her window. "Daddy was mean *all* the time."

"So why'd you leave?"

"Mumma needs her medicine. Nana has some at her trailer."

"Shut up, Courtney."

They've arrived at the house, a little ranch with peeling siding and a roof that should have been re-shingled long ago. A sugar maple, bare branches quivering in the wind, casts shadows over the snowy lawn.

Tina is unbuckling Courtney's seat belt before Nate has parked the truck. "Thanks for the ride," she says. "You can go now."

But Nate doesn't like the look of the house's dark windows. "I think I ought to meet your folks, tell them what happened. I'd go nuts if some stranger brought my kid back home with no explanation."

Tina leads them to the side door, dark green shot through with rust spots. Stepping into the warm room, it takes a moment for Nate's eyes to adjust from the blinding snow outside. It's a kitchen, he finally sees, maybe the cleanest kitchen he's ever stood in. The Formica counters are spotless; the stainless steel sink smells of Dawn dish soap. Unlike his own kitchen, there's no clutter anywhere, no dishes on the drying rack, a streak-free coffee pot tucked away beside the stove.

Tina tosses her and Courtney's jackets on a chair. "Stay here. I'll go see if they're up."

After she disappears down the hallway, Courtney climbs onto the table and opens a box of graham crackers. She crunches away with a somber expression that makes Nate feel it again— that pressure threatening to spill.

He never stops thinking about it. Wondering why, and how. How he didn't see the misery Bridget was in. How he didn't realize how precarious it was, the life they'd built, the only one he'd ever wanted. How he never even considered the possibility of that life disappearing.

After the funeral, his mother offered to take Sophie for a few weeks—three, four at most. Nate agreed. Part of it was just needing time to grieve in private, time he couldn't have had if he were taking care of a seven-month-old. It didn't take long for him to miss Sophie just as much as he missed Bridget. Her baby-milk smell, her round blue-going-green eyes, her sticky, chubby palms. The weight of her in his arms.

But the day he was supposed to go to his parents' house and bring his daughter back home, Nate had sat frozen in his truck, unable to leave his driveway. Chills along his bones, prickles of heat in his forehead. If he couldn't take care of his own wife, how could he possibly take care of a baby? But it was more than that. Worse than that. He kept thinking of Tommy, Tommy's blood on his hands, Tommy's panicked voice as he begged Nate to stop hitting him. Knowing what he was capable of, that violence, that sudden loss of control . . . Sophie was safer with his parents, Nate decided as he sat there inside the suffocating July heat of his truck. Safer away from him. And so a week turned into two, then three, and now here he is, five months later, and his daughter is still living with his parents. Nate wasn't there when Sophie spoke her first word (*bye-bye*). Wasn't there when she took her first steps toward the squiggly pixels of Bob Barker's face.

"You want one?" Courtney shakes the box of graham crackers.

"No, thanks," Nate answers in a raspy voice. He clears his throat. "You ever tried those with Fluff?"

"Who hasn't?"

Down the hall, there's a murmur of voices, Tina's rising and falling like an irate bird. She returns to the kitchen first, wearing a sour expression.

"Mom," she says, "this is the guy. And here's our mother. Deb."

A tired-looking woman, probably a decade older than Nate,

steps into the room. She has the same blonde hair as her daughters, though her nose is longer, slightly off-center.

"Hi there," he says. "Nate Theroux."

Though he expects her to ply him with questions about who he is and where he found her children, Deb merely nods. "Bad weather, ain't it?"

"Sure is." Nate looks at Tina, who's removing Courtney's pink snow boots with quick, almost violent motions. "I found your girls on 227, headed toward Dalton. Car ran out of gas. If you'd like, I can use your phone, call a tow truck for you."

"Oh, no." Deb clutches her blue bathrobe tight around her throat. "My husband will take care of it. His brother's a mechanic over in Caribou—"

"Prescott," says Tina.

"—that's right, Prescott. Anyway, Gary will call and set it up."

There's a shuffle-drag sound of footsteps in the hall, and a slightly-hunched man with a grizzled gray beard limps into the kitchen.

"This the Good S'maritan?" The man's voice reminds Nate of a canoe scraping against river rocks. "Gary Newell. Good to meet ya."

The man's handshake is both strong and gentle, just like Nate's father's, and the Chief's, and all the men he grew up admiring.

"Listen," Gary says, "I'da known these kids was scheming something up like that, I woulda stopped 'em. I was sleepin'. This damn back. You ever broke your back? No? Well, take it from me. Don't."

"Tina mentioned you've been out of work a while."

"Two, three months. Disability helps. Not enough."

Now Tina is wetting a dishrag at the sink, stepping back to the table to clean the crumbs off Courtney's face. The smudge which Nate earlier mistook as a bruise is wiped away to reveal a clean patch of skin.

"Anyway," says Gary, "thanks for bringing 'em home. Can't imagine what I'da done if I woke up and found 'em gone."

"They seem all right," Nate says. "A little cold, maybe, but I don't think they were there that long before I drove up."

"I'm sure they're fine. They're tougher'n they look."

Gary gazes at the girls with humor and quiet wonder, the same wonder Nate feels whenever he thinks of Sophie. The man reaches out to pull Tina close, a one-armed hug she gives into like a sigh of relief, leaning against Gary's shoulder, staying there a moment before returning the dishrag to the sink.

Nate feels a pang at the idea of leaving, even though it seems he had nothing to worry about after all. Kids being kids, running away just to prove they can.

"Tina. Courtney." He bows at the waist, thinking it might be charming, then immediately regrets it. "Pleasure to meet you. You take care now. And no more running off like that. Even if you are eighteen."

Tina finally smiles, revealing a crooked incisor. "No promises."

"Well, I ain't going with her ever again," says Courtney. "She's a real bad driver."

"Thanks again, man." Gary shakes Nate's hand once more. "Take 'er easy."

Nodding goodbye, Nate heads outside, back into the falling snow. He's only made it a few steps down the walkway when he hears the girls' mother call his name. Turning around, he sees Deb on the front stoop in her slippers.

"What'd they tell you?" She pulls the door shut behind her and speaks in a low voice.

"They said they had to get you some medicine," says Nate. "Can I help you with that, go get anything for you?"

"They said that, did they?" Deb bites her bottom lip and stares at the maple. "They're good girls, you know. Don't know why God gave 'em to me."

It's then that Nate notices it—the steady shake in Deb's

hands, so familiar from all the Dalton dry drunks he's known all his life. *Her medicine.* Right. Anger and pity wrestle it out in his mind. He wonders if she asked them to go get the booze for her, if she put it in their heads that she needed the kind of help only they could give. She ought to be held accountable for her mistakes. Her selfishness.

But as the cold wind knocks against his face, Nate remembers what Courtney said earlier—*Daddy was mean all the time.* Who knows what Deb endured before Gary came into her life. Maybe those girls' father cut this woman down to the point where she still can't see straight. Maybe he beat this poor woman as badly or worse than Nate had beaten Tommy.

"They really do seem like great kids," Nate tells Deb, and then he sets off through the snow, falling slower now. The wind has blown the thin clouds nearly to the border of Dalton, so many miles distant, yet not that far away from here. Not too far at all.

Pausing at his truck, he glances back to see Deb still on the stoop. She watches the sky, and in the gathering light, he can see a gentleness on her face, a glimmer in her eyes that hints of dreams she must have had once, dreams she might permit herself to dream again only in the dark hours of night, when the house is asleep and the bottle on the table beside her leers with its hungry mouth.

He opens the passenger door, unlatches the glove box. As he unravels the slippery fabric of Bridget's old scarf, he wonders if he's gone crazy, doing this, giving someone else this poison. As he walks back toward the house, Deb's eyes never leave the brown paper bag in his palms.

"Tell your girls you found some medicine," he says, handing her the bottle. "Tell them you'll feel better now."

As Nate heads back onto the road home, the snow stops falling.

* * *

His parents' small house on Russell Street is bursting with life.

Trudy has been here all day to help Nate's mother make cake and Stromboli, and Nate knows she'll linger to help with the cleanup long after everyone else has left.

"You up for this?" Trudy asks Nate as guests begin to arrive. "Your ma wasn't too sure about this party, putting you through all this damn fuss."

"It's good for Sophie," he says. "She needs it."

"Oh, hell, Nathaniel." Trudy narrows her eyes at him. "Don't be so thick-headed. We're not here for her. Your girl's cute and all, but she's no great conversationalist. It's you that could use a little fussing over."

The guests show up in a clump of flushed cheeks and jackets that smell of woodsmoke and winter. There's Dr. Haskell, his hair thinner than the last time Nate saw him, and Roger and Alice, who tells Nate that Roger's mother wasn't feeling up to coming out tonight—"Shingles," she says, "or maybe just Nora just being Nora." Arlene Nadeau, loaded down with trays of leftovers from the Diner, lets Nate help her take her coat off as she shouts for his mother to clear a space in the fridge for her cold cuts.

And then, unexpected, Rose Douglas, dark hair pulled into a twist. She hugs Nate with a grip he never would have guessed could come from such bony arms, and he inhales the aroma of her mango shampoo while she whispers in his ear—"It's okay about Tommy." And he feels a strange collapsing inward, both the relief of forgiveness and the conviction he doesn't deserve it. "He took off," Rose continues. "Went down to Bangor, said he had to clear his head or some shit. What a guy, huh? Just leaving his two kids like that."

Later, as Nate is dipping a carrot into some ranch dressing, Bruce appears beside him, the man's huge frame casting a shadow over the table.

"Chief says you're coming back," he says.

Nate's stomach flips. "Haven't decided yet."

"Well Christ, figure it out, Boss. If you ain't a cop, what are you?"

"Wish I knew."

All of these people, eating his mother's molasses cookies and drinking his father's cheap beer. The noise, the weight and color of them all—overwhelming. Both a comfort and a worry, a promise and an obligation.

And in the middle of it all, the center around which they all arrange themselves, Sophie waves her chubby arms from her high-chair, the same one Nate sat in on his first birthday. Her curls bounce as Nate's father tickles her feet. She lets out a belly laugh that gets everyone else laughing too, ripples around the room.

When Arlene offers Nate a beer, he declines.

His mother pushes her way through the crowd with a plate of cake in her hands. Her hair is falling out of its ponytail, and her eyes keep flicking around toward Trudy. She takes Nate by his elbow. "Come on, sweetheart," she says. "Come be with Sophie. Her birthday shouldn't be something to mourn."

The familiar fear flicks through Nate as that night comes back to him—Bridget, unmoving, tub stained red. Clammy air, smell of rust. He stood there so long (too long), trying to make sense of it even though his body understood. The frantic call to his father, because that's who he always called when he needed help, and the phone was so heavy; he dropped it, it swung there on the wall as his father shouted his name through the tiny holes in the receiver, tiny holes like dark stars punched out of a hard white sky.

And upstairs, down the hall from the ruined bathroom, his daughter crying out for him.

Save her, save her.

He thinks of those girls from earlier today. Courtney's pink boots, Tina's blue fingernails on the Chevy's windowsill. He wonders if Sophie will ever wear boots like that, if she'll ever come across a stranger on the side of a road and decide, against all good sense, to trust him. And how would that turn out for her?

So many tragedies in this world, so much potential disaster. Endless heartbreak.

Nate feels warm, gentle hands on his back, hears his mother speak his name. She stands on one side of him, Trudy right behind her. Nate hears the laughter of everyone around him, smells their mingled sour-sweet exhalations. The taste of mustard sparks on his lips; the yellow linoleum is smooth beneath his feet.

His father appears on the other side of him, barely as tall as Nate's shoulders, but there. Steady. "Look at your girl," he says.

Surrounded by all these people who have dwelt with him in this town all his life, Nate takes a tentative step toward his daughter. He steps into the center of the room, and he sees how much Sophie's eyes have become like Bridget's—spruce-green, deep and round. And right now, those eyes are watching him—only him—with wonder. Those little fingers reaching, stretching out toward him.

The dam in Nate's chest cracks open. His hands shake, his feet itch to run. Only centimeters between them. A shadow. A breath. He doesn't turn away.

ACKNOWLEDGEMENTS

To my parents: Thank you for every overpriced journal bought from well-lit bookstores, for long rides on back roads listening to Bob Seger, and for inappropriate jokes told over a Scrabble board. Thank you most of all for giving me a love of books and for always believing I would someday be one of the people who wrote them.

For The Fella: Thank you for being unfailingly supportive, for begrudgingly letting me crank the thermostat, and for putting up with my bouts of creative ennui (not to mention the panic attacks). I still can't believe how lucky I am to have found someone willing to marry a writer.

For my sister: Thanks for remembering the same places I do—we've come a long way from stomping puffballs and climbing on giant dirt piles. And thank you especially for giving me the two best nieces a girl could ask for.

Lots of love and thanks to Aunt Sue, who took me school shopping, endured endless "fashion shows," and let me believe I was really cutting her hair.

Thank you to all the friends and family who have followed the trajectory of my writing and done all you could to support me, from reading and sharing my stories to sending me cow-themed well-wishes. You all know who you are.

Special shout-out to Dr. McFaul, the best pediatric cardiologist my family ever could have hoped for.

In memory of Nikki Beaulieu, Richard Bessey, Brenda

McKenzie, and Bob Roberts: You may never read these words, but I will always remember yours.

Thank you to Nat Sobel, who discovered my work and saved me from the querying trenches, and to Judith Weber, who has never stopped believing the inhabitants of Dalton have stories worth telling.

Thank you to Autumn Toennis, the perfect editor for this quiet, place-centric, adjective-ridden debut. Thank you also to Kent Carroll and all the other incredible folks at Europa who put so much thought, care, and love into each work they publish.

An extra special thank-you to Susan Conley, Ron Currie, Jr., Aaron Hamburger, Cara Hoffman, Richard Russo, and Morgan Talty.

An exhaustive but by no means complete list of some of the kick-ass writers I am fortunate enough to have in my life: Darcie Abbene, Julie Brown, Aimee DeGroat, Paulla Estes, Jillian Hanson, Natalie Harris-Spencer, Nancy Hauswald, Sarah Marslender, Judy McAmis, Catherine Palmer, and Judy Sandler. Thank you for your friendship, your insights (literary and beyond), your reading recommendations, your line edits, and your unwavering assurance that I would one day be a Real Author.

I have found paradise in many libraries throughout my life, but I wouldn't be the person or the writer I am today without those that shaped and sheltered me most: Ashland Community, Curtis Memorial, and Patten Free. (If you are reading this and don't have a library card, please go out and get one.)

And finally, for the Aroostook County town that raised me—where all my stories began, and most of my stories return.